PAPA'S CORD

PAPA'S CORD

A NOVEL BY

Mary Pleshette Willis

ALFRED A. KNOPF   NEW YORK   1999

This Is a Borzoi Book
Published by Alfred A. Knopf, Inc.

Copyright © 1999 by Mary Pleshette Willis
All rights reserved under International and Pan-American
Copyright Conventions. Published in the United States
by Alfred A. Knopf, Inc., New York, and simultaneously in
Canada by Random House of Canada Limited, Toronto.
Distributed by Random House, Inc., New York.

www.randomhouse.com

Knopf, Borzoi Books, and the colophon are registered
trademarks of Random House, Inc.

Library of Congress Cataloging-in-Publication Data
Willis, Mary Pleshette.
Papa's cord : a novel / by Mary Pleshette Willis. — 1st ed.
        p.   cm.
        ISBN 0-679-44696-6
        I. Title.
        PS3573.I45654P3   1999
    813'.54–dc21   98-51914   CIP

Manufactured in the United States of America
First Edition

FOR JACK

WITH LOVE

Special thanks to my daughters, Sarah and Kate; my mother, Marjorie Pleshette; my editor, Victoria Wilson; and my agent, Jonathon Lazear.

PAPA'S CORD

ONE

The first time Josie Davidovitch saw her father with another woman, she was just a little girl. She had gone with him to his office on a Sunday morning to make cotton balls and help him sterilize the tools of his trade—speculums and ring forceps, scissors and hypodermic needles.

Josie's father was a gynecologist, a handsome man with dark brown hair and gray-green eyes who gave the impression of strength and grace even though he wasn't very tall. He had a jaunty walk, was quick to dance, and was irresistible when he talked or listened to a woman—leaning forward to hear her better, touching her wrist or squeezing her hand, laughing at her jokes, nodding sympathetically as she confessed her sins. It seemed to Josie that every woman alive was in love with her father—stopping him in restaurants, coming over to him at the theater, flocking around him backstage at the New York City Ballet. Even her friends' mothers were his patients, which meant her friends could boast that he had delivered them. And, of course, Viola, the maid, whose soft wide hips Josie used to hide behind when her older brother, David, chased her into the kitchen. Dr. D. was the father of fertility, the magician who brought and, Josie believed as a child, *made* all those babies.

Josie spread out the sheet of sterile cotton as if it had been cut directly from the clouds, so white and soft that she wished she could make herself small and walk on it barefoot. Her father showed her how to grab a corner and pull a small square and poke it through the circle of her thumb and index finger. As she was happily twisting off the last fluffy cotton ball and watching the jar fill up with the puffs of her labor, Dr. D. whisked her out of the examining room and told her to wait outside. He had an emergency.

Josie sat in the waiting room and picked up a magazine, but she wasn't interested in the pictures and she hadn't yet learned to read. She wanted to see what the emergency was, so she sneaked up to the closed door and listened. "Move your hips to the edge of the table," she heard her father say. "Thatta girl. This won't hurt."

Josie looked through the keyhole and held her breath. She thought she saw a thigh or foot, some piece of flank, but where was her father? She could make out the top of his head, but it wasn't where it was supposed to be. What was it doing between the lady's legs, and what were her legs doing up in those stirrups? Josie knew she shouldn't be looking, that something was going on in there that only her father and the other woman shared. No one else, not even her mother.

Josie ran back to the waiting room and waited. When the woman came out, she was friendly and relaxed. She smiled when she saw Josie and told her how lucky she was to have Dr. D. as her father, how he had delivered all her babies.

"Isn't it time for more?" Dr. D. whispered in his patient's ear, which made Josie feel a rush of excitement she didn't understand. Then the other woman giggled and kissed him on the cheek. He smiled and gave her a gentle pat. If only Josie could be his patient and have babies, he would share all his secrets with her.

There were no locks in the Davidovitch apartment (except for her parents' bathroom) and everyone walked around nude. Until she was eight, Josie carried her clothes into her father's bathroom every morning, where she dressed while her mother slept. There, Dr. D. would regale her with stories about the days when he was a little boy, although a quick glance at his penis made it hard for Josie to believe he had ever been small. He lathered his face with almond-scented cream, then soaped his testicles in the shower until they were white and frothy like coconut snowballs. Albert described his mother, Masha, like a Yiddish saint. She was a tall, handsome woman with a widow's peak, high cheekbones, and a large bosom (which he pronounced *bosoom*), and she cooked like an angel and kept house for a passel of women—three sisters, and two cousins, a maiden aunt, and several nieces. Albert's sisters, Natalya and Lena, were great beauties with oval faces and luminous skin, violet eyes, and ash blond hair. Masha ruled the house from the kitchen, seducing her boychik with brisket and latkes, matzo balls and curative soups.

His father, a quiet, mustachioed man—a black-and-white photo in a Technicolor world—walked out when Albert was twelve, but he came home to be cared for when he grew ill, only to walk out for good when he was well. Smothered with love and *schtupped* with food, coddled and spoiled by so many women, Albert talked about his childhood as if it were a fairy tale, taking Josie every Sunday to the Lower East Side to fish for pickles in the icy brine, eat jelly doughnuts where he bought his bialys, listen to him kibitz with the dairyman who made his farmer's cheese. For Josie, Rivington and Orchard streets were the Magic Kingdom (only the food was better!).

When Josie was thirteen, her father decided it was time for her first pelvic. Why then, she didn't know. But if the big event for most Jewish girls is their bas mitzvah, the big event for Josie was her first Pap smear. Before the appointment, Dr. D. took her to Schrafft's, where, between bites of turkey on crustless toasted white and sips of vanilla egg cream, she wondered if the Irish waitresses with their tightly curled hair, black uniforms, white aprons, and orthopedic shoes had pelvics (or even vaginas, for that matter). But when they blushed and laughed at her father's teasing, Josie thought he must have seen them all.

After lunch, they went around the corner to Dr. Stein's. A sweet-faced, balding man, he spoke in whispers and had baby pink skin and perpetually wet lips. Josie's heart sank. Dr. Stein wasn't nearly as good-looking as her father and she knew that she was getting second best.

"Would you like to observe?" Dr. Stein asked Dr. D. as he ushered Josie down the hall.

"That's all right?" Albert hesitated, debating whether to say yes or no, then decided (although he was sorely tempted) that it was inappropriate (not to observe the examination of his pubescent daughter, but to trespass on a colleague's turf).

Josie wanted her mother. She didn't want to be examined by a stranger. Or a man. She didn't want to be examined at all.

"Just take off your panties and spread your legs," Dr. Stein whispered as he draped her with a sheet.

Josie felt like a sacrificial lamb, a vestal virgin in ancient times.

"This will feel a little cold," Dr. Stein said, snaking the icy speculum inside her and jabbing her with a swab too deep for her to see. She felt splayed, exposed, humiliated, and she couldn't believe this is what her father did for a living.

When Josie was fourteen, her mother told her she'd been married before. "You're kidding." Josie was incredulous. "Did you have any children?" Ruth shook her head. "Was Papa the reason you got divorced?"

"Not exactly."

"Then how did you meet Papa?"

"He was my gynecologist."

Josie couldn't believe her ears. It was hard enough to imagine her parents *doing* it, never mind her father examining her mother, too.

"How disgusting," she said, nearly choking on her egg-salad sandwich. "Papa examined you *before* you were married?"

"Ssshhhh," Ruth said, dabbing mayonnaise and an embarrassed smile off her lips. "He was *my* doctor."

"But you *dated* him." Josie had lost her appetite. "How gross."

"He didn't ask me out *while* he was examining me." Ruth lowered her voice so the other white-gloved ladies at the Women's Exchange wouldn't hear her.

"Well, that's a relief," Josie said. "What did you talk about on your first date? Ovulation and menstrual cramps?"

"Oh, Josie." Ruth called for the check. "You just don't understand."

Ruth Davidovitch, née Hecht, was a lady, always dressed with gloves and shiny pumps, an alligator handbag and cultured pearls. She had rust brown hair that she braided and twisted into a bun, amber eyes that misted when she laughed, and manicured hands that always felt cool and soft on Josie's brow. She had been raised in New Orleans by a father who lost his money in the cattle crash of 1917 and a mother who had high ambitions that her eldest daughter marry a rich German Jew. She was the first woman in her family to graduate from college, but she never believed she was smart. It was her younger brother, T.R., whom everyone thought a genius. A fine musician and brilliant student, he died of pneumonia the year he was admitted to Johns Hopkins medical school.

Ruth's first marriage had been a mistake from the start. "I knew I shouldn't have gone through with it," she said. "But I didn't have the courage to return all those monogrammed sheets." When she married Albert Davidovitch, a Russian Jew ten years her senior, her family disapproved.

"Why couldn't you have married Victor Loeb, like your friend Martha?" her mother complained.

"Because I love Albert," Ruth said. "I thought you'd be delighted to have a doctor in the family."

Ruth learned to cook like a Russian Jew, but no matter how perfect her *petcha* or pickled herring, Albert always said it wasn't as good as his mother's. And no matter how good her borscht, she never lost her infatuation with "Our Crowd" and insisted that Josie take dancing lessons at the exclusive Hortensia Tilden School, in the hopes that she might meet (and marry) a Rothschild or Rosenwald.

Josie fought with her throughout high school, laughed at her pretensions and social airs because she knew without *knowing* that it was her mother who was the sexy one in the marriage, even though it was her father who was in the "business" of sex.

"You're drunk, Ruth," Albert scolded when she had had more than her usual glass of wine and wanted to dance.

"I am not," she would demur, opening her arms as Josie and David stared in embarrassed wonder. If he was in a good mood, Albert would take her in his arms and spin her around the living room to the music of Gershwin or Cole Porter. Only then did they seem to be in love; Ruth was relaxed and sure of herself, never stepping on Albert's toes as he pressed his hand firmly in the middle of her back, leading her from a waltz to a fox-trot, bending her back so her hair touched the ground.

Then the music would stop and Ruth would tiptoe around Albert, deferring to his every whim—not keeping a dress he didn't like, or changing her lipstick if the color was too red. But no matter how hard she worked to please him, he got that irritated look at the dinner table—eyes inching up into his tangled brow, bifocals steaming if she choked on her own spit or sneezed too many times or breathed too loudly or babbled on about something that didn't interest him. He would glance up from his plate, his fork poised in the air, and fix her with such disdain that Josie wanted to throw her arms around her mother's neck and tell her how much she loved her, but instead, she sat paralyzed, her eyes darting from her father to her mother, praying that Viola would break the tension by passing the silver tray of buttered beans, pearl onions, and creamy mashed potatoes.

"You only got one duck." Her father's tone was accusatory, his already-thin lips having long disappeared into a grimace. Josie shot her brother a nervous glance. "You know one duck is not enough for four."

"Of course it's enough," Ruth said, her voice trembling.

"Don't tell me." Albert glared at the crispy bird everyone was longing to eat. "One duck is only enough for three."

"Don't be silly, Albert." Ruth lit a cigarette. "It's plenty. The children don't eat—"

"Are you trying to economize?" he asked, interrupting.

"What's wrong with that?"

"Because we can afford two ducks."

"I know we can, Albert." She lowered her eyes. "I really don't want to fight."

"There wouldn't be a fight if you bought enough food."

"I'm not hungry," Josie said, crossing her legs as her father deftly slipped the shears into the duck's ass and split it up the middle with one surgical slice.

"Why aren't you hungry?" Albert stared at Josie.

"I am." David held out his plate.

"You stay out of it," Albert snapped.

"Will you please calm down." Ruth spoke with the conviction of someone who expected to be smacked.

"Don't tell me to calm down!" he bellowed. "If you'd gotten two ducks, there wouldn't be an argument."

With that, Ruth burst into tears and ran from the table.

Josie sprang up and pushed back her chair.

"Where do you think you're going?" Albert said, placing a large piece of meat on her plate.

"You made Mama cry."

"I'm fine," Ruth said, dabbing her eyes as she came back into the room, avoiding Albert's stares. "Let's eat."

Josie waited for her father to apologize, but he never did. She wondered why her mother didn't ram the duck down his throat. But nobody said a word, and all Josie wanted to do was scream, *Why can't we eat like normal people? All this pressure is killing me!*

Dr. D. might be an angel at work, patient and avuncular, but at home he was a bully. And like all bullies, he had the entire family (including the large black-and-white cat) vying for his attention, purring at his touch, rubbing up against his leg, scratching the furniture. Both Josie and her brother learned early how to tell a good story, time a perfect joke, imitate any foreign accent. The family motto was Make Him Laugh. Just don't step on his punch line or spill your milk.

"Goddamnit!" Albert stood back from the table as David overturned his glass, the milk spilling all over the lace doilies and dripping onto the floor.

"I didn't do it on purpose," he cried, desperately trying to mop up the mess with his linen napkin. "It was an accident."

"D'you know what would happen if there were accidents in the operating room?" Albert leaned forward, the tendons in his neck quivering with anger. "People would die."

"The operating room?" David cocked his head to one side. "I didn't know they drank milk in the operating room."

"You think it's funny?"

"No," David said nervously.

"Then why are you laughing?"

"I'm not laughing."

"Go on! I want you out," he said, ordering David to leave the table.

"But what did I do?" he stammered.

"Go on!" Albert jabbed the air with his finger. "To your room."

"Albert, please," Ruth pleaded.

"Did you hear me?" He pushed back his chair as David scrambled to his feet and ran. Ran for his life as Albert sprang up from the table and gave chase. Josie bolted into the living room as her mother cried, "Stop it, you two. Stop it right now!"

"You Hitler!" Josie screamed, grabbing her father's sleeve as David lay trembling on the floor. "Leave him alone!"

Albert turned on Josie like a gored bull. "What did you call me?"

"I called you Hitler!" Josie screamed, turning on her heel and racing out of the living room, down the hall, through the den, and into her parents' bathroom, where she locked the door.

"Open that door!" Albert banged his fists so hard the walls shook. "I'm counting to three. D'you hear me, Josie? One . . . two . . ."

Josie ignored his cries and turned on the spigots full blast, great clouds of steam rising like the mists above Niagara. She chose the carnation-scented oil from her mother's array of colored bottles and slid into the sweet, hot water, her father's pounding replaced by the sound of her own breathing as she slid beneath the surface, her hair spread out around her head as she floated like a giant fetus.

Everything in the bathroom smelled of her mother—Blue Grass cologne and Lanvin powder, Jergens lotion and glycerine soap. Safe and warm behind the locked door, she was prepared to spend the night curled up on the fluffy bath mat that matched the perfectly folded towels. She floated in her bath until her fingers wrinkled and her feet turned white, the screams from her father having softened to whispers.

"I'd like you to come out now," Albert said politely as Josie squeezed a blob of lotion into her hand. "Do you hear me, Josie?"

"I hear you," she said, rubbing it into her skin. "But I won't come out unless you promise not to spank me."

"What did you say?" Albert said in a tone that belied his efforts to stay calm.

"I said I'd come out if you promised—"

"I heard you." More whispers from the other side of the door. "I promise," he said, with Ruth's audible coaching.

"Do you swear?" Josie asked, dabbing herself with her mother's powder pouf.

"I swear."

"On your children's lives."

He didn't answer. Josie tiptoed closer to the door.

"On my children's lives," he finally answered.

"All right, then," she said, cautiously unlocking the door, fully expecting to be yanked out by her arm and smacked on the rear. But her father did not lift a finger or say a word, and Josie realized for the first time that she could stand up to him as long as she could lock the door.

When she was seventeen, Josie decided to lose her virginity. All her friends had done it, and she was tired of saving hers for "the man she loved." She didn't have a boyfriend or anyone in mind, but she knew her only window of sexual opportunity would be a weekend in August when her parents were going away and she'd still be working at her summer job typing 1,011 recipes for a Jewish cookbook called *What's Cooking in Israel's Melting Pot.*

She met her "intended" at a concert in Central Park, a goofy-looking piano student from the Mannes School of Music. Tall and gangly, with a mop of curly hair, he reminded Josie of a large standard poodle, the kind she ran from as a child because they always jumped her and tried to hump her leg.

Eric Koslow was better looking with his glasses on than off and sexier when he played the piano than when he danced or talked or ate or walked. Somehow, Josie thought if he made love the way he played, it might work out all right. He would arch his supple back over his gigantic hands, which could span two octaves, and arpeggio and trill his way through Chopin and Beethoven, sweating and grunting as he banged out the notes, pumping the pedal with two left feet, humping the piano bench like an overweight jockey, crying out as he crescendoed to the finale.

"How would you like me to cook you dinner?" she said, screwing up enough courage to get screwed. "My parents are out of town."

Josie spent more time planning the meal than worrying about birth control. Should they start with vichyssoise or asparagus vinaigrette? Nothing too spicy or hard to digest. Strawberries or chocolate for dessert to make her mouth taste sweet. But halfway through the first course, she began to lose heart. Eric took huge bites and chewed with his mouth open. Even when he wasn't eating, a dot of spit clung to his lower lip like larvae on a leaf. "Would you like more chocolate cake?" she asked, trying to postpone the moment of truth. "A demitasse with *Schlag*? A brandy. Do you have a joint?"

She led him toward her parents' room—there was no turning back now—and waited for him to "seduce" her. But instead, he tackled her and fumbled with her clothes. Josie's heart was beating so fast, she could hardly breathe and couldn't stop her knees from shaking. It took him forever to get it in, and halfway through she panicked that her broken hymen might stain her parents' mattress, not to mention her guilty conscience for having chosen their bed to do it in. She waited for some epiphany, some sense of loss or gain, but when she looked at herself in the mirror, half-expecting to see her mother staring back, she felt nothing but a soreness between her legs and noticed a raw-looking hickey like a squooshed raspberry on her neck. The only stranger in the house was Eric, whom she politely asked to go home, sickened by the thought of actually sleeping with him. All she wanted was to crawl back into her four-poster bed and suck her thumb. She wanted her mother to smooth her hair from her sticky brow and tuck her in. Just as she was drifting off to sleep, the telephone rang. Josie sat straight up in bed, not knowing where she was, and ran half-blind to the telephone in her parents' bedroom, the sight of the rumpled sheets making her dizzy.

"Is everything all right?" It was her mother on the other end of the phone.

"What do you mean?" Josie said.

"Harriet Abrams just called and said all the lights in the apartment were on."

"What?" Josie was now fully awake, her guilt having slid into anger. "Is she spying on me or working for Con Ed?"

"She was just walking her dog and got worried."

"Well, everything's fine," Josie said. "You woke me up."

"Oh, I'm sorry, sweetie. Just do me a favor?"

"What?"

"Turn out the lights. You know how upset Papa gets when you leave them on."

Josie stood with the phone in her hand. Was there nowhere she could escape the prying eyes of her parents, their noses sniffing every crevice of her life? She put the phone back in its cradle, walked nude through the apartment, and turned off all the lights.

The name of the abortionist was Dr. Sluitch (rhymed with *pooch*). Josie had gotten it from her father, who believed it when she said it was for her friend Leslie Rosten.

"She can't mention my name," Dr. D. said with the gravity of a superior court judge.

"Why can't you do it?"

He looked at her as if she were a three-legged dog. "Me? Do you understand how serious this is? Abortion is illegal. I could lose my license. Go to jail."

"What about Leslie?" There was fear in Josie's voice. "She's the one having the abortion."

"She's the one who was stupid enough to get pregnant."

"It was an accident."

"There are no accidents," he said.

"What do you mean?"

"I don't think anybody gets pregnant who doesn't want to."

"How can you say that?"

"It's what I think."

"Well, it's too late now." She hoped her father could not detect the worry in her voice. "Could she die?"

"There's always a risk," Dr. D. said. He looked at Josie for a long time. "But this man knows what he's doing. He's a good doctor. Just tell her not to eat anything beforehand."

"Will he put her to sleep?"

"I doubt it. He'll give her some kind of sedative, Valium maybe. But who knows. He might give her gas."

Josie fought back her fear. "What if it were me?" she asked, half-swallowing the *me*. "Would you do it if it were me?"

"But it's not you," he said, his gold pencil poised above his leather notepad. "Is it?"

"No," Josie lied, building a brick wall in her head like in the movie *Village of the Damned* as she tried like George Sanders to hide the ticking bomb from her father's X-ray perceptions and psychoanalytical stare. He ripped off the piece of paper and gave it to her. Her hands were shaking so hard that the paper fluttered like the delicate petal of a white anemone.

"Thanks, Papa," she said, swallowing to keep the words from rising in her throat, tripping down her tongue, spilling out of her mouth in a torrent of tears and confession. Wanting and dreading his tearing down the wall brick by brick until her secret was exposed. She could see the whole scene, his disappointment, his incredulity. His questioning how a daughter who had had the benefit of uninterrupted, unadulterated firsthand sex education could get "knocked up," as he referred to unwanted pregnancies—if he only knew it had happened in his bed.

Josie went to the pay phone in the deli around the corner from school where every Friday she ate a pastrami on rye with a pickle, but the thought of food now made her gag. Mr. and Mrs. Klein, two elderly refugees from Nazi Germany, smiled when she came in. They wanted her to eat something, said she looked pale.

"I just need to use the phone," Josie said, walking to the back, where the Kleins kept their supplies—cans of sauerkraut, cases of Dr. Brown's cream soda, sacks of onions and potatoes.

"Of course," Mrs. Klein said as she ushered Josie into the booth, dusting off the wooden seat with a dish towel and settling her down as if she already knew Josie was pregnant. Josie waited for her to leave, but the woman stood outside the glass door, her arms folded as if guarding and eavesdropping at the same time. What was it about Josie that picked up surrogate parents, aunts, and *bubbees* like felt picked up lint? The sight of her father's handwriting with Dr. Sluitch's name made her stomach cramp—not because she was doing this behind his back, but because—his words rang in her ears—she was *stupid* enough to have gotten pregnant. She shakily deposited a dime in the phone and counted to twenty-five as it rang in a place she imagined to be dirty and dangerous, with yellowing blinds the color of tobacco-stained teeth. She was about to hang up when a man answered, his voice high-pitched and reedy, as if he had swallowed helium or had a clothespin clipped to his nose.

"Hello, Dr. Sluitch?" Josie had not asked her father what the abortion protocol was, but she knew enough to be vague. "I'd like to make an appointment."

He didn't answer for a long time. "Are you calling from a pay phone?"

"Yes," she said. "My name's—"

"I don't want to know your name. I can take you this afternoon at five-thirty."

"This afternoon?"

"Meet me at the Esso station in Englewood Cliffs."

Josie's mind was filled with static. Like the snow on late-night TV. She did not know what to ask or do, but she had the feeling if she didn't act quickly, he'd hang up and leave her stranded.

"How will I know you?" she said in a voice that seemed as high-pitched and adenoidal as his.

"You won't see me," he said. "I'll be parked in a black Lincoln Continental. You climb in the backseat and lie down on the floor."

"Lie down on the floor?" she repeated in a monotone, too scared to admit she didn't know what a Lincoln Continental looked like.

"And bring eleven hundred dollars in cash."

"Okay," Josie said.

"Make sure you're alone. Do you understand?"

"I can't bring a friend?"

"No. And don't eat anything."

That's what my father said, Josie wanted to say. He's an obstetrician/gynecologist. Isn't that something? "Will it hurt?" she asked, but he didn't answer. All she heard was a siren and the click of the phone. She sat in the booth for a long time, thinking that the only person she wanted to call was her older brother, but she hadn't trusted him since the day he tried to thrust his gherkin-sized penis between her legs in the bathtub when she was nine and he was eleven.

She had enough money in her savings account to cover the cost of the abortion, money she had been squirreling away from birthday checks, baby-sitting fees, and summer-job earnings to pay for a trip to Paris. She ran home to get her savings book and take the cash out of the bank. Luckily, nobody was there. Viola was in the basement taking the laundress her hot lunch on a tray with a pitcher of orange-sweetened tea. Josie left a note saying she would not be home for dinner.

Now all she had to figure out was how to get to New Jersey, a state that was the geographical equivalent of a Polish joke, where her father once rented a car that neither she nor her brother would ride in because it had Jersey plates. The thing about cheating and sneaking around was that you couldn't ask stupid questions, like "How do I get to Englewood Cliffs?" So she called information in Jersey and asked the operator.

Josie rested her head against the glass of the bus as they crossed the George Washington Bridge. The sun was setting behind the Palisades, and the trees that clung to the cliffs, their roots like fingers clutching the earth, were changing from green to gold. The sky had the sad hue of encroaching winter, smoky clouds evaporating into thin blue air like mist floating above an icy lake. She closed her eyes and tried to feel . . . something. She was good at controlling her feelings, acting *mature*. So good that when she was fifteen she had swallowed so much anger that she developed migraines, paralytic headaches that pierced her brain with blind spots and sent her writhing across the bed, arms flailing, legs flying, longing to throw up and sleeping only when her father slipped a sedative suppository up her butt.

For a moment, Josie forgot the reason she was on this bus and loved the feeling that she was going somewhere alone, without telling anyone why or where. She saw the long black car at the Esso station and felt a chill. What if she died? What if New Jersey were the last state she ever saw? What if she ended up like the woman her father told her about who had been brought to the hospital after a botched abortion and bled to death? Like all his war stories, they were told over dinner, interrupted only by Viola passing seconds or Ruth apologizing for not serving bread.

Josie lay on the floor of the car, feeling every bump on the road and smelling the dampness of the rug and fumes of gasoline. All she saw of Dr. Sluitch was the shiny pate of his head streaked with thin strands of dull brown hair, and a white-on-white dress shirt that cleared the ridge of a frayed tweed jacket.

She closed her eyes when she began to feel queasy, then

opened them and saw the sky rush by with swipes of color from the crimson leaves and spiky stripes of spidery branches. Then the car stopped and the motor went dead. Dr. Sluitch threw her a blindfold and told her to cover her eyes before getting out of the car. She swallowed hard, not understanding, fearful that she would be found in the trunk of his abandoned car in Newark, trussed and gagged like a Christmas pig. She tied the cloth around her eyes with trembling fingers and was overcome by the sickeningly sweet smell of Dune, his eau de cologne, which made her think about the boy she had gotten stoned with from camp who had gone down on her on a putting green in Great Neck, Long Island, and wore the same cheap perfume, which had clung to his hair and fingers like some awful disease.

Josie tried to peek through the patterned kerchief, not breathing but shuffling after Dr. Sluitch into the back entrance of a storefront office. As she adjusted the blindfold, which was sliding down her nose, she noticed the gray-green industrial carpet scuffing the soles of her shoes like bristles from a dirty nail brush. She felt as if she were in a trance or a movie where someone else was playing her. Dr. Sluitch helped her up onto the examining table and eased her legs into the stirrups. She caught an extra strong dose of Dune, which stuck in her nose like syrup, and listened as he washed his hands, trying to drown her fear in the sound of running water. She realized she was still wearing panties when she felt his cold, bony fingers slip beneath her elastic waistband and gently ease them over her hips, slide them down her legs as if he were readying her for seduction, not abortion.

"You can breathe," he said in a lightly accented English that made her think he was Polish or Viennese. "I want you to relax."

Then he pressed his hand gently over her stomach, ran his index finger through the downy hair below her navel that met the curls and whirls of her mons pubis (what her father called pubic hair), and began to caress the baby-soft skin of her inner thighs. She tried to close her legs, but because her feet were stuck in the stirrups, she could only knock her knees together in an embarrassed triangle.

"You're sure you haven't eaten anything," he said as he gently pressed her knees apart and draped her with a sheet.

"Nothing," she whispered, praying he'd give her gas so she couldn't feel him touch her.

She jumped when he slid the cold metal speculum inside her, and remembered hearing her father boast that he always warmed *his* speculum in his hands before inserting it. Dr. Sluitch said nothing and Josie ached for reassurance, kind words that everything would be all right. She breathed deeply and began to float upward like a Michelangelo angel, halfway between a dream and a hashish high. Then she heard the sound of scraping mingle with cries and whimpers. But the pain was more a color than a feeling—red, black, and shards of white splatting and splashing her insides like a Pollock painting, splaying her like a Rembrandt slab of beef. When she awoke from her sleepless nightmare, she was curled around herself, limp and bloody like a mongrel dog.

Josie waited until her mother went to a school board meeting to ask her father if she was abnormal. Whom else could she ask? He was the expert. Ever since the abortion, which she had never told him about, although the weight of the secret was like an invisible cord around her neck, she was sure there was something wrong with her. She couldn't have an orgasm or wasn't sure she'd had one, which meant she hadn't. She waited as her father poured himself a demitasse of strong black coffee and dropped a few pebbles of rock sugar into the cup, stirring with a miniature silver spoon, his pinkie sticking up in the air. He had strong, steady hands and she knew almost by instinct that he was a brilliant surgeon, so assured and precise were his movements when he carved a roast or wrote himself a note in his pocket-sized pad, taking a few practice strokes in the air before jotting down his lists or thoughts in delicate block letters. When he wrote her at camp, she could always read his writing. And the only time she saw him cry was when he slammed his hand in a taxi door.

"What's the difference between a clitoral and a vaginal orgasm?" she asked, sitting up straight and tall. Poised. Always poised. No matter how tormented or embarrassed she was inside.

Her father put down his cup and looked at her as if she had just asked him the time or weather. "A clitoral orgasm is achieved through masturbation," he said. "A vaginal orgasm can only be achieved through intercourse." "And is more satisfying," he added.

"For whom?"

"For the woman, of course."

"But that's not true for a man," Josie said.

He looked at her for a long time. "Why do you ask?"

"Just curious," she said, desperate to confess that she thought she was frigid. "I'd like to see a psychiatrist," she blurted out, hoping she could save herself from specifics.

"Why do you feel you need to see a psychiatrist?"

"I . . . I . . . just do." Josie sank deeper into the down cushions of the couch and saw herself reflected in her father's glasses like a goldfish in a bowl. Her dirty blond hair was parted in the middle and hung limply over one of her heavily outlined eyes. Her lips were full like her mother's, with a beauty mark above the upper lip, as if someone had taken a pencil and twirled it once to leave an indelible spot. Her nose descended from a high, broad forehead in a single line—"like a Greek sculpture," her art teacher, Mr. Henley, had said, his hand on her thigh. But she would have gladly traded Aphrodite's schnoz for Muffy Davenport's upturned button. If only her eyes were blue, not brown, her neck longer, with a cleaner hairline, her breasts fuller. There was nothing she could do about the nipples, which she thought too low and pointy, like the Ubangi women in *National Geographic*.

"You can talk to me about anything," her father said, lowering his voice in a seductive, coaxing tone.

"I know," she said, biting the inside of her cheeks to stop herself from telling him, hoping he wouldn't ask her any more questions before the silence forced her to confess.

"It costs a lot of money to see a psychiatrist," he said.

She didn't expect that. It caught her completely by surprise. Her father had never paid a doctor's bill in his life. "Professional courtesy" was the way he and his colleagues took care of one another's families, except at Christmas, when they exchanged cases of wine, boxes of candy, and Sulka ties.

"Never mind, then," she said, getting up. "I've got to do my homework."

She left him in his fat green chair and could hear him pick up the newspaper as she closed the door to her room, her girlhood room with the wicker furniture and posters of Paris Scotch-taped to the walls despite her mother's objections that she would ruin the wallpaper when she pulled them off. But there they were, stuck just like she was stuck after three months of college at McGill University in Montreal, where she had gone brimming with enthusiasm to study in a "foreign" country, unlike her friends, who all went to Ivy League schools or the University of Wisconsin. She remembered how lonely she had felt when she walked into the Royal Victoria Academy, a grim stone building where only Jane Eyre would have felt at home, the interior dark and cold except for a common room (the only place where boys were allowed) cluttered with heavy leather furniture and pictures of hunting dogs, dead birds hanging from their mouths. Josie had cried herself to sleep, then spent the rest of the semester *sleeping*, and transferred back to NYU after Christmas vacation. "You'll have to live at home," her father had said. "It's ludicrous to pay room and board when we have a nine-room apartment."

Josie lay across her bed and draped her arm over her eyes. She felt like a big black dog was sitting on her chest. She took a deep breath but felt no relief. The apartment felt like an inescapable womb—warm to the point of stifling, dark except for early-morning light. From the age of ten, she had wanted to leave the minute she came home, but except for minor forays to Central Park or turns around the block on roller skates, she was always back by seven, in time to hear Viola announce in her mellifluous Southern drawl, "Dinnah is served."

Josie sneaked out of her bedroom and through the dark hall, peering into her parents' open bedroom. She always knew when they made love, not because she heard any noise, but because it was the only time the door was closed.

The floorboards creaked as she tiptoed past the living room, where her father often read when he had a case in labor and wasn't ready to go to the hospital or couldn't sleep when he came home. The coast was clear.

The front door groaned as she opened it, and Josie felt the rush of air from the elevator shaft as it shot up to the fifth floor. The sound of the door opening and closing, its hollow whistle making her feel instantly lonely, flooding her with memories of the nights she waited for her parents to come home from the theater or a party, staring into the darkness, listening to the elevator on the other side of the wall. The unbearable disappointment when the door did not open; the relief and joy when she heard the sound of their whispers and smelled the smoke from her mother's cigarette.

She sprang from the elevator and flew down the stairs to the street, still wet with rain, and headed toward her father's office on Park Avenue. She walked, half-ran to meet her boyfriend, Chris Wentworth, whom Dr. D. had forbidden to stay in the apartment even though he had let her invite him to their gala holiday party, the event of the year, to which her parents invited all their blacklisted friends—the actors, writers, composers, musicians, and *all the other women.*

"But why?" Josie had asked. "Why can't he sleep in David's room?"

"I don't want him sleeping anywhere in this apartment."

"But why?" she repeated, feeling the strain in her voice as she fought to keep from screaming, *You fucking asshole!*

Albert didn't look up from the newspaper. Ruth pretended not to hear as she balanced the checkbook to the last penny.

"What do you think we're going to do?" Josie was standing under the archway of the door to the den, the perfect place to be in case of an earthquake. "Are you just going to ignore me?"

"I don't have to give you a reason." Albert's lips were thinning, the telltale sign that he was angry. "It's my house."

"It's my house, too." Josie could not control the fury that rose from her gullet to her brain, frying her words like cold water hitting hot oil. "You said I could invite him. Where'd you expect him to sleep? On the street?"

"I don't care where he sleeps."

"Do you really think we'd do anything in this house with you in the next room?" She was entering the danger zone. Red lights flashing. "Yeah, sure." She laughed. "He'll meet me in the bathroom in the middle of the night and we'll fuck in the tub."

"That's it." Albert slapped the paper down on his lap. Ruth turned suddenly, a look of panic in her eyes. "You're such a big shot!" he said. "Always pushing. Always having the last word. Well, smart-ass. Now he can't come to the party at all."

"Albert," Ruth said. "That isn't fair."

"You stay out of it," he said, pointing a finger in her face. She wilted.

"You're such a hypocrite," Josie cried, her voice steely with rage, desperate to win a fight she'd already lost. "All your talk about sex and openness is such a crock of shit! 'You can come to me with anything,' " she mocked. "What a phony you are!"

"Get out!" He was up from his chair.

"And an asshole!" She spit out the words and bolted before he could smack her across the face or shove her up against the wall.

A few seconds later, Ruth came into Josie's room and said, "I'll talk to him."

"He's crazy!" Josie cried. "Sick."

Ruth neither scolded her daughter nor defended her husband, but managed in her own quiet way to convince him that Josie's boyfriend could stay in the office this one time. She knew that Albert's reaction (or *over*reaction) to the boy was a wee bit oedipal, to say the least.

Now Josie's heart was pounding and her teeth were chattering from the cold. It smelled like snow. She knocked hard on the glass-and-wrought-iron door of her father's office and did a little dance to warm her toes. She had to laugh at her father's obstinacy. This arrangement was much better than having Chris stay in the apartment, where they would have had to sneak a kiss. She breathed in through her nostrils and exhaled a cloud of steam. Her heart did a flip as Chris came to the door, pulling a faded Yale T-shirt over his smooth, muscular back, combing his blond hair, straight as flax, with elegant patrician fingers. He had the ruddy complexion and square jaw of a Pilgrim, from whom he was descended, even though his family had lost its money somewhere along the line, holding on to twelve acres of seaside property on Martha's Vineyard that was worth a fortune but would never be sold. He was the ultimate goy, another reason Josie knew her father didn't like him and why she thought him such a hypocrite. Dr. D. liked to pretend he spoke Yiddish and was proud to be a Jew, but he would never set foot in a temple or let her mother hold a seder, because, he bragged, "I hate all organized religion."

The smell of sweat and sleep hit her in the face like the humid stench of the cat house at the zoo, a smell that made her wrinkle up her nose while drawing her closer to the cage. Chris caught her as she jumped into his arms, wrapping her legs around his waist and kissing his mouth, still sticky and pungent from sleep and tasting like sweet-and-sour pork.

He carried her down the hall, which smelled of rubbing alcohol and medicine, past the desk of Dr. D.'s nurse, Miss Orbach, past the examining room, where for a brief moment she considered making love with her legs in the stirrups, past the rows of file cabinets and into her father's inner sanctum, his elegantly appointed consultation room with the antique desk and comfortable leather chair, the sculptures and paintings, the carved boxes and school projects she and her brother had made him over the years. As Chris placed her on the narrow bed with the upholstered bolsters that Dr. D. kept for catnaps, Josie laughed that she was going to make love to this beautiful boy, this gorgeous *shaygets*, in the sacristy of her father's private office.

Serves him right, she thought as she took off her clothes, confident that she wouldn't get pregnant, because her father had given her free samples of the birth-control pill.

TWO

Gus Housman didn't look Jewish. With dark blue eyes and curly brown hair, he could pass—"a Shabbes goy," his father liked to say as he affectionately tousled his tawny curls. It was tempting to be like everybody else in the small Wisconsin town where his grandparents ran the general store and his parents taught school. But when his best friend, Kenny Webster, said, "My dad says Hitler was right; he shoulda killed all the Jews," Gus punched him in the nose.

When Gus was twelve, his father died. He remembered the night because it was spring and he had to play ball the next day. His mother shook him from a lilac-scented sleep to tell him she was taking his father to the hospital.

"What's wrong?" he had said, staring into her worried eyes.

"It'll be all right," she said. "It's probably just indigestion, but his color is bad and I . . ." Her voice trailed off.

"Lemme come," Gus said, pulling on his pants and reaching for a shirt.

"No." His mother was adamant. "You stay here. I don't want Grandma to be scared when she wakes up."

"But Mom . . ."

"Please." She held up her hand.

He would never forget the feel of his father's weight as he helped him down the stairs, across the damp lawn, and into the car, the weight of quiet dignity and disappointment, of wanting to do things he would never do. Like moving to California, getting away from his mother-in-law, having another child. He had dreamed of green lawns and ocean, never having to shovel snow or wear a hat except to protect his balding head from the sun. He marveled at his son's athletic talents, his perfect timing, his speed. In California, he could play ball all year long.

Gus helped him into the car and kissed him, tasting the salt from the cold sweat that had broken out on his face and head. He could still feel the chill and taste the salt, the last memory except for the waxy glow of his father's face, like a waning moon.

"Don't worry," he said with a weak smile, touching Gus's face lovingly. "Go back to bed. You've got a big game tomorrow."

Gus watched them drive away, watched so hard that his eyes hurt. Listened until the motor's hum had vanished like a vapor in the distance. He turned toward the house, a ghostly gray against the inky sky, and ran up the front steps two at a time, up the narrow staircase past his grandmother's room, which smelled of rose water and old skin.

He lay on top of the covers and listened as her rhythmic snore seeped through the wall, and stared into the darkness, seeing only atoms of air and specks of light. He took a deep breath and wondered if he held it long enough, his father wouldn't die. He had the terrible feeling that the only thing that held him from a thousand-foot fall was a flimsy mattress and flannel sheet. He reached for the baseball glove that he slept with every night and buried his face in the pocket. It felt smooth and sticky, aged and kneaded like bread, the smell of leather and neat's-foot oil making him light-headed and happy. He saw the green diamond of the field etched in red dirt and surrounded by clear blue sky and only realized he had fallen asleep when the church bells tolled and the sun danced on his wall. He lay perfectly still, the glove curled on his chest like a friendly cat, and listened to the lonely echo of the bells. He didn't jump out of bed to check if his parents were home or listen for the clatter of breakfast dishes. He lay frozen in the dreadful silence, the final clang hanging in the air like an executioner's ax, and knew his father was dead.

Gus got to California on a baseball scholarship to UCLA. His mother, Edith, only forty when she was widowed, married a furniture buyer from Milwaukee after his grandmother died.

"How're you going to support yourself playing ball?" Edith complained when he was offered a job in the minor leagues after college. "You need a profession."

"Since when is playing ball not a profession?" Gus said.

"It's a game, Gus. Teaching. The law. Medicine is a profession. There's no security in a game. What happens when you can't play anymore or get old?"

"Look at Dad," Gus said, knowing that every time he mentioned him she got that look on her face—hurt, caved in, the pain reemerging like a repressed dream. "He had security and a pension, but he never got old. He'd love it if he knew I had an offer. He taught me the game."

It had been so long since he had seen his father that Gus hardly remembered his face, but when he was out on the field, when he rolled up his socks and put on his cleats, smacked his fist in his glove and ran out on the grass, he felt close to him still. It was his father who had taught him how to throw, to bunt, to hit, to field, who had worked with him hour after hour. What his mother didn't understand and his father could no longer share was that transcendent moment when all the practice added up and everything was at stake and you concentrated, no longer afraid—because you were always afraid when you got up to bat—and your body did exactly what it had been trained to do without thought or design, without hesitation or resistance, and you hit the homer or made the perfect catch, as if the motion were imbedded in your genes.

. . .

When Josie graduated from NYU and got her first apartment on Columbus Avenue, she felt like she'd been let out of jail. Her mother cried as she helped her pack.

"I'm only moving to the Upper West Side, Mom," she said, trying to reassure her.

"I know," Ruth said as she dabbed her eyes with the handkerchief she always stuffed in her sleeve. "It's crazy for me to be acting like this."

"If you want, we could build a laundry chute across the park," Josie joked, knowing how much her mother hated to be alone. How her loneliness made her panic and her panic compelled her to fix and fuss, control and advise, until Josie wanted to strangle her. But how could it be otherwise? Ruth had spent all of her married life taking care of other people, replacing her dreams and ambitions with the tasks of housekeeping, and living through the accomplishments of her husband and children. She was always up when Josie came home from a date, sitting in the living room smoking cigarette after cigarette as she worked her double acrostic, padding down the hall in her slippers to see if Josie was still awake, following her into the closet as she undressed, sitting on the closed toilet seat to chat as Josie took her bath.

The first night alone in her fourth-floor walk-up, Josie inhaled the oily smell of paint, listened to the chatter of Spanish as her Puerto Rican neighbors smoked and gossiped on their stoops, spread herself out in her new double bed (reconditioned from the Salvation Army), and felt like she had died and gone to heaven. She admired the bookshelves she had built from cinder blocks and pine boards, the shiny gleam of her newly scraped and polyurethaned floors. Even the police locks and dead bolts pleased her.

She loved her tiny kitchen, which she had painted taxi cab yellow, and felt a palpable joy when she made her first cup of coffee in her brand-new coffeepot, lovingly pouring it into one of her new Italian mugs that she'd bought in a seconds store on Columbus Avenue. She hated breakfast but had stocked her shoe box–sized refrigerator with juice and eggs, bacon and muffins, knowing she could eat whatever she wanted whenever she wanted or not at all. Without feeling guilty or queasy the way she had felt every morning at home when Viola placed a steaming bowl of oatmeal steeped with raisins and brown sugar on the place mat in front of her. "I'm not hungry," she would say, but Viola would continue to cook French toast or pan-cakes, eggs-in-the-hole or Cream of Wheat, which Josie dutifully picked at but couldn't swallow. It was her father whom she liked to watch as he carefully cut the white brick of farmer's cheese, slid it on his toasted rye, pressed every crumb with the dull side of his knife, ground the pepper, and popped it into his mouth. He made everything look good, even a cup of coffee, which he stirred with superfine sugar and heavy cream, slurping it like an ice-cream soda.

Her parents had told her all through college that her "legacy" was her education and that they expected her to support herself after graduation, until (it was tacitly implied) she found a hus-band to take care of her. Josie settled herself in the lap of an old wicker chair she had found in an antique store in Water Mill, Long Island, and tucked her feet beneath her, the mug of coffee warming her palms as she looked outside at Zingone Market, festooned with bushels of bright red peppers, glistening purple eggplants, green apples, and yellow pears. She took a deep breath and realized her throat didn't catch and her chest wasn't heavy. She didn't feel anxious or like running away. This was *her* apartment, every rent-controlled $104-a-month inch of it, no bigger than her parents' den, but the space belonged to her and no one could enter without permission or barge in without a key.

.   .   .

In the end, Gus didn't take the offer to play for St. Louis, not because he was unwilling to disappoint his mother, but because he knew he'd never be good enough to play in the major leagues.

"We're going to Tijuana," Gary Weinblatt had said the day they graduated. Gus was younger than his friends, having skipped two grades in grammar school, the only nineteen-year-old who was still a virgin.

"What for?"

"To get laid."

They bought a bottle of tequila and some grapefruit juice, then drove south past San Diego and across the border. The whores stood in doorways painted red like their lips, shiny purple like their satin blouses, and black like their hair. The brothel smelled of chorizo and semen, and as Gus followed his "choice" down the stuffy hall and entered her room, painted flamingo pink, and aquamarine, he wasn't sure he would be able to do it. But he couldn't face his friends, who had ostensibly made this trip for him, or wait for his girlfriend, Doris Shapiro, to be ready to do more than jerk him off in the front seat of her car.

He couldn't tell if the prostitute was fifteen or fifty and he didn't want to know. All he wanted was to get off, to let go, to escape the life that seemed to be pressing in on him from all sides—the girlfriend who wanted to get married, the mother who wanted him to go to law school, the friends who had planned their lives out to every penny, knowing exactly how many kids they'd have and at what age they would retire.

He could feel the flounce of the prostitute's skirt between his belly and her twat like the frilly carnival dolls he never won. He closed his eyes and let her lead him silently inside her as she spread her legs wide and tickled his balls with stubby fingers. She smelled of cilantro and lily of the valley perfume, and the slippery touch of her breasts beneath the nylon blouse reminded him of his mother's underwear, the panties she washed and hung on a towel rack near the sink and the lacy nightgown on the bathroom door.

He clutched the pillow and buried his face in the warm brown neck, feeling an excruciating pleasure burst out of him, a surge of heat and power that stopped his breath and made him cry. "Oh God, oh God," he groaned, and felt the walls of the room fall away and the prostitute unhook herself from his cock, which continued to pump and throb. He lay facedown on the bed as she hiked up her clothes and held out her hand.

"Was good?" She smiled.

Gus nodded and pressed ten dollars into her palm.

Josie would never have admitted in 1969 that she was looking for a husband. She had a job, researcher for *Global News*, which meant she fetched coffee for the male reporters and wrote an occasional article, for which she got no byline. She had the apartment, the rent conforming to the formula of costing no more than one week's salary. And she had a best friend, Sylvie, whom she had known since grammar school and who shared the same interest in cigarettes, movies, sex, and rock'n'roll.

"What're you worried about?" Sylvie said, taking a long drag of her Benson & Hedges. She was the first sixties woman to cut her long, parted-in-the-middle hair and style it like Louise Brooks, the first to dress like a "grown-up" in Hermès scarves and Gucci shoes, the first to snort cocaine. "Why *wouldn't* you get married if that's what you're hell-bent on doing?"

"Because I won't find the right guy. Or the right guy won't want me."

"Oh, for Christ's sake." Sylvie picked a strand of tobacco from her tongue with a manicured nail. "There is no *right* guy. They're all a bunch of babies or bigots, winos or whiners. Who needs 'em?"

Josie remembered all the sleepover dates they'd had growing up, the endless conversations and questions about sex.

"No, you can't get pregnant when you're having your period," Josie, the gynecological equivalent of Anna Freud, said, quoting her father. "That's only with dogs."

"What about dogs?" Sylvie said. "D'you think people do it like dogs?"

"Oh, no," Josie said. "My father says you do it on your side. The man and woman lie next to each other and the man *places* his penis inside her." The *royal* penis. He made it sound like some exotic dish—penis under glass.

"Where?" Sylvie looked down at herself.

"In her vagina, stupid."

"But on their *sides*? That can't be."

They hiked up their nighties and lay on their sides, straining to see their vaginas, so far from anywhere. Sylvie was right. It didn't seem possible that you could do it on your side.

"I don't get it," Sylvie said. "Unless the man has a really long thing or *your* vagina is in your belly button."

Gus got Josie's name from his friend Charlie Dyson, with whom he'd gone to Yale architecture school—another scholarship that amazed him, because he didn't think he was that smart. But after graduating, he realized he did not want to design houses for rich people or build skyscrapers for corporations, so he bought a secondhand camera, went down south in '63, made a documentary about the civil rights movement, married and divorced a Philadelphia socialite who was working for SNCC, and moved to New York with a thousand dollars he borrowed from his stepfather. His first "apartment" was a room on Riverside Drive and 107th Street, where his landlady, thin and white as paper, slept near the radiator in the bathroom. It was in New York that he first felt he belonged, because nobody belonged and nobody knew him. He could walk down the street in complete anonymity, pick up a weekend softball game with guys whose only connection was the lines of the diamond in Central Park. He got a job at CBS because a veteran producer had seen his civil rights documentary the one night it played at the Thalia.

"How old is she?" Gus asked when Charlie told him he should call a young researcher named Josie Davidovitch.

"Twenty-two," he said.

"Forget it," Gus said. "I just had a fling with a rabbi's twenty-two-year-old daughter and I swore never again."

"Her father's no rabbi." Charlie laughed.

Gus kept her name in his head but lost the number. Twenty-two was awfully young. Ten years his junior.

"You must experience sex without guilt," his existentialist shrink told him over and over. "Sleep with many women. Experience passion without commitment. You don't have to be in love." Gus called Charlie back and got Josie's number. What did he have to lose?

Gus was out of breath at the top of the four flights of stairs. "You didn't tell me you lived so far up," he said with a smile. Josie loved his face the minute she saw him. Curly brown hair and deep blue eyes. But it was the smile that got her, a warm and generous one that revealed perfect teeth and crinkled his eyes. Not a phony smile; nothing forced, just an opening up, like the sun peeking out from the clouds. She offered him her hand, but he kissed her on the cheek as naturally as a friend she had known for years.

She slipped her arm in his as they headed downtown to a Cuban restaurant in Greenwich Village. In the cab, she noticed he had nice hands—long and graceful, with a hitchhiker's thumb. This was an important turn-on. Not just the hands but everything about him was well proportioned and athletic. He didn't have too big an ass or thighs that rubbed. He walked with a dip and a glide, an extra downbeat on the right and a lope to the left—like a black ballplayer who jogs rather than runs to home plate. The only minuses on her invisible checklist were his socks and his tie—his socks didn't match and his tie was too thin.

Josie hardly shut up all through dinner, talking about her job and the discrimination against women at *Global,* about the free-lance article she was writing on migrant labor, about places she wanted to go, her family, the war in Vietnam. Gus loved the way she jumped from subject to subject like a child tripping across a stream barefoot, cocking her head to one side when she listened with intense dark eyes.

"What's your film about?" she asked.

"The corporate takeover of the American farm. I've been shooting in Colorado."

"I've never been to Colorado."

Maybe I'll take you there, he wanted to say.

When she ordered *"arroz con pollo,"* pronouncing it with a Castilian accent, and the waiter scratched his head and said, *"Arroz con pollo*? You meen cheekin' an' rice," she laughed at her-self, blushed, and grabbed Gus's hand. "So now you know I'm affected."

"You don't have to climb up the stairs to say good night," she said when he took her home.

"It's good exercise," he said, bounding up two steps at a time.

"D'you want to come in?"

"Yes, but I can't. I've got to be up at five."

Josie put out her hand to say good night, but he pulled her into a warm, wet embrace, kissing her with the taste of hot sauce and fried bananas on his tongue. She liked the way he kissed. She liked the way he smelled.

Josie had never been on television before, but there she was on the six o'clock news, the official spokesperson for a group of forty women from *Global* who were suing management for discrimination against women.

"Did anyone ever actually say they didn't think women were qualified to be writers at *Global*?" The CBS reporter pushed his Kewpie-doll face with the dark immobile hair and polished cheeks into the glaring lights and dueling microphones.

"They didn't actually say we weren't qualified." Josie watched herself answer the question on the tube and thought that her voice sounded funny, not really like she imagined herself to sound, but that she looked pretty good except for the furrow in her brow, which the saleslady at Bloomingdale's warned her would be a permanent worry line if she didn't stop frowning. "They said women couldn't grasp the *Global* style."

Another reporter with big white teeth elbowed his way into her face. "But did management ever say—"

"It didn't need to be said. It was understood. There seems to be a gentlemen's agreement at *Global* that men are writers and women their secretaries, fact checkers, or gofers."

She smiled at herself. She liked the bit about a gentlemen's agreement. She was sure she'd be quoted in the papers and couldn't wait to see herself again on the eleven o'clock news.

It would be hard to say if Josie was ambitious or simply vain (the two were not mutually exclusive). Ambition, like aggression, was not encouraged by her father. She accepted his rules with a ball of anger simmering in her belly. Why could her brother stay out all night and boast about his sexual exploits to the prurient delight of her father, while she always had a curfew and felt she had to censor her fantasies? On Cape Cod, where the family went every August, Josie knew the women were the gatherers, the men the hunters; the girls the nurturers, the boys their tormentors. She and her playmates constructed elaborate houses of towels and sheets, dressed up in their mother's scarves and earrings, carried their stuffed animals and baby dolls like papooses on their backs, while their brothers jumped over bonfires, caught snakes and frogs, and roamed the dunes. They all swam in the nude and bodysurfed, played poker and jacks, told ghost stories at the old cemetery, and went to the town hall to square-dance, but the one thing the boys could do that Josie could only watch was to piss out the campfire at the end of night picnics, their faces aglow, their hands wrapped tightly around their cocks, dousing the flames in a great hiss of piss, the acrid smell of urine mixing with the salt air.

Josie got a sinking feeling every time she thought about Gus and wondered why he hadn't called. Was it something she'd said? Had she come on too strong? Was he involved with somebody else?

Gus clicked on the eleven o'clock news and sipped a beer. Next to him was Mona, his associate producer. He had started sleeping with her on location, doing what his Hungarian existentialist psychiatrist had instructed—bedding as many women as he could, so many that he sometimes forgot what he'd said to whom or what one liked and the other didn't. "Women are like the barnyard animals," Dr. Vladislav had said. "They like to be on the bottom." He spoke with an incomprehensibly thick accent, as if he were juggling sour balls with his tongue, and his slick dark hair looked like it had been smeared with bootblack. Dr. Vladislav believed most Americans, particularly men, suffered from magical thinking. "Vhat make you tink you deserve to be hoppy?" he said to Gus the very first session. "Vhat hoppy? You must live like tomorrow never come."

Enough of this bullshit, Josie said aloud after hanging up the phone three times before Gus could answer. What's the worst? He'll say no.

"I'd love to," he said when she invited him to a press screening of *Easy Rider,* all her dejection, pessimism, and self-doubt vanishing with his "yes"; all thoughts of career and politics, sex discrimination and thwarted ambition evaporating like ether. At the screening, the touch of his arm, the smell of his clothes, the sound of his breathing sent off sparks inside her, and as she slid her arm in his, her stomach fluttered. What excruciating pleasure to wait for him to make the first move (although it was she who had asked him out); to know they were going to make love, to want him without reservation.

He kissed her in the cab, his tongue gliding over her teeth, his hand finding her breast beneath the turtleneck sweater. She didn't say anything when he told the cabbie to go to his apartment. The sweet pleasure of anticipation. The blaring silence charged with sex as they stood at opposite ends of the elevator while an elderly couple stared at them as if their sexual buzz were flashing like a neon sign.

Inside the door, he covered her with kisses and pressed himself against her, pulling off her coat and dropping his jacket on the floor.

"I can't." She laughed, remembering the three-date rule.

"Why not?" he said, surprised.

"Because it's only the second date."

"So what?" he said, lifting her into his arms and carrying her down the hall to the bedroom.

Josie had been on the pill for four years, but this was the first time she had wanted to get pregnant, conjuring the child she might have with Gus, imagining a life she had seen in the movies. She lay next to him, sticky with love, and listened to his slow breathing, trying to match each breath with her own, tracing her finger down his long, strong back and touching his soft curly hair without waking him.

She looked around the room, which in the lavender light of morning seemed surreal—no furniture except for the bed and chest of drawers, his jackets, pants, ties, and sweaters draped over door frames and heaped on the floor as if he had lived for the past two years not in an apartment but in a giant closet. It didn't matter that she hardly knew him or that her Jewish voodoo—a belief that if you wanted something badly enough, it would never happen—was always lurking in her dreams. She liked his messiness, his lack of pretense, so opposite to the world she came from, where everything was neat and clean, held together by routine and ritual, the dread of chaos a special glue that kept the world from falling apart.

THREE

"Don't get rid of your apartment *or* your cleaning lady," Ruth said.

"Why do I need a cleaning lady when I'm spending all my time with Gus?"

"I don't want to know." Ruth held up her hand like one of the see-no, hear-no monkeys.

"Don't want to know *what*?"

"Where you're sleeping. I just think you're making it too easy for him."

"Too easy for what?"

"Not to marry you."

Josie shook her head and looked around the large wood-paneled dining room of the Fifty-seventh Street Schrafft's, where she and her mother were lunching before a shopping spree at the Saddlery Company showroom. Ruth's friend Elaine knew the owner and was allowed once a year to hoard purses, belts, wallets, and key chains—wholesale. Josie didn't understand her mother's Pavlovian reaction to bargains, particularly bags that Josie thought were drab and clunky, the texture of the calluses on the bottom of her feet.

"You can shake your head, but it's true." Ruth sipped her Manhattan, a drink she ordered for lunch only at this particular Schrafft's.

"You're talking like we never got the vote, Mom," Josie said with a wobbly heart, remembering how her mother had warned her *not* to knit the black turtleneck sweater for her college boyfriend because he would surely cast her off as quickly as she did the last row of stitches. And he did. Took the sweater and ran. "This is the sixties."

"I don't care what era it is," Ruth persisted. "Some things never change."

Josie took a big bite of the egg-salad sandwich on toasted cheese bread that was placed in front of her by the black-and-white-clad waitress, who could have passed for a nun.

"If you want my advice—"

"I don't," Josie replied, cutting her off.

Ruth ignored her. "If it were me, I wouldn't move in without a proposal."

Thank you, Mom, Queen of Gratuitous Advice, Josie thought as she took a big bite of her sandwich, the warm cheddar bread melting the egg salad; the cool summer crunch of watercress.

"What's the point of my paying rent on an apartment I'm never in?" Josie said.

"A rent-controlled apartment, don't forget."

"Do you know that I go home every Tuesday night to mess it up just so the cleaning lady will have something to clean every other Wednesday?"

"What's wrong with that?" Ruth said. "Good help is hard to find."

Josie was always surprised by her mother's long-held, deeply denied Southern attitudes, remembering the time she objected to Josie inviting a black boyfriend to dinner because "it might make *Viola* uncomfortable."

"Why're you so sure this relationship isn't going to work?"

"I didn't say it wouldn't work," Ruth objected. "I just don't want to see you get hurt."

"My cleaning lady won't protect me." Josie laughed.

Ruth sat up straight in her chair and sipped her Manhattan, the amber tint of the whiskey the same color as her hair. "I think it's very interesting that you're moving in with a man your father and I have never met."

"Interesting"? Davidovitch code for a put-down. "You'll meet him when I'm ready," Josie said, trying to sound grown-up but feeling the way she had when she was a kid and had "disappointed" her parents.

"Ready for what?" Ruth said.

"I haven't met *his* parents," Josie said.

"You said his father was dead," Ruth said, never forgetting a thing. "And his mother lives in Minnesota."

"Milwaukee," Josie corrected. "Maybe I'll bring him to my birthday dinner."

Ruth brightened. "That would be lovely. I was going to suggest it myself, but I thought you'd bite my head off."

Josie licked a dollop of egg salad from her fingers.

"What does Gus like to eat?"

Josie could hardly suppress a smile. "It's *my* birthday, Mama," she said, sounding like a truculent child.

"Well, I thought if he was allergic to something or was—"

"Kosher," said Josie, wanting to see her mother's reaction. "I wanted to surprise you. He's a Hasidic Jew who wears a long black beard and *payess.* . . ."

"Very funny." Ruth shifted in her seat. Another of her hidden prejudices. "How about your favorite? Fried chicken, Spanish rice, spinach salad, and strawberry shortcake?"

Josie thought back to all the birthdays her mother had produced with the style and taste of Ziegfeld—the special dresses she had sewed, the special arrangements she had made with the Good Humor man to meet the party at a designated spot in Central Park. The special lunches, favors and cupcakes for her whole class. The poems that rhymed. The presents . . . always so many presents that Ruth allowed herself to buy for her children but never for herself.

Ruth took the last sip of her drink and fished out the

maraschino cherry, soft with liquor and melted ice, and dangled it in front of Josie. "Want the cherry?" Josie plucked it from her fingers, thinking that if her brother had been here, her mother would have given it to him.

When Josie pulled down the cover on Gus's bed and saw a long strand of straight black hair on his pillow, she thought she should have listened to her mother. Like a forensic expert at the scene of a crime, she held it up to the light, knowing without a shred of doubt that he had slept with somebody else the night before. She swallowed hard, followed the trail of hairs to the sink, the floor, the tub. Who was this person? she thought. A woman or a dog?

"Oh, Gus," she said like a miner's canary before asphyxiating. "Was Juanita here today?"

"No," he called back, unsuspecting. "She comes in on Thursdays."

Josie held the hair between her thumb and forefinger—so easy it would be to let it drop. What an irony, she thought, after I felt guilty for snooping when he was out, riffling through the top drawer of his desk on the pretense of looking for a legal pad, finding pictures of his first wife, a copy of his divorce settlement, a love letter from someone in Germany written in calligraphic script.

Josie came from a family of self-righteous snoops. Her father thought it his right to read anything that was left open, including love letters or diaries; her mother held unopened mail up to the light. Her brother had sneaked into her room when she was talking on the phone or hid under her bed to eavesdrop when she and Sylvie had sleepovers.

"Would you mind coming in here?" she said.

"What's the matter?" Gus was standing in the doorway, his dark blue eyes wide and innocent.

"Whom did you sleep with last night?" she blurted out.

His face went dead. "Whad'you mean?"

"You were with somebody last night." Josie held up the hair. "And it wasn't me."

He couldn't lie. The soon to be familiar tautness in his upper lip gave him away. "Someone I was seeing before I met you."

Josie felt as if someone had pulled a trapdoor from under her feet and, like Alice in Wonderland, she was falling down a tunnel. She couldn't believe this was happening.

"Who?"

"Nobody you know."

"Well, I know her now. Her hair is everywhere—in the sink, on the pillow. What is she? A shedder?"

"You're blowing this all out of proportion," Gus said, taking a tentative step forward, as if he were testing the ice on a frozen lake. "Why're you making such a big deal about this?"

"Because it *is* a big deal. At least to me. I'm not fucking old boyfriends and rubbing your nose in their hair."

Her mother's words stung her brain and rang in her ears. "And to think I gave up a cleaning lady and a rent-controlled apartment!"

Gus couldn't help smiling. "D'you want to leave?"

"No!" she shouted. "Is that what you want me to do?" She could feel her stomach drop, as if she had hit an air pocket at 35,000 feet. But there was no turning back. No place to land. "Look, I'm not interested in wasting time or fucking around," she said, getting up.

"What's that supposed to mean?"

"That if you're not serious, I'd rather know now."

"Whad'you mean by 'serious'?"

"I want to get married and have children," she said, matter-of-factly, ignoring another of her mother's warnings—never propose to a man. "That's what I mean by 'serious.' "

Gus could feel the blood pulse inside his head. "I'm not ready for that kind of commitment," he said.

"I didn't say tomorrow." She moved toward the door and he

noticed how her skirt cupped her ass in a graceful fold, like the sail of a ship catching a gentle breeze. "Listen, Gus. I'm not a good negotiator," she said. "And I'm a terrible bluffer. My cards are on the table." She smiled. "I love you."

She said it so easily, her dark eyes steady and full of light. Just hearing her say it made him want to take her in his arms and kiss her, smooth his hand over the lovely curve of her rear, feel her breasts against his chest, but he just stood there, unable to move or tell her how he felt.

"I'm going," Josie said, walking out of the room.

"No." Gus grabbed her wrist. "Don't go."

She stopped and looked into his face, his navy eyes without guile, the eyes of a man who couldn't lie.

"I just don't want you telling me how to live my life," he said.

Josie laughed. "I'm not telling you how to live your life. I'm just telling you to stop sleeping with the woman you slept with last night."

Gus proposed to Josie at her birthday dinner, which looked more like a party for a twelve-year-old, not a twenty-three-year-old, so many presents and so much fuss. He couldn't remember his own parties or even if he'd had them, but he could still taste the dense chocolate cake his grandmother had baked for him with the icing on the bottom, big globs of crushed pineapple that stuck to the roof of his mouth, and walking up and down the aisles at the Riverside Theater in the new pair of cleats his mother had given him. And the Cubs game at Wrigley Field, where his dad had taken him the year before he died.

Watching the Davidovitch family was like watching a play with every member cast in a special role—her brother, David, the court jester; Aunt Lena, the fading beauty queen; Albert, King of the Mountain; Ruth, the trusting nurse. And Josie, the royal princess.

Their apartment was like a set from a forties movie—everything from the polished silver to fresh flowers, the coasters for the drinks and Viola being summoned to the table by a silver bell.

He worried a little that she was too attached to them, that she still needed their approval for everything, that she would never grow up, but he dismissed his doubts when he realized every time he looked at her how much he loved her, having admitted that he hadn't wanted to lose her the night she threatened to leave. So why as he stared at her sleeping next to him, her leg draped over his thigh, her breath still sweet with birthday cake, was he so scared? Because it seemed too good to be true? That he didn't deserve to be so happy? He pushed his fears away and whispered, "I love you," feeling her turn toward him and mold herself into his body, running her hands over his back and arms.

"I love you, too," she whispered sleepily, returning his kisses and leading him inside her without a word.

They rented a little white farmhouse with green shutters on the edge of twenty acres of potato fields, and Josie pushed the twin beds together so they could make love every night.

The house was like a dollhouse, with small square rooms and miniature furniture, crocheted doilies on the arms of overstuffed chairs that looked like overfed children, fat and squat in a house they had long outgrown. Josie felt like she and Gus were playing house, only it wasn't a game, and if this was the dress rehearsal for marriage and children, she'd been in training since she built her first imaginary house under a card table when she was three.

There was an announcement in the *Times*. "Not the greatest picture of you," her brother, David, had said.

She had registered at Tiffany's, hired Rudy, the omelette maven, to cater the food, hired William Greenberg to make the cake, Madame Roselli at Bergdorf's to design the dress. Ruth called her daily to discuss "the arrangements"—invitations, seating assignments, flowers, whether to book the Plaza or the Carlyle, to be married by a rabbi or a judge.

"Maybe we should elope," Josie said to Gus after her mother had called for the fifth time that day.

"She'll be all right by October," he said, hoping he could last the next three months.

It was only July, but on this Sunday, the only decision they had to make was whether to barbecue hamburgers or pick up baby chickens before heading back to the city.

"Just one more swim," Gus said, pulling her up from the sand and running down the beach to a deserted spot where the breakers seemed perfect for bodysurfing.

He ran into the water and dived under a breaker, his body taut and tan. Josie saw him swim with the next wave, his arms outstretched, his butt bobbing on the surface, his hair slick as a seal's, but at the last moment she felt a tug of fear and dived under it, feeling the water press her down, the sunlight swirl around her head, her hair swish in a whirlpool of sand and salt and bubbles. She sprang up and gulped for air, turning, to see Gus leap up from the sandbar, hike up his trunks, and jump over the riptide to catch the next wave. But he was gone. Josie scanned the surface with her eye—from the beach to the horizon, the horizon to the beach, back again, this time faster, a quick 360-degree turn. But he was nowhere. Swallowed up in the gray-green water.

She began to run, but the water held her back like in a dream where your legs are weighted and you can't move. She screamed his name, but no one answered, and she could feel the panic snake up her legs and around her throat and hear her heart beating in her ears. Then suddenly, she saw his face pop up like a bottle in the foam as he floated near the shore. She pushed herself through the leaden water and reached him as two gay lovers, flushed from their grassy nest like startled woodcocks, flew out from the dunes and gently pulled him up onto the sand.

"I can't move my legs," Gus said in a measured tone.

"You'll be okay," Josie said, kissing his face and shoulders. "Everything's going to be all right."

"I can't feel anything from my chest down," he said.

One of the men ran up to a huge shingled house with a Kennedy-style lawn and screened-in porch and called for help. The ambulance drivers were World War II vets. They carried Gus off the beach as an orthopedic surgeon, still dressed in kelly green golf shorts and an Izod polo, supervised the rescue mission. No one spoke as the ambulance raced toward the hospital, spewing clouds of potato dust over neatly trimmed hedges.

They entered the twilight zone of the hospital, where things are done *to* you and *for* you. No questions asked—as long as you had insurance. They drilled two holes in the side of Gus's head and fastened him to a contraption that turned him on a spit like a roasted chicken. When they took him into X Ray, Josie called her parents.

"There's been an accident," she said, looking down at her exposed body.

"We'll be there as fast as we can," her father said.

Someone handed her a white medical coat and she wandered the medicinal-smelling halls, bought a pack of cigarettes in the basement, even though she'd stopped smoking months ago, and drew the smoke deep into her lungs. Light-headed and confused, she thought she was in the middle of a cartoon. Or in Las Vegas, where there are no clocks and it's always midnight. She paced back and forth outside the emergency room, waiting for them to say Gus was fine, that they could go home and pick up where they'd left off. Then she saw her parents walking down the hall and burst into tears.

"I'm a doctor." Dr. D. strode into the conference room where Gus's X rays were pinned up on a lighted board and shook the doctors' hands. Josie could have been invisible. "What have you found?"

"It looks pretty bad," said the orthopedic surgeon, the same doctor who had been there when they carried Gus off the beach.

"He's dislocated and fractured two vertebrae in his spine." He pointed with an eraser tip to the X ray of Gus's neck.

"We're going to have to operate," the neurosurgeon said, his eyes an icy blue. "We've got to relieve the pressure if we're going to minimize the damage."

"Could he die?" Josie asked as they looked at her, amazed that she was there.

"It's a dangerous operation," the orthopedist said. "Even if he survives and the cord isn't severed . . ." He hesitated. "I doubt very much that he'll be able to walk."

Josie felt her father dig his fingers into her shoulder.

"What about sex and children?" she blurted out.

The doctor shook his head.

"His cord is not severed," the neurosurgeon said two hours later. "But it's badly traumatized and bruised." Josie noticed his surgical booties were splattered with Gus's blood.

"How long until we know if he can walk?" Josie asked.

"In about three weeks."

She searched the surgeon's aqua eyes. "Then there's hope," she said, smiling weakly.

"There's always hope," he said, too quickly. "But I wouldn't expect too much."

There's always hope, she repeated silently as she tiptoed down the hall into intensive care. Gus lay on his back, a crown of thorns oozing blood from his scalp, an ugly tube stuck in his nose. She tried to kiss him, but she tasted anesthetics and antiseptics on his lips. She felt herself sway but willed herself not to faint.

"I love you, Gus." She bent close to his ear and thought she saw his eyelids flutter and a smile flicker across his lips. "Everything's going to be all right."

Josie drove her parents back to the house. No one spoke, not even her mother, who usually filled all silence with chatter. She couldn't bear to look at the bed, the sheets still rumpled and sprinkled with sand, the half-eaten breakfast she'd brought to Gus on a tray, his gray T-shirt on the floor, still smelling of his early-morning run, her birth control pills on the end table.

"You must be tired, darling," Ruth said, starting to make the bed and tidy up the room.

"I'll sleep upstairs," Josie said.

Albert and Ruth exchanged looks, which Josie ignored, but as she climbed the narrow stairs, she felt like the little girl she thought she'd left behind. She lay across the bed, the chenille cover smelling of mildew and the cornflower wallpaper stained with moisture spots and yellow shadows. She wished she could cry, but nothing would come out. No tears or sobs. Only a dull churning in her head like an ancient time machine that let her turn back the clock to another day, reset the future and undo the past. Over and over, she thought, This time yesterday . . . Only five hours ago . . . If only . . . If only . . .

A broken neck? That's what they called it. *Quadriplegia.* The baby-faced orthopedist with the pouty lips never looked her in the eye. *Laminectomy. Fusion. Impotence. Retrograde ejaculation. Loss of bowel and bladder control. Spasticity.* He talked like he was ticking off a grocery list of unrecognizable horrors.

"Can I come in?" It was her father at the door.

"Sure," she said, remembering the same queasy feeling she always felt whenever her father came into her room to "discuss" something, which always meant he was going to criticize her and make her feel bad about whatever it was she had done wrong.

She desperately wanted his approval. Just the mention of "There's something I'd like to discuss with you" made her throat dry up and her chest tighten.

He sat down on the edge of her bed, the room being too small for even a chair, and she thought he looked older than his sixty-nine years, even though his stormy gray-green eyes were ageless. He had had his children late in life—David when he was forty-four and Josie when he was forty-six. Her parents often joked about his past—Ruth alluding to his neurotic attachment to his "sainted" mother; Albert boasting about a mysterious "romantic" past—having worked as a "gigolo" on a boat to Europe, as well as carrying on simultaneous affairs with two showgirls named Iris and Fifi. All part of the Davidovitch lore.

"It would be a terrible thing," he said in his gravelly voice.

"What?" she said fearfully.

"Not to have children." His laser gaze made her want to pull the covers up over her head.

"Who says we can't have children?" Josie said in a controlled voice that belied her panic.

"Josie . . . You heard what they said. He may never be able to have intercourse." (Not *make love* or *fuck* or *rock'n'roll*. Not *boff* or *schtup* or *hump* or *screw*. From the day she had learned the facts of life, it was always *sexual intercourse*.)

"They said we wouldn't know anything for three weeks."

Albert shook his head.

What was it about these doctors? They all shook their heads.

"If Gus can't do the things he's always done . . . If he's stuck in a wheelchair . . . If you can't have children. . . ."

He said it again!

"Wouldn't it be better if he died?"

"I don't want to talk about Gus dying," Josie said, sitting up from a slouch to a rigid posture. "I want him to live."

"I understand how much you love him." Albert softened. "I know what you're feeling."

"I can't imagine life without Gus," she said, thinking to herself that he didn't have a clue.

"You're young," he continued. "You have so much to live for."

"I have Gus to live for," she said, surprised at the force of her voice, but she felt so tired, all she wanted was for her father to leave so she could sleep and dream her old dreams and wake up before the accident, before the walk down the beach. Before the wave.

"I'm sorry, darling," he said, reaching for her hand. "But you shouldn't feel guilty if there's a part of you that wants him to die. I would if it were me."

"But it's not you," she said.

"I'm not suggesting—"

"I know," she said.

Dr. D. stared at her but didn't speak. Josie read his mind: Get out while you can. If he's a cripple, you'd be better off without him. I'm a doctor. I know the odds. Albert rose wearily from the bed and left the room, when all Josie wanted was for him to take her in his arms and stroke her hair, to let her cry and comfort her with words of encouragement and optimism. She listened as he descended the stairs, each step a thud of disappointment.

Josie closed her eyes but couldn't sleep. She tried to rewrite the script. Gus dies, leaving her alone, a widow bride, but she never finds another man who loves her as much or makes her laugh, and she ends up wandering the world like Adèle H., obsessed and crazy. Next draft: Her father's unspoken message—she leaves Gus and flees to some far-off country, only to discover when she comes back that he recovered and married someone else. The thought of him with another woman was worse than him in a wheelchair. She rewrote again. Gus is in a wheelchair, a toddler on each knee, because despite her father's premonition, they *can* have children. Isn't that what's most important? If not . . . Next draft. Gus kills himself, but how? She has to help him. Her father provides the pills, but she is caught and sent to jail.

Josie got up quietly and went downstairs, walked across the lawn, still wet and cold with dew, and drove to the beach. The water was alive with phosphorus; a full moon hung in a sling of haze. Josie listened to the gentle swish of waves as they lapped the hard, smooth sand. The ocean was so calm, it seemed impossible that only hours before it had broken Gus in two. The same ocean that had swept her out to sea when she was five, bobbing in her tube like a piece of flotsam, her parents so small from her seaward perch, running back and forth, their arms flapping above their heads like birds, inaudible screams blowing in the wind, her father diving into the surf and swimming toward her, caught like her in the riptide. She could still feel him grab her and flip her onto his strong, slippery back and swim like a giant turtle back to shore.

Josie looked out over the ocean and thought how beautiful it was, how if Gus died, he would never see it again. She wanted him to live.

Gus dreamed he was running down a hill, his legs spinning like a wheel, propelling him forward, so fast that he didn't see the wall. It hit him smack in the face, so hard and sudden that he saw stars. Then red. Bright red. Like blood.

He awoke in a panic and blinked his eyes. He was paralyzed. He had somersaulted out of the wave like he'd done a thousand times, but this time, instead of water, there was only sand.

He felt no pain, felt nothing but a hollow ache. An emptiness just like he'd felt the night his father died. Only now, he thought to himself, I can't even kill myself.

The last person he wanted to see was his mother, Edith, but

there she was bending over him when he opened his eyes, her angular face a mask of lines like a charcoal drawing. He had never thought of her as pretty, although the photos of her as a young bride showed a gentle woman with large blue eyes and a wide-open smile. Like his.

"You'll be all right," she said, her voice strong and steady. "I don't care what they say."

He closed his eyes to escape her.

"Look at me, Gus." His mother's face was so close, he could smell her breath, dry leaves and Pepsodent. "You've got to think it every day, every minute. You're going to be all right. You're going to walk. I don't care what they say. If the odds are a hundred to one, you're the one! You just listen to me, Gus. You've got to will it."

"Where's Josie?" he asked, searching the ceiling, his peripheral vision only reaching to the top of the door, her exhortations exhausting him.

"I'm here," Josie said, stepping forward and bending down to kiss him, the smell of her like fresh peaches. He felt a wave of desire, except he couldn't tell if it was a sexual response or the catheter. "I just picked your mom up at the airport."

"Not the greatest way to meet," he said.

"Does away with a lot of small talk." Josie laughed, wishing her future mother-in-law wasn't there. "How're you feeling?"

"I'll wait outside," Edith said, rising to her full height, a regal woman even if her hair and dress were drab as toast.

"That's okay," Josie said, feeling the tension rise. "You just got here. . . . Unless you're tired, in which case I'd be happy to drive you to the house."

"Take your time," Edith said. "I'm fine."

"But if you'd like—"

"She's fine," Gus said loudly, his voice the strongest muscle he could use. "I'll talk with you later, Mom. I'm not going anywhere."

Edith bent over him and touched his face, her hands calloused from so many years of doing her own housework and fixing things around the house, even though her second husband, Ed, always offered to help. Ed Davenport (just like the upholstered couches and nubby gold chairs he sold at the Boston Store in Milwaukee) was a benignly pleasant man whom Gus hardly knew, even though he'd been married to Gus's mother for as long as she'd been married to Gus's father. But from the day he moved in with her, he never tried to take his place, acting more like a boarder than a husband or stepfather. Gus couldn't imagine his mother having sex with anyone, even though he realized with a start that she was only a few years older than he was now when his father died.

"How's Ed?" Gus asked, trying to picture his stepfather but only seeing an overstuffed chair.

"He's all right," Edith said without much interest. "He wanted to come, but I told him to wait."

"That's okay." Gus wished he could escape his mother's gaze, feeling for the first time the inescapable constraints of his paralysis, his head literally tethered to the frame that held his neck in traction.

"Just remember what I said, Gus. Every day. Every minute. Don't listen to the doctors. They don't know a thing."

Josie couldn't eat. In just two weeks, she had lost twelve pounds, unable to swallow the meals her mother and Edith competed over.

"I don't put sugar in my coleslaw," Ruth said.

"And I can't eat my steak so rare."

"I think we should get a dishwasher," Ruth announced over coffee one morning after rehearsing her argument with Josie for a week.

"I don't think we need one," Edith said. "I don't mind washing dishes."

"No," Ruth insisted. "How about a portable KitchenAid?"

"I have a G.E.," Edith said. "Took me twenty-five years to get one, so I know what I'm talking about. Read every consumer report on the subject." Josie listened with fascination. This was the most animated Edith had been since she arrived. "The *old* KitchenAids were excellent. But the new ones aren't so good. Like everything. I still have the same double oven I had when I married Gus's father. Every year, my friend Minny tells me, 'Edith, get a new stove, for God's sake. Whadda you hangin' on to the past for?' The past? What's so bad about the past? They made things better then, made 'em to last."

"That's interesting," Ruth said, not wanting to give in so fast. "They leave my glasses clean and shiny."

"No streaking?" Edith frowned. "I hate it when they leave a film."

When Josie saw the beatific smile on her mother's face as the new KitchenAid (she won this round!) started its gentle whoosh and the tension ease between Edith's shoulders as it clicked into the dry cycle, she understood that all those shiny plates and iridescent pots made them both feel safe. She watched them go about their chores—matching socks, separating laundry (the darks from whites), scraping carrots, making endless lists on pads and torn envelopes—and saw that there was a certain comfort in it. Simple goals to accomplish, even if, like digging in sand, the hole immediately filled up again and at the end of the day there was nothing to show for it but an orderly house and an attic stuffed with hidden clutter and pain.

On the twenty-first day after the accident, Gus squinched up his face and willed the big toe on his left foot to move. He had been working every night to make a connection, feeling an electrical tingle; unable to see his feet but sure that he could send a message from his brain down through the tangled trunk of nerves to his big toe. He knew the minute he made the connection, just like he'd known the minute he swung a bat and hit a home run.

Before it sailed out of the stadium. Before he could even see it with his eyes.

"I told you," Edith said as she watched his toe take a little bow. "I knew you could do it!"

Every day, there was a little improvement. Every twitch and spasm gave Josie hope that Gus would walk again. Every pinch and poke that hurt or burned made her happy that he had feeling.

"The urologist thinks Gus will be able to have erections," Josie announced loudly at the restaurant where she was meeting the family. All heads turned as Albert glowered, David laughed nervously, and Ruth and Edith hid behind their menus. "He thinks we'll be able to make love."

"Sssh," Ruth whispered. "You don't have to yell."

Josie felt an undertow of embarrassment swirl around the table, but she didn't care. "Isn't that wonderful?"

"This may not be the best place to talk about it," Albert said.

"Why not?" Josie was not to be deterred.

"Because your frankness is making your mother and Edith uncomfortable."

"I'm sorry." Josie felt her excitement collapse into shame, the same shame she had felt when she ran out to greet her uncle Carl in a skimpy nightgown when she was twelve and her father ordered her back to her room to put on a robe. "You're too old to walk around half-naked," he'd said. "You're beginning to develop."

"So?" Josie'd said, feeling her perky little nipples, which until recently had looked like the slits of day-old kittens' eyes, deflate and flatten like a slow-leaking balloon. "I'm not walking around half-naked."

"I'm just telling you, Josie. It's time you wore a bra."

Below the waist was his business, but above it was her mother's, so the next day, Ruth had taken Josie to the corset shop around the corner, where a bent-over woman with hands like twisted branches asked Josie to take off her shirt.

"Let's see what we've got to work with," she said, taking the fabric tape measure from her jowly neck and cinching it across Josie's chest. Josie's nipples, hard as pebbles, throbbed with pain.

"It's okay," Ruth encouraged her. "We're all girls here."

"I don't want to." Josie cupped her hands over her breasts. "I don't want to wear a bra."

"But why?" Ruth seemed taken aback. "I'd think you'd be thrilled."

Josie shook her head. "I don't need one."

"You don't want to get stretched out and saggy." The corsetiere smiled a crooked smile. "It's very important to start off on the right foot."

"But it's not a foot," Josie said, pulling on her blouse and running out of the store.

The only place Josie could relax was with Gus in his cramped hospital room. Outside the hospital, everyone looked normal, young, and healthy. Everyone could walk. Even in the commercials on television—all those muscled bodies jumping into lakes, playing volleyball and touch football on the beach. The world was now divided into them and us.

"Don't get too excited," the orthopedist said when she met him in the parking lot on her way to visit Gus. "Most quads don't live past forty."

"He's a para, now," Josie corrected him. "He can move his arms and shoulders."

"But not his fingers or hands."

"Why're you telling me this?" Josie said angrily. "He's getting return. Regaining feeling and movement. I'd think you'd be encouraged."

"I've been around too long to assume anything will be more than what it is," he said, sounding just like her father.

"What does that mean?" Josie had never liked this man, but

now she hated him. Hated that he was healthy and arrogant and thought it his right to *tell* her what she hadn't asked to know.

"It means he may be able to move his big toe and shoulders, but nothing else. You're very young," he said, eyeing her uncomfortably. "You have a choice."

"What're you saying?" Josie couldn't believe she was having this conversation with the man who'd saved Gus's life. "That I should leave him? Put a pillow over his face? Why would you say anything now that he's getting return?"

"I'm just telling you that Gus will always have problems. With an injury like this, he will never be normal."

"Normal." She pulled back. "What's normal?"

Every night, she dreamed Gus was walking, running, swooping her into his arms, and then she'd wake up and feel a rock in the pit of her stomach and fight to breathe.

"I wish we could go home." Josie broke down, tasting her tears as they dripped onto Gus's chest.

"We'll go home," he said, caressing her hair with a tight fist that looked like a claw, the result of atrophy, which, like rigor mortis, had set in only weeks after the accident. "It's going to be all right. I promise, Josie. I'm going to walk, and we'll have kids, just like we planned."

She looked into his eyes, still clear and sure despite the shadow of fatigue and pain. "I hope so," she said, believing him but knowing nothing would ever be the same. And for a second, there was no before or after, no future and no past. Everything was present. At least when they were alone together.

But not when she dreamed. When she dreamed, she was always alone in a car without brakes, gliding down a hill in the middle of nowhere between unrecognizable cities that combined tall buildings with rococo opera houses, large piazzas with stark medieval castles. Then she was out in the country on a steep hill above the sea and the car began to pick up speed. She pressed her foot all the way to the floorboard trying to stop it, but the brake wouldn't catch and all she could see was the waves crashing below like a scene from *Rebecca* or *Suspicion*. Josie woke up wet and shivering, unsure where she was. Then she remembered as she unraveled the bunched-up sheet around her feet, and she pulled the mildewed bedcover up over her head and curled herself around the hollow in her chest.

"What's the matter, Mama?" Josie walked into the kitchen, where Ruth was wiping the kitchen counter with one hand and drying her eyes with the other. Albert had gone back to the city and Edith was visiting Gus at the hospital. She would be leaving soon to go back to Milwaukee to begin teaching after Labor Day, but she had already booked a return flight for the Jewish holidays. Josie couldn't believe the summer was almost over, but the potato fields, the only barometer of time passing, were full and leafy, their earthy clods of buried treasure ready to be harvested. When Gus and she first saw the house, the fields were a geometric maze of little bushes with delicate white flowers.

"Why're you crying?"

"Oh, it's nothing," Ruth said, stuffing the tissue into her sleeve as she continued to swab the counter.

"Tell me," Josie insisted. "What's wrong?"

Ruth hesitated. "I don't want to upset you."

"You're the one who's crying. . . ."

"I just got a call from Martha Loeb," Ruth said, her posture stiffening at the mention of her rival's name, the same "friend" who had married Victor Loeb, whom Ruth's mother had coveted for her.

"Catherine's getting married." Ruth caught the sob in her throat. "On the same day you and Gus . . . On *your* wedding day." Her lips trembled. "How could she do that? How could she be so cruel?"

"But it's not my wedding day anymore, Mom."

"But still. Of all the days in the year." She looked at Josie, her eyes flashing with envy. "Doesn't that upset you?"

Josie hunched her shoulders. "Upset me? I don't know. It's just a day like any day now that my wedding's on hold."

"On hold?"

"We're thinking maybe Christmas, but who knows."

"But Josie. How can you even *think* of getting married now?"

"What do you mean how can we *think* of getting married? That hasn't changed."

"Everything's changed!" Ruth said, her anger spilling over her tight lid of control. And then hearing herself, she began to back-pedal. "It's just that marriage is hard under the best of circum-stances. Even your father and I—" She stopped, lowered her eyes. "Once, for a while, he was . . . well, we couldn't . . . I mean . . . He had physical problems," she whispered. "Sexual problems."

"I don't really want to know," Josie said.

Ruth's neck reddened from the base of her pearls to the deli-cate point of her brow. "I'm sorry, Josie." She shook her head quickly like a pigeon shaking off water. "I shouldn't be saying this to you. I love Gus. But when I think of all the problems . . ."

Her mouth began to tremble again. "It's terrible to see your children suffer. You'll never know the pain a mother feels until you have your own children. . . . But now—" She stopped herself, mourning the grandchildren she thought she'd never have.

"It's okay, Mom. I understand," Josie said, wrapping her arm around Ruth's shoulder, rubbing her back.

Shouldn't it have been the other way around? The mother comforting the daughter. The grown-up taking care of the child. But it had always been like this, except when Josie was sick. Then Ruth had nursed her with the assurance of Florence Nightingale, the confidence of Marmee. It was Ruth who had caressed her feverish brow with her long, cool fingers, held her head with a wet washcloth as she heaved into the toilet, extracted the finest splinter with the skill of a brain surgeon, read her *The Secret Garden* and *The Little Princess*, scraped apples and spoon-fed her chicken soup. One of Josie's fondest memories was going with her mother to Atlantic City to take the sea air after a particularly bad winter of strep throats and scarlet fever. They stayed in a big hotel on the boardwalk, in a room that overlooked the slate gray ocean, and slept in a double bed with fluffy pillows. They were awakened every morning by a waiter in a short white jacket with gold epaulets and shiny black shoes who brought them breakfast on a large silver tray with pink linen napkins, fresh juice wedged in ice, a basket of muffins with all kinds of jellies, and a single red rose in a crystal vase. Josie had never seen her mother so relaxed. Lying in bed with her long auburn hair spread out on the pillow like a woman in a Corot painting, far away from Albert's critical silences and dictatorial demands, not having to compete with *his* flamboyant past. She had her own stories of growing up in New Orleans, eating mile-high pie at the Pontchartrain, crawfishing late at night, sneaking out to drive her father's car when everyone was taking their siesta, and, unable to stop, driving around and around until she ran out of gas.

Sometimes Josie felt they were more like sisters than mother and daughter.

"Don't say anything to Papa about what I said," Ruth said now with a sheepish grin. "Okay?"

Josie thought, What an irony if the great baby doctor, the sex maven who had all the answers to all her questions, couldn't get it up.

That's all anybody talked about at the Taylor Rehabilitation Center, where Gus was sent in mid-September. Death and fucking. Tough love and nooky.

"They do this test to see if you can do it." His roommate, Clyde, held his finger over his trach tube so he could talk. High on acid, he'd broken his neck diving off a roof, thinking that he could fly and that the puddle below was a lake. "It's like sticking your dick in a blender," he said. "If dats your thang, go for it. But it ain't nothin' like pussy. I can tell you that."

Josie couldn't wait to escape the smell of disinfectant and stale urine, the broken bodies, crutches, wheelchairs, bedpans, catheters, metal braces, tilt tables, and walkers. The only people who didn't mention sex were the doctors, the only normal bipeds in this whir of wheels. They acted like sex wasn't important if you could dress yourself (with or without a buttonhook), lift yourself from the bed to a chair, feed yourself without jabbing yourself in the eye.

Josie stood behind Gus's wheelchair on the corner of First Avenue as the November wind whipped off the river, freezing her hands on the metal handlebars. She tried to hail a cab, but the minute a driver saw the chair, he flipped on his OFF DUTY sign and sped off. "You fucker!" she screamed, all her rage and terror exploding as Gus slumped deeper in his chair.

Life was now reduced to obstacles and functions. How to get the wheelchair up the stairs. How to wheel it down the hall. How to get into the bathroom. How to take a shower.

Josie pushed Gus into the bedroom and suddenly felt shy.

"Come here," he said, pulling her into his lap and kissing her on the mouth. He still smelled of the hospital, stale and soggy, and his body was like a sick young boy's. "Help me onto the bed."

She scooped him up under the arms and lifted him onto the bed.

"Undress me."

Josie unbuttoned his shirt with trembling fingers. He looked like a sand sculpture after the waves have washed half of it away.

"It's okay," he said, gently pulling her close to him, cradling her head in the crook of his arm. "Don't be scared."

"Aren't you?" she said, holding back the tears.

"Terrified."

Gus ran his stick fingers over her face, down her neck, and between her breasts. She kept her eyes closed and returned his caresses, feeling his bones jut out beneath his skin.

"Do you feel this?" she said as she traveled cautiously below his nipples, twirling her finger around the curls above his navel.

"It feels good." He smiled and helped her pull off her clothes.

Slowly, awkwardly, they began to make love like two strangers, wanting to please and terrified of disappointment.

"Just relax," he said, knowing that she was in a panic.

"That's like *trying* to be spontaneous," she said. "I don't know what to do."

"Don't do anything," he said. "We don't have to perform."

Perform? Josie thought. What about *function*?

"It's going to be all right," he said, kissing her eyes, her nose, her lips. "Just give it time."

All Josie wanted was to fuck and forget. To escape. To be carried off. To be ravaged. Lying next to Gus, so thin and weak, in the twilight of their bedroom, the shadow of the buildings moving across the wall like a giant sundial, the stack of pictures from Memorial Day weekend unopened on the shelf, she felt as paralyzed as he. And for the first time since they'd been together, she felt alone.

He could feel the heave of her chest and soft curve of her hips pressing against his groin, and the touch of her skin and downy hair on her back made him stir, made him want to crawl inside her and be reborn. Whole. He wanted to comfort her and be comforted by her.

"It's going to be all right," he whispered in her ear as she rolled over and buried her face in his neck, running her fingers down the pencil-thin scar on his back.

"What a great incision," the neurosurgeon had said when he came to see Gus after the operation.

She felt him harden against her belly. She didn't dare ask or look to see what he was feeling. She didn't really know what to do, but when he took her hand and pulled it over his penis, she laughed and said, "I don't remember it being so big."

"Every cloud has a silver lining," Gus said as he pulled himself on top of her. She felt him fill her like a warm, familiar friend. But after a few thrusts, he collapsed with exhaustion.

Josie missed his penis, the first penis she had known and loved without embarrassment or hesitation. Not that she was scared of penises. She'd grown up surrounded by them, literally with them in her face—her brother primping and preening in front of his mirror; her father bending and bathing, secretly touching his balls through the pockets of his pants; the boys at school dances, their hard-ons pressing against her thigh; the flasher in Central Park who carefully wrapped his uncircumcised penis in a clean white hankie.

But in those days, it seemed that penises were always in the way, rude and intrusive, begging to be touched, talked to, and tucked in. This strange pendulous thing that seemed to have no purpose but to annoy. This silly thing that one minute just hung there and in a flash could stiffen and grow, swaying to the left or right with the slightest touch, transforming itself from benign appendage to dangerous sword. It was better not to look, to avert the eyes. Josie always felt the same push/pull—wanting to touch but flinching at the touching, dying to suck but revolted by the thought.

"I've missed you," she said, and waited for him to get hard again.

Gus remembered the first time he came. He'd been touching himself all his thirteen years, but it wasn't until he saw a guy in the bull pen pretending to jerk off a bat that he figured there was something more he could do.

He took off all his clothes and lay across his bed. His mother wasn't home yet and his grandmother was playing bingo at the Jewish community center. He loved being naked, loved running his hands over his smooth, narrow chest, pinching his nipples, caressing the tight muscles of his belly, and twirling the curls above his groin. He felt his eyes moisten and breath shorten, his skin tingle and the weight of his cock begin to fill with blood as he purposely resisted the urge to touch himself, to wrap his hand around himself and stroke. Just a little longer, wait, not yet, he chanted to himself, imagining the soft pointed breasts of his mother's friend Janice and the girls in his class who brushed against him in line. He could hear the neighbors' children playing next door, their shrieks of laughter mingling with the smell of summer that wafted through the window, a warm, heavy smell of manure and honeysuckle, wheat fields and warm milk. He remembered how safe and private he felt naked in his room, the sun spilling over his feet like warm water, the titillation and mortification at the thought of being caught, his breathing growing heavier as he closed his eyes and wrapped his hand around his cock, impressed by its size. Then he visualized the motion of the ballplayer's hand as he stroked the bat at first slowly, then faster and faster until he felt a mysterious pressure deep inside his stomach and balls, a pressure so strong that it almost hurt as it built and built until his head seemed to detach from the world and he heard someone cry and felt an explosion that was so exquisite, so strong, so divine, he thought he'd been shot to the moon and was falling back to earth through stars and clouds; wondering if he were dead until he felt something warm and sticky between his fingers and on his belly.

Josie didn't remember when she started liking sex, then loving it, then needing it, then panicking when she didn't get it. But she knew she was panicking now.

"I just don't understand why it's taking so long," she said, almost apologizing to Dr. Vladislav, Gus's old shrink, whom she had decided to visit because he was the only doctor she knew her father didn't know and also because he had been trained as a neurologist . . . but in Hungary!

"It all haf to do wif lebel-a-sesation," he said so quickly, she had to work to understand.

"What?"

"Lebel-a-sesation," he repeated.

"Oh," she said. "Levels of *sen*-sa-tion?"

"Lemme esplane. . . . I haf a patient—berry nice man—berry handsome—he fucka da girls all night, but he canna come. He go into basroom and hitta his balls wif nylong brush and then he come. Vhell, dis man haf created lebel-a-sesation no voman could possibly satisfy. Understand?"

Josie shook her head.

"I gif you nother esample. I haf voman—berry pretty, berry nice. She haf problem wif da men. No feel nossing. No come. I tink dis lovely voman. Eezer she smell or vagina too big. I send her to genicologogist."

"To what?" Josie was still picturing the nylon brush man.

"A genicologogist," he repeated. "Like your fazer."

"Oh," Josie said, understanding now.

"He get five fingers in zere. Vell! Only a horse could satisfy zis voman. She haf operation on vagina and everyzing be fine."

Josie stared at Dr. Vladislav, his teeth so crooked that they looked braided, a hairpiece that listed to the left, as if someone had dropped it out of a window and it had accidentally landed on his head.

"What does this have to do with Gus and me?" she asked.

"It take nerves longer to stimulate lebel-a-sesation for sexual activity zhan for valking or brushin' teeth. You be on top?"

"On top?"

"You like being on bottom wif legs in the air, no?"

"No. I like being on top a lot, too."

"Dat vhat you do until Gus strong. You be ze man."

"That's it?"

Dr. Vladislav's voice was stern, without a hint of humor. "You get ice cubes and warm eggs. You put zem between scrotum and shaft. You listen to Dr. Vladislav. I know dese tings."

Sunny-side up or over easy, Josie wanted to say, not knowing whether to laugh or cry. But when Gus gave her an engagement ring on Christmas Eve, she burst into tears.

"I don't want to wait anymore," he said, thinking they were tears of joy. "Let's get married."

"I don't know," she said, not wanting to tell him she wasn't ready, that she was still in love with the man who only a year before could run up four flights of stairs and carry her to bed like Rhett Butler. How could she admit that she wanted to spend her life with *that* man, wanted to have *his* children? That when they made love, it was *that* Gus whom she pictured in her head?

"It's okay," he said. "There's no rush."

"I'm sorry," she said. "It's not that I don't want to. . . . It's just . . ." She hesitated, not wanting to hurt him. "I hate the way I feel."

Gus wished *he* could feel. Or cry. It was hard enough relearning how to stand and walk. How to get to a bathroom without shitting in his pants. If he admitted how scared he was, he'd never make it. Like a soldier in the field, if he gave in to the fear, he'd be shot. He had to keep on going, pushing himself beyond self-pity and exhaustion. He had to finish his film.

"It would be harder for me," the orthopedic surgeon had said when he was still in traction. "I'm a surgeon. I need my hands."

"Fuck you," Gus shot back. "Whad'you think I do? Make films on my back?"

He was sick of doctors and rehab hospitals. Sick of crutches and falling on his knees. She needed time. But for him, there was no time, only will. To survive his body—this petrified slab of muscle, this short-circuited trunk of electric current—he had to bury his feelings, shove them down so deep, he wouldn't know they were there at all.

In the middle of the night, he slid closer to Josie, her body

sweet and heavy with the smell of sleep, and felt his penis swell.
Felt it connect to the dream that had awakened him where he
was running out to center field, his legs loose and buoyant, his
feet bouncing off the grass like pogo sticks. He smiled that he
could be so quick to react to her, knowing her body better than
he knew his own. He kissed her neck and nipples, waiting for her
to push him away while inching closer to his touch. He rolled
between her legs and kissed her navel, caressing her breasts with
his hands, moving his tongue down the soft blond hair on her
belly. Without waking, she ran her fingers through his hair and
gently pushed him down. She moaned as he kissed her inner
thighs, the trembling tendons of her hips. "Don't stop," she
whispered.

"*Harei ata m'kudash li,*" the rabbi intoned, and Josie, who had
never been to temple nor had a seder at her home, repeated in a
tremulous voice, "*Harei ata m'kudash li.*"

They were married in her parents' apartment after a vacation
in Mexico, where everything had worked—Vladislav had been
right after all, although in Mexico they passed on the ice cubes
because no one wanted to drink the water—and after her own
trip to an avuncular psychiatrist whose name Josie stole from her
father's address book, having no choice but to trust he wouldn't
tell him and would respect her patient privilege before bowing
to the medical fraternity of paternalism.

"Do you know how many people I see who don't know how
to love?" he had said when she told him she wanted to get married but was scared. "D'you know how many people can't say it
or feel it? Who come to me to learn how? I'm not just talking
about sex. I'm talking about feelings."

She felt comfortable in his office, the Persian rugs on the polished floors, the sun streaming in through leaded-glass windows,
the heavy leather couch like a giant walrus with the clean "analytic napkin" carefully placed at the head, the mahogany chair

with carved legs and armrests. He was an elegant man with a light Viennese accent, and he wore a vest and watch fob and sported a handkerchief in his breast pocket. "Do you love this man?" he asked.

"Yes, I do," she said without hesitation.

"Do you think if this accident had never happened, you wouldn't be facing a world without questions?"

"No, I don't," she said, wondering why her father and mother were always bad-mouthing their psychiatrist friends.

"Then you will do what is best for you," he said. "And there is no one in the world who can tell you what that is." Then he stopped and smiled. "I have a story. A true story. When my father was dying, I went to the hospital and sat by his bed. I held his hand and asked him if he could tell me something about life, something I could remember when he was gone, something that might help me. And he opened his eyes for a moment before he died and said as I am speaking to you now, 'Life? Life is very peculiar.' "

The wedding was not the "star vehicle" Josie had always dreamed of—the long white dress, antique veil, and satin shoes. Ruth had suggested she borrow Catherine Loeb's dress, "a perfectly beautiful Chanel, knee-length and only worn once." Josie didn't know if her mother was economizing or acting out of a subliminal disappointment that her romantic image of the perfect bride had been blemished by a groom who looked more like a prisoner of war than the marzipan groom on the top of a cake. But Josie did not object or think anything strange about borrowing her mother's rival's daughter's dress. She was used to hand-me-downs and saw no reason to buy something new and expensive. It was a Chanel, after all.

Gus walked stiffly on two canes, his legs like the Tin Man's, his balance precarious. Josie glanced at the faces of the guests—the faces of her childhood—and saw them frozen in terror that he might fall, holding him up with their eyes, hardly breathing until he steadied himself and stood underneath the chuppah. Josie gripped her father's arm and waited for her old piano teacher to play Mendelssohn's "Wedding March." She could feel the tension in the room—joy mixed with questions, questions laced with admiration, admiration tinged with doubt. Her bouquet of baby's breath and sweetheart roses trembled as she walked toward Gus, his lighthouse smile drawing her in like a dingy to safe harbor.

"This is a celebration," the rabbi said. "Of love and survival. Gus and Josie have endured a test most couples never have to take. They are a testament to strength and courage, the love of *other* more than self."

Josie was only half-listening, only half there. She had waited so long for this moment that she wasn't sure it was really happening. Then she caught a glimpse of herself and Gus in the mirror above the mantel—the same mantel that she had stared at every time she made out with her boyfriends on the couch in high school, the loud ticktock and gong distracting her from her rising blood pressure and incipient orgasm—and saw that they were joined together in a gilded frame.

Gus crushed the glass with his cane, and as they kissed, Josie realized he was crying. Even her brother was crying as he hugged them both and said how much he loved them. Ruth dabbed her eyes with an antique hankie that had belonged to her mother, and Josie's best friend, Sylvie, threw rose petals in the air. *Mazel tov! Mazel tov!* The sound of champagne bottles popping. The trill of laughter. The only people *not* crying were Josie and her father.

"You didn't want a big wedding, did you?" Ruth whispered as Josie was about to cut the cake. "You wanted to be married at home."

"Yes, Mama," Josie reassured her. "I wanted a celebration. Not a big to-do."

Years later, when her brother got the million-dollar bash, his wife the long white dress, string quartet, and five-tiered cake, Josie realized she had been lying.

FOUR

He first noticed it while doing a C-section, a simple procedure he had performed a thousand times. A slight tingling in his fingers, a weakness in the right hand. He once calculated that in his forty-two years of practice he had delivered more than six thousand babies and remembered as if it were yesterday the first delivery he had done on his own. He was a resident at Harlem Hospital and was called to a tenement on Lenox Avenue and 138th Street. The woman was having her seventh child. Just like a cat. Unafraid, instinctive. He didn't have time to get her down the five flights of stairs, so he spread newspaper over the kitchen table and had the oldest child, a skinny girl no more than ten, boil pots of water. Her other children floated like shadows around the tiny, cramped apartment while her husband smoked cigarette after cigarette on the fire escape.

He remembered the look in her dark brown eyes, the smile across her soft, wide mouth, the pride and sense of wonder, the love she felt for *him* as he helped her deliver her son, his black head slick as marble, his skin a lovely shade of mocha cream.

Dr. D. did not want to give up obstetrics. It was the part of his practice he loved the most. Not the babies—they were all pretty much the same—but the women. He loved them all, especially when they were in labor—the Italians and Jews, who screamed the loudest; the Puerto Ricans and Dominicans, who cried out for their *mamis;* the Japanese, who hardly made a sound; the Swedes (and *most* gentiles), who did it naturally.

He wanted to practice until he died, but he was too good a doctor to hang on that long. If he limited his practice to gynecology and gave up surgery, he could probably go on for another five years.

Josie sat in the waiting room of the Midtown Fertility Clinic, listening to the sounds of children playing in the school yard across the street. She was ashamed to be there, ashamed that after eight months of trying, she still wasn't pregnant.

"Just relax," her gynecologist had tried to reassure her. "Drink a little scotch and warm milk before you go to bed. You're a healthy young woman, Mrs. Housman. You're just worried because of your father."

Josie leafed through a magazine as she waited to be called and in a conscious daydream was transported back to her room on a gloomy day in February when she was studying for a college art history exam.

"What're you doing, darling?" It was her father calling. She loved it when he called her "darling."

"Studying for an exam."

"Would you mind coming down to my office?" he said. "I have a patient here from Gabon who doesn't speak a word of English."

Josie's fluency in French was a source of pride and vicarious pleasure for Dr. D., who had spent a summer in France working for the Pasteur Institute when he was a medical student. He had a wonderful accent and remembered enough to charm a waiter or a Parisian shop girl, but, like his Yiddish, it was mainly bullshit.

The woman who sat on the opposite side of her father's desk had skin so black, it looked purple. She wore a dark maroon fabric with yellow ocher swirls and black zigzags wrapped around her head and body, like the bedspreads college students in the sixties (who didn't live at home!) tacked up on their walls. She smiled when Josie said *"Bonjour,"* then turned to Dr. D. in anticipation of the information he was unable to make her understand.

"Tell her she is fine," he said. *"Normale,"* he pronounced in his perfect French accent.

"Mais non." She frowned. "I have not been able to conceive," she said in French. She spoke quickly, in an accent that was rounded and musical, belying the distress that shadowed her sad coal eyes. "Ask the doctor if he can help me have a son."

Josie turned to her father, his brightly patterned Italian tie peeking out from his white medical coat with pens and stethoscope in the pocket. He looked very handsome in his doctor's outfit, much younger than sixty-seven. His full head of hair was still brown except for his sideburns, which were only flecked with gray, and his eyes, deep and understanding, were soulful and attentive.

"She wants you to help her have a son," Josie translated.

Dr. D. laughed, but Madame Mobaso shook her head. *"C'est très sérieux."* She turned back to Josie. *"Si je n'ai pas un fils, mon mari me mettra à la porte."*

"Her husband will kick her out if she doesn't have a boy."

"That's ridiculous," Dr. D. said.

"I'm not going to tell her that." Josie could feel a tug of irritation that her father could be so dismissive of a culture he knew nothing about.

Madame Mobaso quickly added in French, "In my country, it is a disgrace to have only daughters." She rested her hands on the edge of Dr. D.'s desk and Josie noticed how small and delicate they were, the moon-shaped nails as pink and shiny as the inside of a conch, the gold bracelets dazzlingly bright against the moist luster of her satiny black skin. She sat very straight, like a princess, even though Josie could tell she was crumbling inside.

"Je vous en prie," she said to Dr. D. "If I do not give him a son, I will be replaced by another."

Josie hesitated. What did she mean by "replaced"?

"She's begging you, Papa. She's not the only wife. . . ."

Josie's father was quiet for a moment; then he reached across the desk and took Madame Mobaso's childlike hands in his and, looking directly into her eyes, said in a voice that could have calmed a stampede of wildebeest, "I will help you. I will help you have a son."

Madame Mobaso held her breath, then turned her round onyx face, lips parted voluptuously over Chiclet-white teeth, and waited for Josie to translate.

"Merci," she said, her eyes black pools. *"Merci, Monsieur le docteur."* She squeezed Dr. D.'s hands. *"Grace à Dieu, j'aurai un fils dans un ans et je l'appellerai Albert."*

"She's going to name her son after you, Pop. You could probably work out a deal to be the chief witch doctor, too. Have a couple more wives."

Dr. D. took a prescription pad and scribbled something on it. He handed it to Madame Mobaso and spoke in his doctor's voice—assured and direct, never condescending. She liked that about her father. Even when he was mad, he never talked down to you. Madame Mobaso sat perfectly still, not turning her face to hear Josie's translation, as if the act of listening might make her fertile.

"You must take one of these pills on the tenth day of your cycle," he explained. "In the morning. Before you eat. Then for the next fifteen days, you must continue to have sexual intercourse every day in the morning in the posterior position."

Josie translated as fast as she could, not wanting to feel what she was feeling, like this was some kind of bizarre ménage à trois with her in the middle. Why was she always in the middle of two people who didn't speak the same language? In the posterior position? Doggy-style? For a second, she wasn't sure how to say that.

"Dans la position postérieure," she said as her father smiled his approval.

Madame Mobaso did not understand. Josie quickly remembered her Rabelais. *"La bête à deux dos."*

"Ah, oui." Madame smiled bashfully as she folded the prescription and slipped it into the folds of her toga.

"Merci." She almost bowed to Dr. D. *"Merci, mademoiselle."* She took Josie's hands and squeezed them warmly, which made Josie feel a rush of pathos as Madame Mobaso, who had seemed so dejected when she first came in, now floated out of her father's office like an angel of hope. Josie prayed she would give birth to a son in nine months and not be kicked out of the royal hut. Or fed to the lions.

"Bonne chance," Josie said as her father gently ushered Madame Mobaso out of his office. "What did you give her?" she asked when he came back.

"Sugar pills." He shrugged. "Who knows. They might just work."

"I can't find anything wrong with you, Mrs. Housman," the doctor said. He was young and handsome, with a chiseled face and blond hair. He looked more like a mannequin from Abercrombie & Fitch than an infertility specialist, which made Josie feel even more uncomfortable and Lilliputian—not to mention the picture of his perfect goyish family, three blond children with matching headbands and a model-beautiful wife. "Your husband's sperm count is a little low, but nothing serious," he said. "*Technically,* he could still impregnate you."

"What do you mean by 'technically'?" Josie asked, thinking that ever since the accident, everything physical seemed technical. "How low?"

"A good sperm count is about sixty. Gus's falls in the forty-five range."

"Forty-five?" Josie nearly shouted. "That seems *very* low."

"Forty-five *million.*" The doctor laughed.

Why did he think that was funny? Josie felt her face flush.

"It only takes one." He smiled sweetly, and all Josie wanted to do was punch him in the nose.

"If it takes only *one* and he's got forty-five million, how come I can't get pregnant?"

"We don't know," the doctor said. "We don't even consider it infertility until we've been trying for a year."

We? Josie thought with irritation.

"It's been only eight months." He folded his hands and placed them on the desk in front of her. She noticed how perfectly tapered and strong they were, with clean, clipped nails and smooth white knuckles. She could see the blue veins through his translucent skin and thought they looked like the relief maps she had made in school of the Nile Delta and the Fertile Crescent. She felt a wave of desire for him and imagined kissing his hands, feeling them slide over her body. Maybe *he* could get her pregnant.

"I don't think you're infertile," he said, moving his hands onto his lap as if her gaze had some telekinetic power. "I just think you're upset."

"Fucking A I'm upset!" She blew up so quickly that he reared back as if she had spit in his face. She apologized, apologized so profusely, the doctor seemed visibly annoyed. "It's all right," he said, but she knew he was lying, just trying to get her out. "Infertility can be *very* stressful."

"I'm sorry," she repeated, and backed out of the office.

She wandered down Fifth Avenue, not sure where she was going. Back to work? Home? To her father's office only two blocks away?

She entered the park at Eighty-fifth Street, near the playground where she had frolicked as a child, past the brace of magnolia trees that she and Sylvie called their "summer cottage." Down to the Great Lawn, where the weather station loomed over the lake like a witch's castle. Into a hidden pocket behind the transverse wall where she had been bitten by a squirrel when she was three. Suddenly, the whole world looked pregnant—women with big bellies and voluptuous breasts. Dogs with swollen teats. Everywhere she looked, there were toddlers and infants. Baby boys and baby girls. Nannies and mommies. A churning, spawning, writhing reproductive stew.

Josie found an empty park bench and sat down so hard, the wooden slats and flat-headed nails dug into her bones. Her mind was a swirl. A leaf being sucked down a drain. She could take almost anything—Gus's lurching, falling, the weight of him on her shoulders, sex with her always on top, cleaning up when he had an accident, rushing to open doors, worrying when he was late. Worrying when his face got that sad look like there were clouds and rain over his eyes. Knowing there was nothing she could do to fix it or make him better.

But not to have a child? The thought made her dizzy with pain, and for the first time since the night at the hospital and her walk on the beach, when she lay awake alone in her bed and made a bargain with God (or the devil) that Gus should not die, she felt lost and trapped.

"I've got great news." Sylvie burst into Josie's office. "Remember that publishing guy I used to date? Well, I told him you and Gus had tapes from the hospital, and he's really interested in meeting you."

"What for?"

"He thinks there's a book."

"About the accident?"

"Absolutely." She drew her hands across the sky. "The love story of a century . . ."

"Yeah, yeah." Josie chuckled. "We could call it *Paralysis Lost*."

.   .   .

The last time Josie had been to the Four Seasons was on her thirteenth birthday. Her father had gotten a choice table near the pool because he had delivered one of the owner's babies, and as much attention was paid to the doctor as to the birthday girl. But Josie didn't care. She was used to his being the star, which by close association conferred a certain status on his family. There was never a mention in the *Times* of a movie star or stage actress, a chance encounter with a dancer, singer, socialite, or model whom Ruth didn't identify as "Papa's patient." So it was no surprise that when Josie was introduced at a party to the composer/conductor Leonard Bernstein, she didn't say how honored she was finally to meet the great maestro, but shook his hand and announced, "I think my father delivered your children."

She saw the way everyone stared at them as Gus lurched into the Grill Room—embarrassed stares and lowered eyes, a combination of fear and pity, discomfort and curiosity. Gus walked with a scissor gait, as if there were weights attached to his ankles and metal coils threaded through his thighs, a Rube Goldberg myoneural mishmash that could break down at any second and send him crashing to the ground. Josie was used to his stops and starts, his sudden falls, which left his knees and elbows bruised and bloodied—a giant toddler learning how to walk—but whenever they were out in public, she could feel the tension in the room, could hear the silence as people held their breath at every step, poised to jump up and help him, resenting how uncomfortable his disability made them feel.

Ted Wyman looked like a walking, talking specimen of taxidermy, his buffed-up chest snug against his dark blue Turnbull & Asser shirt, his too-small head a lollipop above a stiff white collar. Josie figured his clothes cost more than a year's rent for their rent-controlled apartment. He spoke with a Gatsbyesque lockjaw, the scion of an old publishing family, and as he called for the waiter with a wave of his signet ring, Josie appreciated Gus's lack of clothes sense, although it had always annoyed her that he wore the same blue oxford shirts, chinos, and tattered tweed jacket 365 days of the year.

"Sylvie told me about the tapes," Wyman said, tasting the wine and nodding for the waiter to pour. "How'd you come to make them?"

"When I was first hurt, I couldn't move my fingers," Gus said. "I bought a tape recorder so I'd have someone to talk to when Josie wasn't there."

"Vicious surf," Wyman said. "I was thrown that same weekend. Sprained my shoulder." He rubbed his arm with an inordinately small hand for such an ursine man. "Still hurts me when I play tennis." Josie felt the cold white wine slide down her gullet and settle in her empty stomach. "My polo days are over."

Poor you, Josie thought. "Do you really think there's a book here?" she asked, wanting to order.

"I think it's an incredible story," Wyman said. "A love story with the immediacy of a documentary. Were you married when it happened?" He ran his eyes quickly over Josie's sweater.

"No. Engaged."

"Not many women would do what you did."

"What?" Josie smiled. "Marry a cripple?"

For a moment, he seemed taken aback and quickly called for the menus. "I know my girlfriend wouldn't have stuck by me."

"Wrong girlfriend," Josie said, fixing Mr. Wyman with sloe eyes and thinking, If only it had been *you* who broke your neck and Gus who sprained his shoulder.

"I don't think anybody can say what he would have done," Gus said, steering the conversation into safer waters. "Nobody plans to break his neck."

"Nobody plans for anything these days." Wyman held the wine in his mouth before swallowing, and Josie wondered what his sperm count was. "But I think there's a market for inspirational love stories. Against all odds. With a beautiful young woman at your side."

Josie wondered what people thought. What their fantasies were. *Lady Chatterley's Lover* or *The Story of O*. When she first went back to *Global* after a three-month hiatus, a coworker whom she had never liked accosted her at the coffee wagon, put her big hands on Josie's shoulders, and said, "Boy, you sure must be horny." For someone who swore and loved dirty jokes, who thought constantly about sex and rarely looked at a person without imagining them nude, who had made pornos in her head from the first time she ventured alone to the Pussycat Theater, Josie was shocked. Why did people think they could say anything to her now? That they could unburden themselves, confess their fears and "share" their feelings. In the hospital, people had lined up to tell Gus their problems like he was their father confessor, their paralyzed priest. A truly captive audience. Women she hardly knew now assumed a certain intimacy with her, telling her about their failing marriages or hopeless affairs. It was as if the *normal* world had an investment in their being heroes.

Write a book about their accident? Why not?

"I think there's a movie here, too," Wyman enthused, popping a bacon-wrapped shrimp into his mouth. "Like *The Men*."

Josie preferred Marlon Brando in *A Streetcar Named Desire*. "*The Men*?" she said brightly. "My favorite movie!"

Two days after Teddy Wyman made a deal with them to write a book (for twice the money Josie was earning at *Global*), Josie thought she might be pregnant. Her BBT chart, a graph of dots and lines corresponding to her body temperature, was elevated, or, more simply, she was late with her period.

This was another moment she had dreamed of, rehearsed, and replayed a thousand times. Like the scene in *It's a Wonderful*

Life when Donna Reed tells Jimmy Stewart that she's pregnant—
"George Bailey lassos stork."

She remembered every movie that had to do with pregnancy—
even unwanted—*Fanny*, *A Place in the Sun*, *A Taste of Honey*,
Georgie Girl, *The L-Shaped Room*, *Seven Brides for Seven Brothers*
(her favorite—all those strapping red-haired brothers holed up in
Montana!).

Josie felt a rush of excitement, a frisson of anticipation when
she pictured telling Gus and her parents that she was going to
have a baby.

Ezra Eliason began going to the Stanley Isaacs Neighborhood Center to play checkers with his grandfather, an enormous man who still spoke Russian and loved to cook. There,
in the large sunny room where it looked like God had tipped
a bottle on its side and the only people to have slipped through
the neck were over eighty, he would listen to the *alter Kockers*
reminisce about their past, making the hard times seem like
good times, the street fights with Italians, Irish, and Poles
like block parties. He felt closer to them than he did to his
own father, who only *talked* when he was yelling, bursting into
Ezra's room and screaming at him to turn down the *fucking
music*, cuffing him around the head for smoking dope, then
slipping him a fifty the next morning because he didn't
want him going back to the old neighborhood to buy his
shit. Ezra liked it better in Brooklyn than Ronkonkoma, where
he had moved with his mother and younger sister when his
father began making money in the air-conditioning/forced-
air-heating business, following the burgeoning middle class into
the suburbs.

Smoking a joint, dropping a tab of acid as he rode the train
to the city, he forgot about school. He couldn't do it, the
words in his head never coming out the way he heard them;

his tongue doing funny things with vowels and dependent clauses. But he was good with things—old cars and boats, tape recorders and stereos. The last gift his mother had given him was a super-8 camera, but he hadn't touched it since she died.

He looked a lot like his mother—a full, voluptuous mouth, olive complexion, and high cheekbones. Neither short nor tall, but what would be described as "average," he exuded strength and health and athletic prowess. He had a slightly pigeon-toed walk and shock of dark brown hair, which he combed nervously with his peasant fingers. But what made him so appealing was neither intelligence nor wit, but a certain shyness mixed with an irresistible sexual confidence.

He started sleeping around when he was just fifteen, and he knew from the first fuck that he was really good. Talented. Far from his father's bullying, safe from his mother's illness, he felt free and, at the same time, in control. He liked to do it with his eyes open, looking straight into his lover's face, watch her squirm and part her lips, hold on to him as he plugged deep into her body, flipping her over and doing it from behind, sitting her on his lap and sucking her tits. He liked to watch his lovers cry out "I love you" while he buried his face in their luscious folds and tasted them as they squirted in his mouth like little clams at the shore. He liked to wait as long as he could, diving deep into their warmth, his thick brown hair black with sweat, his back glistening, his ass wet as the day he was born, coming with a surge of power that felt as if he were breaking the sound barrier. Except he never said a word, just whimpered like a puppy.

Albert stood out in the sea of elderly people who came to the center. Unlike Ezra's grandfather and most of the men who shuffled through the halls in pee-stained khakis and baggy sweatsuits in neon hues of purple and turquoise, Albert always wore an elegant silk tie and Jaeger jacket. Ezra appreciated nice clothes, even if his father accused him of being "a fairy" when he bought his first designer suit.

"What the hell are you doing?" Albert barked at Ezra as he held up the camera.

"Leave him alone," Lena chided her brother. "He's making a movie." She smiled at the camera.

"I'm sorry," Ezra apologized. "I should've asked first."

"What kind of movie?" Albert asked, his eyes narrowing with suspicion.

"I don't know yet."

"Who're you making it for?"

"I'm applying to film school."

"What's your name?"

"Ezra." He stuck out his hand.

"Ezra who?" Albert gave him a firm handshake and stared him in the eye.

"Eliason. Sol Baumann was my grandfather."

"Oh." Albert softened. "You're Rachel's son."

Ezra nodded.

"I loved your mother. She was a wonderful woman," he said as he threw the dice onto the backgammon board and moved the thick round pieces from point to point.

"How'd you know her?" Ezra asked.

"She was my patient."

"Everybody was his patient," Lena said, throwing double sixes on the board.

Albert looked up into Ezra's handsome face, recognizing the same huge brown eyes and luscious lips his mother had had. "I even delivered you."

"No kidding." Ezra's eyes lit up.

"You were a breach, as I recall. Your poor mother was in labor for thirty-six hours."

"I wouldn't know." Ezra laughed with the same melodious laugh as Rachel.

"Hurry up and move," Lena said, shaking the dice impatiently in the leather cup.

"How is she? I haven't seen her in years."

Ezra didn't answer for a minute, shocked whenever anyone didn't know his mother was dead, upset to repeat a fact that made his voice crack. "She died last May," he said, shaking his head and coughing to stop the tears.

"I'm sorry," Albert said. "I didn't know. What of? Cancer?"

Ezra nodded.

"Whatever happened to your father?" Albert asked, remembering a coarse, gruff man who had said after the delivery, "Sew her up real tight."

"He remarried."

"So soon?"

Ezra nodded, a hint of discomfort passing over his eyes like a stray cloud over the sun.

"Younger woman?"

"Is it all right if I film you?" he asked, changing the subject, wondering if the doctor knew that his father had started having an affair right after his mother's double mastectomy and had left Ezra to take care of her.

"So, what do you want to know?" Albert sat up in his chair, waiting for Lena to set up another game.

"Where were you born?" Ezra asked, bringing the camera up to his eye.

"At French Hospital. I was the first of my mother's children to be born in a hospital. My sisters were all born at home."

"Where'd you live?"

"On the corner of Crystal Street and Belmont Avenue."

"In East New York," Ezra said.

"You know it?"

"I grew up near Pitkin Avenue."

"No kidding." Albert knew he liked this boy.

"Do you remember it?"

"Do I remember it?" Albert's eyes were dancing. "Like yesterday."

"So tell me," Ezra said as the camera began to roll.

Josie told her parents the minute they came into the restaurant, before they'd ordered drinks or looked at the menu or nibbled a crust of bread.

"I think I'm pregnant," she almost shouted.

"Oh, darling." Ruth sucked in her breath and brought her hands to her mouth. "How wonderful!"

"Are you sure?" Albert asked with professional coolness.

"I'm a week late and my breasts are sore."

"But have you had a urine test?"

Josie suddenly felt insecure and stupid for telling them so soon. She wasn't *sure*. It could all be a trick. She'd read about false pregnancies, miscarriages, ectopic pregnancies.

"I'm sure you're fine," Albert said, reading her mind. "But it's smart not to say anything for the first three months."

"Oh, stop it, Albert." Ruth reached across the table and grabbed Josie's hand. "You'll be fine."

Josie remembered the night her father had come into her room to kiss her good night and she had asked him if when she grew up and had a baby he would take care of her. "Oh, no," he said quickly. "I'd be too involved. I mean, if anything went wrong, I'd be too close."

Too close? Wouldn't she want her father close if anything went wrong? Wouldn't she want her doctor to be involved? For years, she dreamed up all sorts of dramas where her father would have to deliver her—on a plane where there were no doctors; on a Caribbean island before the banana boat arrived from the mainland. All kinds of dramatic scenarios in all sorts of exotic places, but no matter what the scene, the hero was always her father, the savior with the little black bag.

Josie got up to go to the bathroom, feeling a heaviness in her groin. "Let me be pregnant," she prayed as she sat down on the toilet, not wanting to look at her panties. But look she did, and there it was—the dreaded spot, the red-brown splotch, the smear of disappointment, the scarlet *I* for infertility. She wiped again to make sure, shoving the toilet paper up with her finger, hoping it would come out clean but knowing from her cramps and monthly pallor that her "friend" was now the enemy. Why did I have to say anything? she asked herself, feeling an overwhelming attack of Jewish voodoo.

"What's the matter, darling?" Ruth asked, seeing the tears brimming in Josie's eyes, recognizing the tightness around her mouth.

She shook her head, knowing if she spoke, she'd cry.

"Are you all right?" Ruth caressed her shoulder as Gus took her hand.

"What's wrong?" he asked.

"I don't feel very well."

"We'll get the check." Gus called for the waiter.

"D'you feel queasy?" her father asked. "Morning sickness—"

"I'm not pregnant," Josie burst out, anger and disappointment colliding in an explosion of humiliation and pain. "I got my period."

"Oh no," Ruth cried. "Maybe you're just spotting."

"I don't want to talk about it," Josie said. "I want to go home."

"It's okay, sweetheart." Ruth handed her a tissue. "It took me six months to get pregnant with David."

"I've been trying for a year."

"And then I miscarried once—"

Josie felt a surge of jealousy that her mother was a mother, and she remembered a letter her father had written Ruth on Cape Cod when she had had a miscarriage and he was stuck in the city, David was at camp, and Josie and her mother were alone. "Sometimes there are apples that do not grow round and juicy and red because they're not healthy and must fall off the tree before they can ripen." Ruth's lips had trembled as she read and big pearly tears splattered on the light blue onionskin. Josie hadn't understood the metaphor, but she had touched her mother's cheeks with a chubby hand and told her not to cry. But now, all she could see was that tree filled with luscious fruit and one shriveled prune.

"Have you had an infertility workup?" Albert finally asked.

"They say there's nothing wrong. That we should keep on trying."

"Or think about adopting," Gus said.

"Adopting?" Ruth looked horrified. "Why would you want to adopt if you could have a baby of your own?"

"Because we want a family," Gus said.

"But d'you know how long it can take to get a white baby?"

"Who says we have to adopt a white baby?" He fixed Ruth with his dark blue eyes, which now looked like black ice. "There are plenty of kids who need families. African-American and Spanish, orphans from Korea and the Philippines."

Ruth looked at Gus as if expecting him to say, Only kidding, but Albert knew he was serious.

"Do you mean to tell me you'd adopt a Negro child rather than have a kid of your own?" He leaned forward and hunched his shoulders toward his ears the way he did when he drove a car, riding the gas pedal with a leaden foot, clutching the steering wheel with white knuckles. Josie could feel the storm brewing, the boat tossing in the wind. And she already felt seasick.

"I didn't say that," Gus said, unafraid of Albert's temper. "We'll keep on trying, but yes, I'd adopt a black child. Do you have a problem with that?"

"You're goddamn right I do!"

Ruth slid her hand over and touched Albert's arm.

"Why?" Gus said softly.

"Oh, come on. You don't think it'd be harder to raise a black child than a white one? Adopted kids have enough problems to begin with. And you're talking about raising a *black adopted* kid?" He made both words sound unpleasant.

"I didn't say it wouldn't be hard."

"So what's the point?"

"There is no point. We want a child. We want a family."

"We're not adopting anything right now," Josie said, getting up from the table. "I want to go home."

"Why do you have to bring up the adoption shit?" she screamed over the wind that rushed into the open cab window. "You were baiting him."

"Is that what you think?"

"Yeah, that's what I think. If it had been me, he would've told me I was full of shit."

"Do you think I'm full of shit?"

Josie looked at the streetlamps reflected in neon puddles. It had started to rain and the city looked shrouded in mist like the old Sherlock Holmes movies. "I don't know what I think," she said, feeling like a teenager seated between three parents—her mother and father on one side, Gus on the other. Bound by a cord to her father that connected her to loneliness, a sinkhole that left her feeling sterile and alone, she threw the other end to Gus, who caught it and tied it with a love knot, pulling her free until it broke with the force of the wave.

Josie buried her head in her hands. Gus moved closer, looping his arm around her neck and pulling her close to kiss her ear. "It's going to be all right," he whispered. But instead of comforting her, his optimism made her stiffen. "How can you say that? How can you talk so blithely about adopting a child? Without talking to me. I don't want to adopt. I want my own."

"I'm sorry," he said, sliding away. "I don't feel the same way about it as you do. Adoption isn't a problem for me."

Josie hit her head against the side of the cab, the strap digging into her temple. "Why does everything have to be so hard?" she said. "Why can't something be easy?"

"Who says it has to be easy?" Gus spoke evenly. He had an instinct for calm when other people were crazy, which was why he was a good reporter, knowing how to fade into the background and ask the one question that would make people open up and reveal themselves.

"What do you mean?"

"I mean nobody has it easy. What makes you think you're more entitled to being happy than the next guy?"

" 'Entitled'?" Josie growled. "What's wrong with wanting to be pregnant. I've only wanted it my whole life. *To* BE *pregnant.*"

"What're you going to do with it after you have it? Give it up for adoption?"

Josie twirled around so fast, she was surprised when Gus seized her wrist before she hit him. "Fuck you!" she cried.

"Fuck you, too!" he screamed, and then felt sick. "I hate it when you get this way."

"What way?"

"So out of control. So angry. You're not the only one who wants a family. You're not the only one who is upset. You don't think I wonder if it's me? If the accident—" He stopped himself, not wanting to look back. What was the point? Who knew if the accident had anything to do with their not being able to conceive? He knew he'd gotten a woman pregnant before when he was working on his civil rights film, and she'd called to tell him she needed money for an abortion. "You act like it's only you, like there's only one way. There isn't. There're lots of ways to have a child. And one's no better than the other."

"It is to me."

"Why?"

"Because adopting is . . ." She hesitated. "I don't know . . . is second best."

"You sound just like your parents."

"What do you mean by that?" Josie hated to sound like her parents.

"Positive. Judgmental. Opinionated."

"When did you start hating my family?"

"I don't hate them. I hate the myth."

"What myth?"

"The Davidovitch family myth. That you're the best. The best cooks, the best wits, the best dressers, the best relationship with the kids."

"What's wrong with that?"

"It's fucked-up, that's what's wrong. Because look what you have to live up to and why. Look what happens when you think you can't. Second best? Who gives a shit. Life isn't all blue ribbons."

Gus was scared of Josie when she got this crazy, as if some hidden pool of anger buried deep inside her could explode at any minute like a geyser spewing oil.

He had seen it once before when an article she wrote for *Global* had been spiked by her editor and he heard her screaming into the phone from the other room, interrupting her boss at every turn, pushing him, insulting him, losing all control. Or when she'd burned an apple pie she was making for Thanksgiving and turned on him like a rabid dog when he suggested picking up another at Greenberg's rather than starting over from scratch. He could still see her crying that there weren't enough apples, dumping flour and sugar into a bowl, a cloud of starch dusting the kitchen; her shoving the (second-best) pie into the oven, her mind as twisted as the braided crust. It wasn't her fight and determination that scared him; it was her desperation.

. . .

Albert knew why he found Ezra so appealing. Because he reminded him of himself. The way he listened to a story with his eyes full of humor and gentleness, never ingratiating or obsequious, always interested and understanding. He wasn't a talker. In fact, he had great difficulty with words, mispronouncing and transposing syllables. "You talk like English is your second language," Dr. D. said. "Don't you ever read?"

"I go to movies," Ezra answered without apology.

That was the other thing Albert liked about him. He didn't pretend to be someone he wasn't. Didn't fake knowing what he didn't know.

"Have you ever been down to the Lower East Side?" Albert asked.

"Is the Pope a Catholic?" Ezra laughed. "I used to get stoned under the boardwalk in Coney Island, take the train to Manhattan, go dancing at a disco on West Broadway, pick up a chick and roll out of bed in time to get a jelly doughnut at a little bakery on Delancey."

"You *schtup* a lot of girls?" Albert asked.

"I do okay. Why do you ask?"

"Prurience." Albert smiled.

"What's that?"

"Lewd curiosity."

Ezra shrugged.

"How about lunch at Russ & Daughters?" Albert said, already tasting a warm bialy with cream cheese, the mention of Delancey Street making his stomach rumble.

"I can't," Ezra said. "I've gotta get back to the Island."

"How long are you going to work for your old man?"

"Until I get into school."

"He's not gonna make you a partner?"

Ezra looked at Albert like he was crazy. He hated working for his father every second he was there, but anytime he'd ever tried to do something else, he'd always failed. Like the barbecue franchise he was sure was a winner until the recession hit and he lost every cent of his father's investment. So he figured that if he just kept his mouth shut and did what his father said, sidestepping his outbursts and put-downs, he'd be all right until he could go to film school. When that happened, he was never coming back.

FIVE

The "baby" that Josie and Gus created was called *The Wave,* a 190-page book that recounted their ordeal (in alternating chapters) and the triumph of their love.

Josie wrote her part as if she were describing someone else, a phantom woman tripping across the stage like the ballerina in *Prelude to the Afternoon of a Faun,* only to be snatched from her gauzy dream like Maria Tallchief in *The Firebird.* But there was nothing balletic about the publicity tour Skylark arranged, sending them from one end of the country to the other. Selling themselves, their book, their courage, their love. Their *exhaustion.*

In Cincinnati, they did a morning television show with a talking monkey and a dancing bear. "Who was the Borscht Belt comic who said, 'Never come on after the animals'?" Josie asked as they staggered back to their hotel before the next round of interviews.

That night, she dreamed they were on *The Tonight Show,* where Johnny Carson and Ed McMahon were waiting in their sherbet-colored suits, their suntanned faces smiling, the band playing "He-e-e-e-ere's Josie!" and just as Gus stepped onto the stage, he caught his toe on the rug and went flying across the screens of 60 million viewers. And then she remembered as she awoke that he'd come close to falling off the set in Houston when the host of the local talk show, a Billy Graham look-alike, asked him to show the folks back home how he could walk.

"I thought we said no *demonstrations?*" Josie reminded Gus as they wandered the halls of the giant Yankee Doodle Motor Lodge, searching in vain in a labyrinth of identical rooms and halls and maps that said "You are here," but where, they didn't know.

"I've got to pee," Gus said, beginning to panic, his weakened bladder threatening to explode.

"Just hang on," Josie said, fumbling with the key. Jamming it into the nearest door and praying it would open.

"I'm not going to make it," Gus said, unzipping his fly and beginning to scream, "Help! Someone help us find our room!"

Within seconds, businessmen in boxer shorts and patterned socks were falling into the hall, their crew cuts matted and pointy from lying on polyester pillows and floral sateen coverlets as they watched TV and guzzled beer. "What the *hell* is goin' on?"

For ten days running, Gus and Josie told and retold "The Gus'n'Josie Story," pressing all the buttons that would bring their audience to tears and send them running to the nearest bookstore. Josie began to feel a little queasy that her big break was a broken neck, but she secretly hoped a good review in the *New York Times* would prove their book had literary merit and wasn't merely an exploitation of their (very) bad luck. Every morning, she picked up the paper with trembling fingers and turned to the book review, fantasizing that Gus and she might be touted as the next Diana and Lionel Trilling.

"Judging from the photo on the jacket," the review began, "they were a handsome, vital-looking couple before the accident. But he is smiling a bit too vehemently and there is a hint of panic in her eyes." Josie thought she was going to throw up. " 'When you come right down to it, Gus wanted to survive, not to illustrate the indomitability of the human spirit but to get back to his undistinguished life and pleasures.' In other words, who gives a shit about a guy in love who breaks his neck!" Josie crumpled the paper into a ball and threw it across the room.

"Did he spell our name right?" Gus joked.

"How can you joke about this? The fucker's reviewing the jacket photo, not the book."

"What do you want me to do, *cry*? The guy's a putz."

"A putz who just happens to write for the most powerful paper in the world," she cried.

"I don't give a damn who he writes for." Gus headed out the door. "Today's news wraps tomorrow's fish."

The minute Gus was gone, Josie retrieved the crumpled paper and uncrumpled it, flying like a moth back into the flame, a kosher chicken watching itself bleed to death—slowly. She read the review again. And again. "Undistinguished"? "A hint of panic"? "A bra made of doughnuts to fit her doughnut-sized breasts." What did he mean by that? She looked down at her chest, feeling a rush of hatred, a flush of shame. To be panned by the *Times* was a fate worse than death. And for her looks? Who in New York (and the world) didn't measure his worth (and everybody else's) by what was printed in the *Times*? Did it matter that friends and family were outraged, that the phone didn't stop ringing all day long? (Josie wondered if a rave would have elicited so much excitement.) She stayed up all night imagining a long and painful death for the reviewer, woke up the next morning with a stone the size of Plymouth Rock in her stomach. All her life, she had dreamed of being a star like the famous actresses and dancers her father had cared for, to be taken seriously like the blacklisted writers (without having to go to jail) who came to the house, to hear her parents boast "my daughter the writer," like they would have boasted "my son the doctor" had David gone into medicine.

She didn't want to go outside, imagining her enemies chortling over their croissants and coffee, clucking about her being slammed. Barbara Walters canceled their appearance on the *Today* show, Skylark pulled the plug on their publicity budget, and the paperback rights were sold in the low four figures. But not *everybody* lived (or died) by the *Times*. Some people didn't even read it. The literary establishment may have spurned *The*

Wave, but Hollywood's legs were spread wide open. It was a love story, an accident story, a "will he walk or fuck again?" story, a true-life adventure. In other words, the quintessential Hollywood movie.

"I love it!" the producer Howard Weiner cried as he waved to everyone who walked into Elaine's, where he had taken them for lunch. "I laughed. I cried. I fell in love with you both. Please let me make your movie. Oh, pleeze, oh pleeze. I'll make it dance. I'll make it sing!" Sing, maybe, Josie thought as Gus lurched toward the men's room. But dance?

Suddenly, their life was a property. Producers would say anything to prove they were the best (though not necessarily the brightest). Josie had never seen so much pushing and priming, kissing and sucking up.

"I hope you don't settle for television," one producer said. "This is *definitely* a feature."

"They're offering you fifty grand for the film and television rights," their newly signed agent, Marvin Feingold, said, calling them from the Coast. "And another fifty if you write it."

"But we've never written a screenplay before."

"For fifty thousand, you can learn," said Marvin.

Josie had never been to Los Angeles. The only thing she had ever heard about it was that it was terrible. The place from where her parents' blacklisted friends were banished and to where their television friends migrated in the fifties and made large fortunes.

Her brother, David, had moved there a year before and was living in a grove of eucalyptus trees high above Laurel Canyon, kicking off his custom-made English shoes for soft Italian loafers, hanging up his Paul Stuart suits and donning jeans and linen shirts open to the waist. He left advertising to produce. That's what everybody *did* in L.A., even though they all *wanted* to direct.

L.A. felt to Josie like a foreign country with a different language and currency. Even the brightest beach day on Cape Cod was dark and dreary compared to the glaring white light of L.A., like the pop of a million flashbulbs. Gus drove her from the ocean to the Santa Monica Mountains, up the Pacific Coast Highway, and out to the Valley. Josie had never seen so much sprawl or malls, so many houses squooshed so close together, so many pools and flowers. She couldn't get over the garishness of the flora—the crimson bottlebrush trees, hot-pink bougainvillea, bright orange-and-purple birds of paradise; the heavy scent of candytuft, mimosa, and jasmine.

Another shock was the people. All smooth and brown, with perfect teeth and hair. Even *she* felt crippled in this town. But the biggest shock of all was that nobody knew her father. No one looked up midsentence and said, "Are you related to Dr. D.? He delivered all my children." No one even cared.

"Let's blow the whole wad and rent a fabulous place in the hills, with a pool and a sauna, and a panoramic view," Gus said as they wound up Tower Grove Drive in their rented Pinto. "I never lived in anything bigger than a room when I was here. Only saw Bel Air when I picked up somebody's maid in the cab I was driving."

"I don't know," Josie said as they walked through a five-thousand-square-foot "ranch" with orange shag carpet, smoked mirrors, a fireplace big enough to roast a goat, and a driftwood candelabra that looked like a menorah in a pear tree. "I'd kind of like to live at the beach."

"You don't want an indoor/outdoor shower, an outdoor/indoor barbecue, an Olympic-size swimming pool, and a private bomb shelter?"

"Do you mind?" Josie said. "Is the beach a problem for you?"

Gus shook his head and smiled. "As long as I don't surf."

So they rented a bungalow in Ocean Park, a block from the beach and around the corner from Jerry's Liquor Store. Josie scraped and polyurethaned the floors, bought wicker furniture from Pier 1, and ate her granola every morning watching their next-door neighbor, Barry, a blond Adonis aikido master, stand on one leg and stretch the other one up over his head.

"Will you look at this?" Josie said, calling Gus over to the window as Barry bent himself over like a hinged door and stuck his head through his legs. "The only guy I know who can give himself a blow job."

The whole place was like a circus. Lincoln Boulevard, a street so ugly, it was almost beautiful—a jumble of stores, car dealerships, Taco Bells, Arby's, McDonald's, wallpaper outlets, tile stores: anything and everything you never needed but couldn't live without.

"You've written an inspiring little book," their producer, Langston Jones, said as he drummed his fingers on his black marble desk, clean and shiny without a single scrap of paper or pen to clutter the surface. "But it's too small for a feature and too big for TV."

Bigger than a bread box, smaller than Yugoslavia, Josie thought.

"It's got to be big, dramatic. Cataclysmic." He gestured with enormous hands that looked like he was wearing asbestos mitts. "Orgasmic!"

Gus and Josie shifted in their leather Corbu chairs, sunk two feet below the carpeted platform on which Langston sat like the great and powerful Oz.

"Here's a suggestion." He held up his electric-fan hands. "Just a suggestion . . ." But before he could finish, Gus's leg began to jiggle violently like one of those Magic Fingers beds Josie loved to feed with quarters in cheap motels. "Stop it!" she yelled, slapping her hand down hard on Gus's knee as if disciplining an obstreperous dog (their own private sick joke to show the world they didn't care).

"Clonus," Gus explained to Langston, who looked blithely at his dancing leg, as if everybody in Hollywood were spastic. "Ever since the accident," Gus tried to explain, but Langston wasn't interested.

"What if the two of you are on a yacht in the middle of the Atlantic Ocean?" he continued. "And you're on your honeymoon. You're fucking your brains out. And a tidal wave is brewing."

Josie waited for the punch line.

"And the audience knows it, but you don't!"

She kicked Gus, gently, but he didn't respond. Then she realized she was kicking the leg that didn't have any feeling.

"You mean like *Jaws*?" Gus said.

"Like *Jaws*?" Langston repeated, trying to wrap his soggy brain around the title. "Like *Jaws*!" He clapped his hands together, remembering the movie. "Yes! *Jaws!* You got it."

"Except instead of a shark," Gus added enthusiastically, "it's a tsunami!"

The minute they stepped out of the refrigerated coolness of Langston's office and into the blasting heat of the parking lot, where, to Josie's delight, they had their own *personalized* parking spaces, she blurted out, "What the hell was he talking about?"

"It doesn't matter." Gus laughed. "By the time we hand in the first draft, he will have forgotten."

Josie had no idea how to write a screenplay. Gus didn't know much either, although he had written the narration for all his documentaries. So they bought a book called *How to Write a Screenplay* and a pack of index cards.

"We write every scene on a different card and stick 'em up on the wall," Gus said. "Then we plot out the story and divide up the scenes. You write one; I'll write the other."

"That's all?" Josie asked incredulously.

"Why not?"

For a month, they arranged and rearranged their file cards,

sometimes organizing them with color-coordinated tacks, sometimes switching the order from horizontal to vertical. They
"worked" all morning in the bungalow they shared with James
Earl Blake, a director who hadn't done a picture in ten years but
who played his baby grand and looked strikingly like Clifton
Webb with a pencil mustache and ascot. By noon, they were
starved and tired of listening to Blake play "Für Elise," so they
bopped over to the commissary, where they picked at their
Cobb salads and sipped iced tea like the best of the studs and
starlets, heavy hitters and wanna-bes.

"This is ridiculous," Gus said after another week of staring at
the file cards, with nothing to show on the page but food stains.
"You write scenes one through three and I'll do four through
seven. Then we'll switch and edit each other. No matter what,
we grind out twenty-two pages a week and we'll be done in six
weeks."

"Not bad." Langston riffled the pages of their first draft. "Not
bad at all. But you passed on my tidal wave idea?"

"We thought it'd be too expensive," Gus quickly added.

"That's okay. I really liked the scene with the hooker," he said,
patting the script as if it were a lapdog.

What scene with what hooker? Josie started to say, but Gus
jabbed her in the ribs, knowing that Langston tended to get confused after lunch.

"I have a few notes," Langston said, folding his hands behind
his head and stretching himself out like he was sunbathing at the
pool. Josie noticed his large chiseled features and thick mane of
silver hair, his silk suit in light tones of gray, his navy satin tie.
He exuded a kind of sexuality that bordered on obscenity. Josie
imagined him auditioning starlets on the casting couch, his cock
as hard and craggy as his face.

Langston leaned forward, lacing his phallic fingers together.

"What I'm trying to say is breaking your neck in the surf isn't very *filmic*."

Josie held her breath. "I'm thinking if we get Bob Redford, we set it in the mountains and do an avalanche. Throw in some ecology. Bob's really into nature. If it's Paul Newman, we do it in a racing car."

"And he gets out of bed to win the Indy Five Hundred," Gus added with mock enthusiasm.

Josie floated out of her body and hovered like a blimp over the white carpet, clean as freshly driven snow, and drifted past the Rauschenberg, Walasse Ting, Diebenkorn, and Georgia O'Keeffe the studio had bought for Langston. Then paused to gaze at the photos of his children, big and beefy like the no-neck monsters, and a silver-framed autographed photo of Governor Reagan.

"Look," he said, stretching out his long legs until his Gucci shoes peeked out from under the marble slab. "It doesn't really matter how it happens. It's only a movie."

Ruth and Albert were due to arrive at LAX at 2:53. Josie set out to meet them at 1:30, allowing almost an hour and a half to drive to the airport, even though their house at the beach was only thirty-five minutes away. She had inherited her father's lack of navigational skill, or, more aptly, his pathological tendency to get lost in a car. The summer of Gus's accident, Albert had come within inches of driving off Montauk Point when he got lost in the dark trying to find Gossman's Restaurant. "Albert, stop!" Ruth had screamed as he backed up in a panic to make an illegal U-turn and nearly drove off the road into the ocean. Josie remembered thinking as the waves crashed below that if they should perish, the morning headline would qualify for her personal collection of morbidly funny newspaper clippings: FAMILY DROWNS WHILE FIANCÉ RECOVERS FROM SURFING ACCIDENT. Right up there with: DRIVERLESS, CIRCLING CAR RUNS OVER OWNER or TRICK PIANO IN TOPLESS BAR CRUSHES MAN IN FLAGRANTE DELICTO; WOMAN SURVIVES.

It wasn't until she saw the signs for Newport that Josie realized she had passed the airport by about fifty miles. How could she have gotten so lost? She'd even written the directions down: Lincoln to Sepulveda, Sepulveda to Century, Century to airport (on right).

But here she was on the San Diego Freeway, going seventy miles per hour with Van Morrison singing "Brown Eyed Girl," without the slightest inkling that she was going the wrong way.

Okay, she said to herself. Don't panic. But it was already too late, and she could feel the onset of her Auschwitz fantasy—tachycardia, sweating, shortness of breath, the dread of ending up in the ovens.

She had to get off the freeway and turn around. But how? And where? The signs kept rushing by—Balboa, Laguna, La Jolla.

Just do it! she said, clutching the steering wheel and shooting across three lanes of highway, barely missing a Greyhound bus and bouncing down an exit ramp going fifty.

Now what? she thought as she tried to read the signs, all unrecognizable streets named after flowers—Poinsettia, Dahlia, Oleander. Not a soul on the street.

Josie's heart was racing faster than the cars above her head. It was already 2:30. She'd never make it. Her father would be furious. She looked into the shimmering heat and in the distance, like Don Quixote tramping across *la pampa*, she saw a man—an apparition? A mirage? Josie squinted (she'd become a very good squinter since moving to L.A.) and saw a Mexican gardener walking toward her.

Josie unrolled her window and felt a wall of heat hit her in the face. "Excuse me, sir, could you tell me how to get to the airport?"

The man smiled sweetly but didn't answer.

"LAX," Josie yelled over the roar of trucks and zooming cars.

He hunched his shoulders together shyly and scratched his head. "No speak English," he said.

"*¿Dónde está* Ellay, Ah . . ." Shit! What was the word for *X*? Like the beer . . . Dos . . . "*¡Equis!*"

"*Ah, sí.*" The gardener broke into a wide grin and pointed. "*Norte.*"

Josie saw a dust-covered sign for 405 North across the street. "*Gracias, muchas gracias,*" she cried, swinging her car into the road, waving adios to her Mexican savior. Suddenly, she heard a terrible crash, the crunch of metal, the sound of her tailpipe scraping asphalt. Sparks were flying out of the asshole of her car; her left headlight was hanging from a single thread like a gouged-out eye. She patted herself all over. No cuts or broken bones. Maybe she was dreaming. She willed herself to look across the street, where the car she'd hit, a yellow Datsun, lay idling in a bed of zinnias, its tires spewing dirt like black confetti.

Now I'm going to get beaten up, she thought. Just because everybody's always smiling and saying "Have a happy day" in this town doesn't mean Angelenos won't hurt you.

But the woman walking toward her wasn't angry at all. She looked genuinely concerned. "Are you all right?"

"I'm really sorry," Josie gushed. "I'm supposed to be at the airport picking up my parents."

"Oh dear," the woman said.

"Are you all right?" Josie touched her arm.

"I'm just fine." She smiled. "It happened so fast, I didn't know what hit me."

"I'm so sorry," Josie apologized again, making the mistake of glancing at her watch. It was already three o'clock. "Now whaddo we do? I've never been in an accident before," she said, feeling weak at the knees.

"Me either." The woman giggled, wrinkling up her button nose. "I think we exchange things."

"Telephone numbers?"

"Gee, I don't know. Maybe registration and driver's licenses."

"That sounds right," Josie said, taking a deep breath and steadying herself against her car. "Let's just take it a day at a time."

"Oh, wow." The woman clasped Josie's hands and looked at her with loving eyes. "My name is Cindy and I'm an alcoholic."

Albert was pacing back and forth in front of American Airlines, looking at his watch every other second, his lips a thin black line, his eyeglasses cloudy with anger.

"Jesus Christ!" he exploded as Josie ran panting toward him.

"I'm sorry," she burst out. "I got lost."

"What the hell happened to you!" He wasn't listening. "We've been waiting here for over an hour!"

"I got on the wrong freeway. Or the right freeway going the wrong way," she sputtered. "I had to get off to ask directions and a Mexican gardener pointed me into the back of a car."

"Are you all right?" Ruth's voice was laced with worry. Josie realized she hadn't even been thinking about her mother, who looked so fresh and summery in her cotton skirt and Belgian play shoes, her crisp white blouse and white summer beads.

"Where's the car?" Albert growled as Josie tried to wrestle the valise from him. "Leave it," he said, pulling it roughly back with an iron grip.

"No, let me," Josie insisted, tugging at the bag.

"I said, 'Leave it.' " He pushed her away.

Josie felt the tears well up and burn her eyes, her throat constrict, a sob catch in her chest. "I said I was sorry," she choked out. "I didn't do it on purpose."

Her father peered at her over his glasses, saying without an ounce of sympathy what she had heard her whole life. "You know what I think about people who are late? I think they're hostile and controlling, and if I'd known where the hell you lived, I would've taken a cab."

Josie felt her excitement curdle like sour milk in the back of her throat and the butterflies in her stomach turn to stone.

This was Ruth and Albert's first visit to L.A. since Gus and Josie had moved more than a year ago. David had moved a year before that to coproduce *The Gates of Heaven,* a multimillion-dollar film set in the Yukon that he was sure would be his break. "Mama and Papa never came to visit me," he whined. "And I've been living here longer than you. Papa could give a shit about what *I* do."

"Maybe because there's no word for *freelance* in Yiddish," Josie joked.

Since Albert had given up obstetrics and was practicing only gynecology these days, he had run out of excuses why he couldn't come to L.A. When she and David were growing up, he often missed birthdays and school plays, even Christmas one year when a woman was having a baby. But since he was no longer on call, he had agreed, with Ruth's prodding, to come to the cast and crew screening of *The Wave,* which had slipped unceremoniously from feature status to TV movie when Langston passed (only in Hollywood did *pass* mean "fail") and Larry Levin, the senior VP of production at NBC, and son of one of Ruth's wealthy German Jewish friends, had picked it up in turnaround.

"What I love about your script," Larry had said when he was trying to buy it, "is it's not your run-of-the-mill *affliction* movie. It's sexy. It's got soul."

"Two great parts," said his sidekick, Monty, a short, balding man who looked like his designer suit had been painted directly onto his tight little body—the Mutt to Larry's Jeff.

"Two Emmys." Larry creamed them with compliments and

stroked them with promises as Josie listened quietly to the "boys" talk about sports and the ratings as a kind of foreplay to the pitch. And when it was all over and everybody had become best friends, Larry made a joke about Monty's little feet and Monty made a joke about Larry's little hands, and soon everybody was laughing and joking and thinking about everybody else's little dick.

Josie glanced at her father in the rearview mirror as they drove to the theater. He had stayed mad a whole day after her airport debacle, giving her the silent treatment, which made Ruth so nervous, she blathered on and on about Larry Levin's mother. "She had the most incredible engagement party," she reminisced. "I'll never forget that house in Oyster Bay—porches all around the house. Gardens of roses. A lawn down to the water. Nothing like *good* taste and *old* money. . . ." Albert stared out the window at the wasteland of freeways and tract housing, the black skyscrapers in Century City sticking up into the robin's-egg blue sky. Josie thought his skin looked sallow, his silky hair thin and mousy, his sparkling eyes dull. Everything about him seemed distant and alone.

Yet the minute they walked into the theater and a woman ran up to him, grasping his hands and saying, her face aglow, "Dr. D.? I'm Diana Petersen. Do you remember me?" he was transformed from a stooped-over old man to a jaunty boulevardier. "Of course I remember you, Diana," he said, lighting up. "How're the children?"

"Not children anymore," the woman crowed. "Adam's twenty-one and Elizabeth just started college." Then she turned to Josie and said, her face pink and happy, "Your father was the most wonderful doctor. Today, women are so worried. They have all these tests." She turned back to Albert. "We never worried with Dr. D. We just knew he'd take care of us."

.   .   .

The lights dimmed and credits rolled. Josie reached for Gus's hand as the music—violins and cello—played a lachrymose tune and on the screen, Gus (or rather, the actor *playing* Gus) ran along the beach and dived into the water. Josie could feel her heart begin to pound as Gus (the actor) disappeared beneath a wave and popped up, wet and exuberant, bolted from the sea, and jogged up the beach to a parked camper where Josie (the actress) lay sleeping. Josie scanned the audience—cast and crew, her brother, her parents, and Gus—all with eyes glued to the screen. She felt embarrassed as they (or rather, the actors *playing* them) began to make love and then, postcoitus, jumped back into the Atlantic, which was really the Pacific, but who knew?

The camera cut to THE WAVE, then segued to Gus swimming madly to catch the swell as it crested and broke. . . . Josie suddenly felt woozy. She didn't want to pass out at her own debut, but she thought she might get sick if she didn't turn away.

"Are you all right?" Gus whispered as she put her head between her legs, feeling her eyebrows tingle and nostrils flare.

"Yeah, fine," she said, willing herself upright again, reminding herself that this wasn't real. It wasn't *really* Gus being thrown into the sand, or *really* Josie caressing his cheek and telling him everything would be all right. None of this was real. It was surreal. She was watching the reenactment of the worst thing that had ever happened to her. She was witnessing the death of her romance, reliving the moment that had killed her dream. She spent the rest of the screening in a state of catatonia, dreaming but knowing she was awake. Then everybody started clapping and patting her on the back, squeezing her shoulder and enthusing. "Terrific." "What a movie." "So moving." "It'll get a fifty share."

The next day, they had three offers to write three more docudramas, the hottest form of television entertainment—an amalgamation of fact and fiction, truth and dare, poetic license and outright lies.

Josie was thrilled. They had arrived. Which one to write first? The script about the woman accused of killing her children or the one about the lesbians who have a turkey-baster baby and are forced to give up the child because the reactionary community claims "paternity"? Or the one on infertility, which Josie wasn't sure she wanted to do.

"I don't want to do any of them," Gus said in the middle of the night. "I want to make documentaries. And I want to move back to New York."

"Wait a minute." Josie clicked on the light. "We're just getting started."

Gus shook his head. "This isn't for me. I hate the business. I hate the place."

"What about me?"

"You can write anywhere."

"And not make any money."

"We've always made money."

"Not me. This is the first time I've had a shot."

"At what?"

"At making it."

"You call this 'making it'?" he asked.

"Since when did you get so high-and-mighty," Josie exploded. "You had no problem selling our story to the highest bidder. So now we've got a chance to reap the benefits."

"There are no benefits for me if I don't like myself when I get up in the morning. And don't holler at me!"

"I'm not hollering at you. I'm yelling."

"Well, cut it out! I'm not telling you what to do."

"The hell you're not. We're a team."

"Not anymore."

Josie stared at him. "Whad'you mean?" she asked fearfully.

"A *writing* team," he said a little too quickly. "That's what I mean."

"That's not what you said."

"Whad'you want from me, Josie? I don't want to write this shit. I don't want to live in Hollywood. That doesn't mean I don't want to live with you."

"Why's it always me who has to make the sacrifices?"

"Sacrifices? What the fuck have you sacrificed?"

"Nothing." Josie could feel the soles of her feet sizzle from the hot coals she was treading on. "I didn't mean it like that."

"Then what did you mean?"

"Nothing."

"Bullshit, nothing! I know you too well. What're you trying to say?"

"I'm doing well. I'm getting work. I'm making money."

"I'm not stopping you."

"Yes you are. How'm I going to get work if we move back East?"

"There are planes, you know."

"So why can't you make your documentaries from here?"

"Because I don't like the way I feel here."

"Maybe that's got to do with something else."

"Like what?"

"I don't know."

"Sure you do. Why else wouldn't I like myself?"

"I didn't say that. I just said—"

"That maybe I have another reason not to like myself. What could that be? I wonder."

"I don't know." Josie could feel the noose tightening. She wanted to run.

"Yes you do. It's the baby thing." Josie's stomach twisted. "We've just brushed it under the rug."

"There hasn't been any time."

"That's not why." Gus hated bringing it up as much as she did. "It's because you think it's me."

"I never said that."

"But it's what you think. You're pissed because you think it's my fault that we can't have a baby."

"I don't know what I think," Josie said, reaching for the cigarette she'd hidden in the binding of *Ulysses*.

"I thought you stopped."

"I did," she said, lighting up and inhaling so deeply, her head began to spin.

"What're you doing?" Gus knew she'd already been cheating. He could smell it on her breath despite the peppermint toothpaste and cinnamon gum.

"I'm smoking a cigarette. It won't kill me. Look at your friend Dick Ellis. He's got lung cancer from radiation. Never smoked a day in his life."

"I don't want to fight," Gus said, turning his head away like a wolf that bares its neck in defeat.

"You never want to fight, Gus. You just like to start them."

"Fuck you!" He had never hit her, but he wanted to now.

She looked at him through a haze of nausea. "I'm sorry," she whispered. "I didn't mean—"

He turned away, shaking her hand off his arm. "I said I was sorry," she repeated in a childlike singsong, wanting him to say, All right. It's okay. I understand. She *was* right. He hated to fight, having grown up in a household where his parents never fought, just drove around the block when they were mad at each other or whispered in staccato voices behind closed doors. But not fighting didn't close the invisible gully, the narrow crevice that had grown between them, which he felt every time she rolled over on her side, her back to him even as he rubbed her head and shoulders, waiting for her to inch closer to him, wishing he could make her feel hopeful and passionate, but feeling her float away, imperceptibly, like an ice floe cracking off from the berg, silently blaming him for their infertility. Not wanting to talk about adoption.

They lay like sculptures beneath a sheet that felt as cold and smooth as marble. Josie imagined the medieval crypts in France with sleeping knights and virgin princesses carved in stone. She could hear him thinking even though he hardly breathed. She could read the silence like a language only they understood, each molecule a word. What are you thinking? she wanted to say, but she didn't want to hear the answer. Or if he answered, Nothing, she would know it was a lie. They had never mourned what they had lost. Never acknowledged it, so busy getting back to where they had been, climbing the grassy knoll to what had seemed a time of perfect happiness.

Josie rolled over onto her side and stared into the darkness, her eyes catching specks of light like fairy dust or fireflies. Mold yourself around me, she wanted to cry. Hold me like a spoon. Comfort me. Let me comfort you. If only we could cry. But Gus remained frozen, a curtain of hurt and disappointment hanging between them, a dark cloud of sadness blocking their light.

"I'm sorry," she whispered, feeling a tear seep out of her eye and roll across the bridge of her nose. And waited, waited with the same dread she felt whenever her father didn't speak to her or she watched her mother walk stoop-shouldered and cowed around the apartment. Or when they sat in silence around the table while Albert ate and dabbed the corners of his mouth, Josie so twisted inside that she could hardly swallow, her heart so heavy that she couldn't breathe, her eyes throbbing dry tears.

"I'm sorry, too," Gus said, rolling over and pulling her into the soft hollow of his belly, wishing he could cry in her hair.

"I've got a great assignment for you," said Josie's new agent, a man who affected an air of superiority in the skin trade he so successfully negotiated. He wore wide-wale corduroy slacks, button-down shirts with bow ties, and still carried his green Harvard book sack to distinguish himself from the throngs of hustlers who worked for William Morris and ICM. Pushy and arrogant, ambitious and tough, he had assured Josie she would make him rich, but he made her feel as if he were doing *her* a favor every time he took her call. "A MOW about prostitution," he said. "I got your fee up another twenty-five hundred and they've agreed to pay all your expenses."

Expenses? Josie wondered what those expenses could be. "What *about* prostitution?" she asked.

Her agent didn't speak. He reminded her a little of her father (they even had the same first name), but the agent had no charm or sense of humor.

"It sounds great," Josie said, pretending she hadn't asked a question. "All I ever wanted to know about prostitution but was afraid to ask." She laughed.

"I'll send the contracts out tomorrow," he said in a very businesslike way, and hung up the phone.

SIX

Albert couldn't stop thinking about his mother. He would wake up from a dream where he was back in the house on the corner of Crystal Street and Belmont Avenue and think for a moment that he was still a young boy. He would smell Viola cooking breakfast and be transported to the large sunny kitchen where his mother stood on hobbled legs–never properly healed from when she fell through a skylight hanging up the wash–cooking mushroom and barley soup, kugel and strong tea, their huge black cat, Juk (which meant "beetle" in Russian), brushing up against her ankles.

At first, his thoughts were fleeting, but then he found he looked forward to these times, planned his evenings around going to bed. But after forty years, he could no longer sleep with Ruth, feeling as she climbed in next to him that she was an intruder taking up memory space that he was saving for his mother; the smell of stale smoke and night cream sent him down the hall to David's old room, where he could be alone.

He pulled over his shoulders the multicolored afghan his mother had crocheted, the wool smooth as silk after so many years, and conjured her face like the lady in the moon–her large deep-set eyes, dark and brooding, the widow's peak that framed her brow, the rich brown hair swept back and fastened with tortoiseshell combs, a few silky strands curling like ribbon down her neck. Her large, soft bosom. Then he remembered the day she almost died, a sad old woman sitting in a chair staring into the garden of the old people's home where he and his sisters had put her, and he felt his heart crumble, his soul crawl inside itself. A shell of guilt. "Why did you save me?" she'd whispered as the ambulance sped her to the hospital, where her stomach was pumped and she would be kept alive to stare at dead forsythia and rotting roses for another two years. "Why didn't you let me die?"

Josie had decided to do her prostitution research in New York instead of L.A. It didn't matter if she "worked" Eighth Avenue or Hollywood and Vine. Gus, too, was going away–to Utah, where he was filming with his friend Dick Ellis, racing against time and money before Dick died. "I feel like a crab is eating my insides," Dick said as they drove through the barren land of the high desert, 150 miles downwind from where the government had tested their atomic bombs in the 1950s.

"Are you in pain?" Gus asked, concerned about his friend but happier than he'd been since the accident to be doing again what he loved best, making a documentary about something he believed in, far away from the bullshit and hype of Hollywood.

"How would you feel with a crab eating your insides, schmuck?" Dick laughed and tousled Gus's hair like his father had done when he was a kid. He had been a robust man with a mass of curls before the chemo and radiation had turned him into a bald shadow who shuffled like the Ancient Mariner, making Gus feel athletic by comparison.

"We're quite a pair," Dick said as they crept slowly into the best restaurant in Salt Lake City, where white people with permed lavender hair and peaceful smiles on their bland faces stared at them like dybbuks blown in with the dust. "Reminds me of the old joke about the Siamese twins who go to a little town where the circus is playing and one says to the other, 'Why don't we look up that cute little whore we fucked last year?' And his brother answers, 'D'you think she'll remember us?' "

Later, he tucked Dick in and helped him bathe, patting him

dry like a sickly child. He watched him inject himself with morphine and waited until Dick's breathing slowed before he dared close his eyes. Gus wondered what his father would have thought if he were alive to see him crippled, his legs so stiff and tight he had to fight through rods of steel to make them move. How he had loved to watch Gus run, had gone to all his games, lived vicariously through his son's grace and fluidity, he himself never having been so lithe and strong.

Gus closed his eyes and dreamed he could walk again without canes or fear of falling, though even as he dreamed he knew it wasn't so. Then he saw his father standing in the middle of a lake, waving for him to join him. "Hey, Dad," Gus said, feeling his body lighten. "You're here."

"Come on." Gus's father beckoned.

"I can't," Gus said. "I'm up at bat."

Then halfway across a mint green lawn, Gus stopped and turned like Orpheus looking back at Eurydice and saw a halo of light in the middle of a pool where his father's bald head had sunk like an irradiated stone.

Josie had no idea what to expect when she rang the bell to Sheri Montenegro's Riverdale apartment, but from her basso telephone voice, she imagined her to be big. How big, she didn't know. She had gotten Sheri's name from an old New York friend who had worked for the DA and was now on the board of a nonprofit organization that Sheri, who herself had risen from the ranks of streetwalker to madam, had founded to help women get out of *the life*.

The door swung open and there before Josie stood a woman at least six feet tall, with a massive head of red curls and green eyes, who must have weighed two hundred pounds. She filled the door frame like Man Mountain Dean or Mrs. Claus on steroids, but she walked on spike heels with the grace of the hippo ballerina in *Fantasia*.

"Come on in," she said, ushering Josie into an airy apartment that looked out on the Hudson.

"What a great apartment," Josie said, admiring the view. She'd often wondered who lived in these Tudor-style apartments when she had passed them on trips out of the city.

"I lucked out," Sheri said. "It's rent-controlled." Josie followed her to the baby blue moiré-covered couch, where Sheri sat herself in a pouf of down like a giant hen spreading her feathers over her eggs.

"So you're doing a script on prostitution," she said with a smile. "Is there a part in it for me?"

Josie didn't know if she was being tested. Everybody wanted to be a movie star. "Wouldn't you rather direct?"

Sheri laughed. "I'd be good at that," she said. "Domination was my thing."

Josie could already feel herself getting excited. She had never been so close to a real pro, or more correctly, a genuine ho. "I'm going to ask you a lot of dumb questions," she said apologetically.

"There are no dumb questions," Sheri answered. "Just dumb people. I'm so sick of listening to politicians talk about rehabilitating prostitutes, when it's the whole society that's fucked-up. We watch war movies on TV, see people getting beat up. But we freak out when two consenting adults wanna fuck?"

"For money."

Sheri looked at Josie with disbelief. "Isn't that the American way? Take a natural resource, add the cost of labor, and sell it for a profit? Nobody has the right to tell me what I can and can't do with my body. If a Vassar grad came to me and said, Hey, Sheri, I'd like to sell my body; can you help me out? I wouldn't tell her to do something else. I'd support her choice. But if a thirteen-year-old kid came to me and said the same thing because she'd been kicked out of the house and had nowhere to go or any other means of support, I'd say that kid was a victim, and I'd do everything I could to keep her out of the life. We're all raised from birth to be quiet and tender and hold out for the highest bidder."

"Who's raised to hold out for the highest bidder?" Josie asked.

"We are," Sheri said. "Women. From the time we are born and wrapped in a little pink blanket, we're expected to put out. When Jackie O holds out for the richest husband, she's called a shrewd businesswoman. When a young chick from the suburbs hooks up with a fat slob twice her age for a house with a pool and a Bloomingdale's charge, it's called marriage."

"Are you saying we're all prostitutes?"

"I'm saying it's a white man's world."

"I can't argue with that," Josie said, taking out her steno pad and ballpoint pen. "But what I'm interested in is you."

"In me?" Sheri widened her eyes in mock surprise and folded her manicured hands under her chin. "You wanna know about me?" Josie nodded. "Whad'you wanna know?"

"How you got started."

"In the dressing room at Alexander's," Sheri said without hesitation. "I was always going there to try on clothes. I'd spend hours trying on the most beautiful dresses, and when the saleslady came over, usually suspiciously, I'd say that *Mummy* was waiting for me downstairs in the limo. So one day, this little schmuck, some clerk, comes in and says he'll pay me ten bucks to watch him jerk off. Well, ten bucks to watch anything was okay by me. The next time, he said he'd give me a dress if I blew him. That wasn't such a big deal. I'd been doin' that for nothing since I was fourteen." Josie looked up in surprise. She hadn't known what a blow job was until college. "Listen, honey, where I grew up, there wasn't a kid who didn't know about sex and prostitution. Half their fathers were in the mob. Their brothers were boosters and their uncles were pimps. The best-looking women with the nicest clothes and fanciest jewelry were hos. My whole world was hot." She smiled at her pun. "If you bought a TV, you knew it was stolen; if you wanted something and couldn't afford it, you traded it for something else." She motioned with a sweep of her pink pearl fingernails around the room, where every corner and table top was filled with crystal whatnots and embroidered pillows, family photos in silver frames, cut-glass vases with silk flowers and ostrich plumes. "I always liked pretty things."

"So you did it for things?"

"I did it for money. Money's power. And it doesn't matter if you sell your body or you sell your soul, the girl on Eighth Avenue is no more a whore than the woman in Scarsdale or her stockbroker husband who's *churning* tricks on the street."

"Except the girl on Eighth Avenue's got *no* power," Josie said, impressed by how smart Sheri was.

"And the guy on Wall Street is probably her john."

Josie flashed to her disgusting uncle Joe, who used to take her to lunch at the Harmony Club every Christmas and then to Bonwit's, where he bought her expensive Lanz dresses in exchange for a gooey kiss and a pat on the ass. "I'm not judging anybody," Josie said delicately. "But it's not the same. Everybody's got a choice. You didn't have to be a hooker."

"I *liked* being a hooker," Sheri said with pride. "And I was good. At the top of my game, I was pulling down three grand a week, traveling to Vegas and Puerto Rico with clients who were politicians and big-time business tycoons." She reached for a gilt-framed photo of herself at El Morocco. "Wasn't I beautiful?" she said, admiring the picture. "Fifty pounds lighter, ten years younger . . . I was some piece of ass," she said longingly as Josie lifted the picture out of her hands and examined it, hardly recognizing the woman who stared back with a "fuck you" expression on her face and platinum hair.

"I like you better now," Josie said.

"Get off it." Sheri snatched the picture from her. "I looked great."

"You looked hard."

"I *was* hard. How else do you think I made it from the street to running my own house?"

"How?"

"One fuck at a time," she said, throwing back her head and laughing, her red curls bouncing around her cheeks like Christmas tree ornaments.

"You never had a pimp?"

"Not after he broke my jaw. I didn't need a pimp. I knew real early that I had an ability with men, particularly men with money. The girls who need pimps need a father, a mother, a lover. Anybody who'll say 'How's tricks?' "

So that's what it means, Josie thought to herself, understanding the expression for the first time. "How's tricks?" she repeated.

"Except with a hooker, nobody cares. You know how many girls are killed by their johns?" Josie shook her head. "In New York last year, over fifty. But they all say she was just a whore, like that doesn't count. Half the time, they don't even investigate. The johns don't care about you, either. They walk in ready. Half-hard. They're not interested in making you feel good. You're like a washing machine, a dryer." She undulated her tire-size hips in a circular grind. "You don't think, I'm doing this for me. You think, Hurry up and come so I can get some sleep."

"Who're the johns?" Josie fantasized Robert De Niro or Marcello Mastroianni.

"Mostly schlumps, married guys whose wives won't go down on them. Politicians who can't get it up. I had one guy, a Greek shipping magnate, who wanted me to tar and feather him. He had this cute little lisp." Sheri cocked her head to one side and opened her big green eyes like Shirley Temple in drag. "He'd pull out his little pink penis and start playing with himself while I told him what I was going to do. Then he'd say in this lispy voice, 'Oh, pleathe, Stheri, will you tar and fethar me, now?' "

Josie laughed.

"There are a lot of freaks out there," Sheri said. "I had another guy who used to lie in a coffin and I'd start to cry, 'Oh, Philip, you're dead. Why're you doing this to me!' Then he'd sit up, I'd scream, and he'd come. Usually the richer they are, the freakier. I had a priest who wanted to pay me five hundred dollars to sew his foreskin up around his penis and another five hundred to open it up."

Josie grimaced. "Did you do it?"

"No." Sheri laughed. "I can't sew."

"You said your speciality was domination."

"Most people don't understand that the art of domination isn't pain. It's the fear of inflicting it." Sheri rose from the couch like the Jolly Green Giant rising up from the corn and ran her hands over her size-eighteen frame, her powder blue angora sweater hugging her forty-five-inch breasts. "You don't spank the shit outta some guy like in the pornos; you take off your shoe and bring it close to his face. Then you make him get down on his hands and knees and beg to kiss your heel." Sheri took off her delicate Cinderella slipper and placed her trunklike leg on the coffee table. Josie had no trouble imagining it as a john on all fours. She was mesmerized. Like a child who doesn't want to go to sleep and begs her mother to tell her one more story. "Oh, honey, if these thighs could talk." Sheri beamed and Josie imagined two large fresh hams. "Was it ever fun?"

"Fun?" Sheri thought for a while. "When I was stoned and had their money in my pocket, it was fun. But the problem was, I never met anybody interesting turning tricks. Not anybody who talked about *stuff*. I mean, all anybody cared about was who had the best cocaine or the most money or the biggest car."

Sounds just like Hollywood, Josie thought.

"I remember one year, I wanted to organize an Easter-egg hunt for the kids, but nobody wanted to get up before noon."

"You have kids?" Josie asked, feeling a pang whenever she was reminded how badly she wanted her own child.

"Yeah, a son."

"What about his father?"

"What about him?" Sheri looked suspicious, as if Josie had wandered into a place where she wasn't welcome.

Josie decided to try a different tack. "Well, lemme ask you. How was sex different with him?"

"It wasn't work."

"But how could you go from a trick to your man?"

"The same way a gynecologist looks up ladies' twats all day and then comes home and makes love to his wife."

Josie smiled. "I always had trouble with that, too. My father's a gynecologist."

"That had to be a trip. . . ." Sheri raised her eyebrows. "You've got to keep your lives separate. Sex is up here." She pointed to her head. "People talk about how most whores never come. Well, how many *happily* married women never come? I could get it on with a trick if I'd made my money and was still in the mood for some action. If I was relaxed and feeling good. I'd go over to the Hilton and meet some guy, have some drinks, and dance. Then I'd tell him I was a hooker and he'd say, 'Ah shit, never mind. Let's have some fun.' "

Josie pictured picking up a stranger at the Hilton and felt a twinge of pleasure. If he were handsome and sexy . . . That was her fantasy.

"So what happened? I mean, why'd you stop?"

"I had a real tragedy." Sheri fiddled with a silk-tasseled cushion. "My father died." She swallowed hard, as surprised by her sudden rush of feeling as Josie was. "It nearly killed me. . . . I adored my father. I was twenty-five, at the top of my game, and I felt like I was living in this big bubble, looking down at myself doing all these things that had nothing to do with who I was and—there's a saying in the business. When the life leads you, it's time to get out. I couldn't cut myself off from myself after my father died. I had nowhere to hide."

The atmosphere in the room suddenly changed, as if the

lights had gone out and the temperature had fallen. "What did you do?" Josie asked quietly.

"I tried to kill myself. Called the suicide hot line and they put me on hold." She guffawed. "Can you imagine? Here I am with a gun in my mouth and they put me on hold? I remember thinking, Shit! There's no future in suicide. Fuck them! I'm gonna live. . . . So I sold my black book to one of my girls, packed up my stuff, and took my son to the Bahamas." Sheri stretched out her massive legs and threaded one of her long painted nails through an auburn curl. "I remember sitting with him on the beach and noticing this little birthmark on his left shoulder blade." She reached out as if to touch an imaginary child. "And I thought to myself, Oh my God. What the fuck have I been missing?"

Josie didn't want to go back to her parents' overheated apartment. She had wanted to stay in a hotel, having an expense account for the first time, but had felt so guilty when Ruth said, "I don't understand. You're not comfortable in your own home?" that she caved in and found herself at 2:30 a.m. in her wallpapered room with the wicker furniture and four-poster bed, listening to the buses switch gears beneath her window, their headlights dancing across her ceiling; her mother following her into the bathroom to keep her company while she soaked in the tub, her father barely talking as he sat for hours in his big green chair reading the *Lancet* and the *New England Journal of Medicine*.

Eatin' angel, on the stroll, white liver, goin' out, goin' down, goin' round the world. Golden showers, delirium sex. Scat, scum, come. Josie's head was still spinning with scenes of weirdos and whack-offs, mafioso princes and Puerto Rican pimps. It had turned her on, fueled her imagination, sparked her memory of *Belle de Jour*.

As she entered a luncheonette near the Inwood subway station, the smell of greasy steam and burned coffee stuck to her like a humid summer day. She slid into the red Naugahyde booth, sunken like a hammock from so much use, and traced her finger over the table, the silver specks in the Formica no longer shiny, but permanently dull from years of wiping.

She was tempted to order a bacon cheeseburger with grilled onions, a double order of french fries, and a chocolate shake, but she knew her parents had made an early reservation at an Italian restaurant, where she dreaded going, as her father had now taken to barking at waiters and yelling at clerks. Going out with him was like playing Russian roulette; you never knew when he would explode or embarrass you in public like a spoiled child who throws a tantrum in the middle of a department store.

Josie sipped a cup of coffee and peered across the restaurant to the counter, where a handsome young man, long-limbed, with a tangle of blond hair, was sipping a Coke. He stuck out because he was so fair, like the Marlboro Man had stepped off a billboard and wandered into the Bronx looking for a room and a cup of joe.

Josie scanned the bleached hairs on his forearms and let her eyes glide over the faded work shirt stretched tightly across his back. She imagined rubbing her hands lightly over his perfectly tan, pimple-free shoulders, moving slowly down his faded jeans, so tight that as he straddled the stool, she could make out every sinew and ripple of his thighs. Then she saw herself swiveling the stool around so that he was facing her, draping herself over his lap and unzipping his fly. A perfectly stiff uncircumcised penis popped out like a child's jack-in-the-box, and he pushed her head into his crotch with strong calloused hands. He made no sound as he thrust harder and harder in her mouth, until she began to get a crick in her neck and climbed up onto his lap, wrapping her arms and legs around him and twirling so fast on the stool that she got dizzy. He turned and stared now, as if her fantasy had been communicated telepathically. Embarrassed, she rose quickly and paid her bill, then walked out, her heart pounding as she ran to the subway and down the stairs, jumping into the waiting train a second before the doors closed. She breathed a sigh of relief to be with people reading newspapers and not one another's minds and settled herself near a grime-clouded window.

At 138th Street, a gangly black man who smelled of hair pomade, shoe polish, and starched white cotton sat next to her. Instinctively, Josie gathered up her legs and turned away, aware as she did so that her buttock and thigh were touching him. She could see his profile reflected in the window, sticky with grime, as the train barreled downtown, whizzing past stations, steel posts, and low-hanging beams, the electric sizzle of the rails sending off sparks, which made Josie feel she was thirteen again, riding downtown to take her Saturday piano lesson, where she played Bach with her arms bent inward to hide her breasts because she was sure her handsome wavy-haired piano teacher was looking at them, breathing on her hair as he corrected her fingering, grazing her thigh with his leg like the black man was doing now. She pictured herself following him to the Hotel Theresa, to a room with dim lights and a big brass bed, rubbing his sweet-smelling pomade all over her body and watching him enter her—black on white like the keys of a piano—in the smoky glass mirror above the bed. She started as the train lurched to a stop, then watched the man step onto the platform and weave through the crowd, dipping to the right in a graceful glide, the way Gus used to walk before he was hurt.

"I can't hear you," Albert snapped at the handsome Italian waiter who had meekly recited the specials. "Tell me again, but not so fast."

The young man with large doe eyes leaned forward deferentially. *"Penne con rosmarino e pancetta,"* he said in a frightened voice. *"Scaloppine di vitello con funghi e—"*

Albert waved him off dismissively. "I can't understand a word he's saying."

Just because you can't *hear* doesn't mean we can't eat, Josie was tempted to say, but she didn't want to ignite the anger that smoldered beneath a surface of constant irritation. Ruth looked exhausted, like the mothers at the supermarket who push their snot-dripping kids through aisles of junk food, pulling Mallomar cookies and Froot Loops, Cheez Whiz and neon pop off the shelves to stave off hysteria. As usual, Josie felt it was up to her to be the entertainment, to keep things rolling so the King of Hearts wouldn't chop off any heads.

"This woman was really incredible," she enthused as the waiter cautiously poured the wine. "She used to be a madam, but since leaving the life—"

"The life?" Albert asked, interrupting her. "Whad'you mean by 'the life'?" It was a challenge, not a question.

"That's what they call it. The life. You've never heard that expression?"

"No, have you?"

"I just used it."

"But did you know it before?"

"No, but what's the difference?"

"I'm just interested in how much you know."

Ruth looked up nervously, the emphasis and rhythm of the conversation presaging disaster.

"Anyway," Josie continued, trying to protect herself from imminent attack. "Sheri's started this nonprofit organization to help prostitutes get off the street. There's absolutely no place where these women can go when they quit. . . ." She hesitated.

"Whad'you mean?" Albert prodded.

"There's no services for prostitutes. Nothing like AA or NA."

"That's not true."

"Just pick up the Yellow Pages and see for yourself. There's something for alcoholics, for drug abusers, sex addicts, battered wives, battered husbands, but nothing for hookers."

"So what?"

"How can you say that?"

"Because these women are whores." He pronounced the word "hoo-ores."

"These women are *people*."

"Who've chosen to do something that's demeaning and dangerous—not to mention illegal."

"So they don't count?"

"Whad'you mean, 'don't count'?"

"That nobody cares what happens to them. Sheri told me at least fifty women a year are murdered by their pimps or tricks, and half the time, nobody even investigates. They say, *like you*, she's just a *whoo-ore*."

It was a mistake to mock him.

"Since when is this Sheri your new best friend?" he taunted.

"Why're you so contemptuous of somebody you don't even know?"

"You interview one whore and suddenly you're an expert."

"I never said I was an expert. Why does everything with you have to be an argument?"

"You're the one who's arguing. I'm just not moved by the hooker with the heart of gold."

"Why must you belittle a woman who's trying to help other women?"

"I help plenty of women," he said self-importantly.

"We're not talking about you, Papa. We're talking about Sheri Montenegro and the script I'm writing."

"I guess I don't care," he said, calling for the waiter.

"I guess not," Josie shot back, feeling white rage burn the back of her throat like regurgitated milk. "I guess all you care about is yourself."

Ruth spoke for the first time. "That's enough, Josie."

"What did you say?" Albert looked up from his menu, his hearing suddenly as sharp and angry as his eyes.

"I find it truly amazing that anyone who spends his life taking care of women can be so unforgiving."

"And I find it amazing that a daughter of mine could be so aggressive."

"You say *aggressive* like it's a dirty word," Josie said. "Just because I won't take your shit, I'm aggressive."

"And a pain in the ass!" Albert exploded. "Of both my kids, you've always been the worst."

"Shhh! Both of you!" Ruth looked furtively around the room at the other diners.

"The worst? So, I'm the worst." Josie spat out the words, ignoring her mother and the waiters who peered out of the oval glass from the kitchen. "You know what you are, Papa? You're a big fucking bully. And if a woman's not flat on her back with her feet in the stirrups, she's a threat!"

Josie didn't know what happened next, but she heard the dishes rattle as she stood up from the table and saw the wine bottle teeter on the edge of her plate. "I'm leaving," she said, turning on her heel.

"No, Josie, please." Ruth grabbed her hand. "We haven't even ordered."

"I'm not hungry."

"Albert, please, ask her to—"

"Let her go," he said, beckoning to the waiter, who cowered near the bar, visibly relieved that Albert's wrath was not directed at him.

"*Sì signore.*" He hung his head like a dog expecting to be hit.

"I'll have the veal. . . ."

The worst. You've always been the worst! She gulped in mouthfuls of cold air and felt the tears sting her cheeks. "You fucking asshole," she howled. "How could you say that!" She hurtled down the street, oblivious to traffic and red lights, walking without direction in long, angry strides, not wanting to go home or face him in the morning, but fearing his dark silence and ostracism more. She walked past stores and houses and churches and museums, all part of the patchwork of her past—the trees on Park Avenue lit up for Christmas, the Empire State Building bathed in green and red, the fountain in front of the Plaza Hotel glistening like diamonds. If only she could hail a cab and go straight to the airport, but where would she go? Not back to L.A., a place that suddenly seemed weird and lonely because Gus wasn't there, and she couldn't call him, as he was hopping from one dinky town in Utah to the next, staying in motels right out of *The Petrified Forest*. She longed for Gus, his steadfastness. His understanding. His unconditional love. The *good* father, she thought fleetingly as she kept walking and crying and baying at the moon, replaying the scene in the restaurant and remembering all the times she'd fled from the apartment—that nine-room womb—to smoke cigarettes in front of the Guggenheim and brood alone in a double feature at the RKO, always limping home with a lump in her throat and a car wreck in her head, fending off her mother's pleas to "make up" with cries of outrage, "Why should *I* apologize to *him*?" Until she couldn't stand the silence anymore, the oppressive tension, and found a way to "make nice," like the good girl she'd been raised to be. She thought of sending him a gift of African violets or anemones (his favorite flowers) with a note that said, "I may never understand your anger, but I will always love you," but why wave a white flag to ease her torment when she knew if she apologized, which she always did, he would write back, "I love you, too, darling," and they would stumble along, sidestepping the rage, waltzing around the frustration until the day he closed the door and would not let her or anybody in.

It was midnight when Josie tiptoed into the apartment, but

seeing the lights ablaze and hearing the phone ring off the hook, she knew instantly that something terrible had happened.

"Where've you been, Josie?" Her mother's voice was strained and frightened. "I've been calling you for hours."

"What's wrong?"

"Papa's had a stroke."

"Oh God." Josie felt sick to her stomach. "Where are you?"

She raced out of the apartment, imagining the worst—her father paralyzed, mute, drooling—and ran ten blocks to Mount Zion Hospital, her heart pounding in her head, her mouth dry with fear. Thoughts of James Dean and Raymond Massey in *East of Eden*. Had their fight caused the blood vessel to pop? She followed the yellow brick line in the basement to a corridor of cubicles where she heard her father bellow, "Get me out of here, Ezra. I want to go home."

"Well, at least you can talk," she said, bounding into the room.

"Josie!" Albert's eyes brightened at the sight of her, their dinner fight forgotten or burned out. "Will you help me here?" He struggled to sit up but listed to the right like a steamer caught in shallows. The young man who tried to steady him had a strong, broad back and a wonderful head of thick brown hair, which he casually brushed out of his eyes as he eased Albert back onto the cot.

"I wanna go home," Albert protested in a husky voice.

"Will you stop it!" Ruth said angrily. "You're not going anywhere. You had a stroke."

"A minor incident," he protested. "I'll be all right."

"Will somebody tell me what happened?" Josie asked.

"He fell down," Ruth explained. "On the way out of the restaurant, he started to keel over. Then he collapsed like he'd been hit by lightning."

"I never lost consciousness," Albert corrected. "I faltered. Nothing more."

"We tried to reach you, Josie."

"I know," she said, feeling guilty. "Are you a doctor?" she asked, turning quickly to the stranger, who seemed to know her father well. "No, I'm Ezra," he said, reaching out his hand.

"He's the guy who's making the documentary," Albert said. "I told you."

"No you didn't," Josie said, looking into Ezra's strong, open face, his soft brown eyes smiling at her as if he knew her. The voluptuous mouth. He had to be seven or eight years younger than she, but there was something about him that seemed mature. Confident. Experienced. She shook his hand, liking the strong grip and smooth, dry skin. "Who for?" she asked.

He stared at her, not understanding.

"The film," she said. "Who're you making it for?"

"I'm applying to film school."

"Oh really, where?"

"UCLA. USC."

"Not NYU?"

He shook his head and ran his eyes over her mouth and neck, lingering on her breasts. He had stared at the picture of her in Dr. D.'s office, the one where she wore a polka-dot bikini and was sitting on top of a cellar door with GARBAGE graffitied across the top. She was smiling as she pressed her arms together to make her breasts look larger as they spilled out over the skimpy top. But the beauty mark (invisible in the photo) was a surprise—a little teaser above her lip. An invitation. He was aware of holding himself back from leaning over and flicking it with his tongue. She looked better in the flesh, not much older than she was in the picture, although her hair was shorter and darker now and her eyes a little sad.

"What the hell is taking them so long?" Albert shouted. "I'm telling you I'm fine."

"Just stop it, Albert," Ruth admonished. "You're not fine."

"I'd be better off at home."

"You can't go home. You've been admitted."

"Stop telling me what I can and can't do!" he snapped at her, and tried to sit up again.

"Albert, please," Ruth looked helplessly from Josie to Ezra. "Tell him to lie down."

"Dr. Davidovitch." A bespectacled woman doctor came into the room. "We'd like to do a CAT scan."

"I want to be discharged," he said.

"I can't do that, Doctor. You've had a transient ischemic attack and we want to keep you here overnight."

As soon as she was out the door, Dr. D. sat up, holding on to Ezra's arm. "What she's saying is that if I have another stroke, I'll be a vegetable. And if I'm a vegetable, the last place I want to be is in Mount Zion Hospital."

Before he could make another move, a nurse's aide swooped in and started to wheel him down the hall. "They're a little backed up at the CAT, Doc, but you're next in line."

The hospital hall was cold and drafty. "What the hell's going on?" Dr. D. shouted. "I'm freezing my nuts off!"

Ezra laughed, but feeling Ruth's icy stare, he stopped abruptly.

"Calm down," she said curtly.

"Don't tell me to calm down, goddamnit!"

"Don't talk to me like that," she shot back, and then burst into tears.

"I'm going home," he said, beginning to unfasten his hospital gown.

"Oh, Albert," Ruth pleaded, then turned to Josie. "Make him stop."

"How can I—"

"Ezra," she beseeched. "He'll listen to you."

"Listen, Al." Ezra spoke in a quiet, understanding voice. "You're driving the women crazy. Why don't you just chill?"

"Chill? I'm already freezing!" He turned to Josie. "I need your help, Josie."

"What do you want me to do?"

"Help me get dressed."

"You're sure you want to do this, Papa?"

"I'm sure."

"What if you have another stroke?"

Albert looked her square in the eye and said without a moment's hesitation, "If that happens, you let me die."

"This is terrible," Ruth wailed. "You can't do this."

"Hand me my clothes." Albert turned to Josie, ignoring Ruth's cries. "Steady me, Ezra. Let me hold on to you."

Ezra stooped down so Albert could hook his arm around his neck while Josie grabbed his shirt and pants from under the gurney, unraveling the familiar suspenders, and helped him into his corduroy jacket. His left side sagged, but with Ezra's help, he could stand. Draping his other arm around Josie's shoulder, he could move his feet in an unsteady shuffle. Josie found Ezra's hand and looped her fingers into his, feeling a warm current flow up her arm and into her belly.

"Are you okay?" Josie said to her father as she and Ezra half-lifted, half-dragged him toward the exit.

"Let's go," Albert said, girding himself as he lurched forward, like a windup toy with one last surge of power.

"You can't do this," Ruth repeated wanly, standing off to the side. "It isn't right. . . ." Her voice trailed off as they hobbled out into the cold December air, Dr. D. holding on to Josie and Ezra, focusing all his attention on getting out, escaping, propelled as much by anger as by fear. Oblivious to cold or wind, they staggered to Fifth Avenue—Josie the rudder, Ezra the sails—where Ruth, defeated in her fight to stop him, hailed a cab. Ezra climbed in first, dragging Albert like a sack of potatoes; then Josie fell in.

"We made it," Albert cried triumphantly, as if he'd just

escaped the Nazis. "We're free." He pulled Ezra and Josie into his chest, kissing them both on the top of their heads. "Thank you," he said, holding them in a tight embrace, so close that Josie could feel Ezra's warm, sweet breath on her face. As the cab pulled up to the house, she realized she and Ezra were still holding hands.

SEVEN

Josie had never thought about sleeping with anyone else when she was going steady, and marriage seemed about as steady as you could get. But since her trip to New York, she had found herself thinking a lot about Ezra, imagining his soft, promiscuous mouth and stubby fingers exploring her body; holding on to his smooth, broad back as he made love to her from above; kissing the lovely hollow between his high cheekbones and the dark shadow of his beard. Sometimes, she saw his face when she felt Gus kissing her thighs, or pictured him staring down at her with intense silent eyes as she soaped herself in the tub. Sometimes, she melded the two—Gus and Ezra—into one perfect lover, and the second before Gus came, when his body tensed and his moans seemed to rise from some dark mystical place, she closed her eyes and saw Ezra rearing above her like a prize bull. If she was cheating on Gus, it was only in her head, and she could justify it all as research for her script. She reread her notes about Sheri's sexual past and the interviews with another hooker named Opal, a cocoa-colored wisp of a woman who looked like a sparrow, who had told her in explicit detail all the things she would and wouldn't do. "Won't let 'em fuck me in the ass," she said. " 'Cause it hurts when I fart. Some of 'em likes to do it under my arm. That's cool. But the best is my portable pussy. I jes strap it on and the johns don't know the difference. Course, you gotta take good care of it. Sit it up in the douche and take it to the doctor twice a week to check for crabs and lice."

What was it about these women that moved her? That made her want to be their friend? Their sexual biographies compared to hers were grotesqueries of character and experience. They had done it all at terrible risk and degradation. All outcasts who in the world of sexual commerce still held a certain power. It was that power, or illusion of power, that turned Josie on. To be the boss, to lift the veil that shrouded a life of *love without fear,* the title of the book she'd stolen from her mother's lingerie drawer and read in the locked bathroom when her parents were out—her first pornography, a marriage manual for better sex! To listen to Sheri and Opal talk about the men who paid them to do the things their wives wouldn't do. To learn that *nobody* did it on their side like her father had told her. To fantasize without guilt or feel constant pressure to confess, as if having secrets were a sin. These women had no secrets except for loneliness and fear.

"Ain't nobody lonelier than a whore," Opal said. "Don't go to lunch with friends like you. Don't go to the theater or sit in the park. Gets up at six, when everybody else is coming home. Shits, shaves, and showers, buys makeup and prophylactics on her day off. Watches the soaps and eats canned soup. Stays out from ten till five. Comes home, showers and douches, and falls back into bed."

Profile of a Prostitute went into production the day Dick Ellis died. He had gone to the Yucatán in the belief that the sun would make him well and had fallen asleep in a hammock overlooking the Caribbean, never to wake up again.

"That's how I'd like to go," Gus said as he and Josie drove up the Coast Highway to Ojai, where Dick was being buried in a valley of avocado and lemon groves. "Lying in the sun in a hammock overlooking the sea." He turned to Josie. "We could use a vacation, you and me."

"Not now," she said too quickly. "I've just been offered another script."

"Can't you put it off a week?"

"Not really. No."

"I feel like we're strangers," he said.

"You're the one who's been holed up in an editing room for five months."

"Why're you getting defensive?"

"I'm not defensive." She could feel herself tense. "I just can't get away now."

"Okay," he said, retreating into silence as the wind and sunshine rushed in through the car window. He remembered when they had first arrived in California to write their script and he had taken Josie on a trip up Highway One and shown her a whole new world she had never seen. The Pacific Ocean. Big Sur, Mendocino, the Russian River. She'd thought everything was wonderful and marveled at the huge green hills that curved like graceful thighs down to the sea, clung to a tree to peer fearfully at the waves crashing against the craggy rocks below, nestled close to him in the cabin near Nepenthe, which she said reminded her of camp.

They had always been so close, more intimate than most couples since the accident, although not always in ways conducive to romance. Right afterward, he'd hated having to depend on her for everything—to go to the bathroom, shower, shave, dress, undress, be lifted up whenever he fell. Somehow, they'd gotten through. But now, he didn't know what she was thinking, except he felt she wasn't thinking of him. He wrote it off to worry about her father. She was right to be concerned. He'd never told her about the conversation he'd had with Dr. D. when her parents had visited them in L.A. "What would you do if you couldn't work?" he'd asked. "I don't know," Gus replied. "I haven't thought about it. What about you?" "I'll kill myself," Albert said point-blank. "But you've got so many other interests," Gus said naïvely. "The theater, ballet, travel." Albert knit his brow and smiled a crooked smile, as if to say, Don't give me that shit. "What about Ruth and Josie and David?" "They'd survive without me," he answered without emotion, then turned away, as if his mind was already made up and it would do no good to argue.

"I'm sorry," Josie said, feeling a weight inside her heart. "I didn't mean to be so short."

"It's okay," he said, squeezing her hand. "It's just that I miss you."

"Maybe when I get back, we'll go somewhere."

They drove through a narrow valley of fruit trees and flowers so sweet, the air smelled perfumed. "I think we should call some adoption agencies when we get back." She turned to Gus. "I don't think we should wait anymore."

He pulled the car off to the side under a giant acacia tree. "You're sure?" he said, smiling.

"I'm not sure about anything," she replied, shaking her head and feeling that familiar *sinking* in her stomach, the dip of a swing falling back to earth. "But I want a baby." And then without any warning, she started to cry.

"Come here," he said, pulling her into his chest and smoothing her hair. "It's going to be okay."

"When do you ever say it *isn't* going to be okay?" She laughed, resting her cheek in the crux of his neck, his sharp collarbone pressing into her ear.

"I love you," Gus said, kissing her gently on the eyes. "I hate to see you so sad."

"I'm not sad," she lied. "Just ambivalent. I still want to have a baby of my own."

"Who knows what's going to happen?" he said with a sense of relief that this was why she seemed so far away. "You could still get pregnant."

Indiana in March looked even flatter on the ground than it did from the air—nothing but fat wide squares of brown and puce, a patchwork of fields that time had faded dull and dry. Not a tree or bush to break the horizon—only big shiny silos in black and navy blue that stuck up like giant penises into the cloudless sky, as if defying the earth's warmth and roundness.

Josie drove from Indianapolis to Craryville—no way she could get lost, as there was nothing on the map but straight lines. She was here to research her new script, the story of an amateur circus whose high-wire team, all corn-fed, honey-haired, pink-cheeked teens, had gone out drinking after the opening show and been in a car crash, killing two and leaving a town bereft, devastated, and perplexed by the question of whether the remaining teammates should go on with the show.

"What a concept," the producer had raved. "An American tragedy with *series* potential. I'm thinking of calling it *Flying High.* . . ." Then he cracked his knuckles. "Get it?"

"I get it," Josie said, not knowing until she was seated in front of the circus board in a town that looked like Maple Grove that her producer had failed to secure the rights for either the story or the circus and it was up to her to get them now.

"This is a real pleasure," said Lowell Brockton, the president of the circus board, a square-jawed, handsome blond with periwinkle blue eyes and a thin judicial mouth, greeting her cordially. "We really appreciate your comin' all the way down here to talk to us."

"No problem. I was so moved by your story, I wanted to meet you all," Josie said, feeling suddenly like Woody Allen in the Easter supper scene of *Annie Hall.* (Although she was hardly dressed in *payess,* she sure wished she hadn't worn gold jewelry or Perry Ellis shoes.) Seated around the table at circus headquarters were six men whose faces looked like they'd been chiseled out of Mount Rushmore. No smiles or blinks of the eye, arms folded uniformly across the chest. Josie had pitched to men in shirts unbuttoned to their navels, women tucked so tight that they could hardly smile, and cokeheads who sniffed and disappeared into the bathroom, but she had never pitched to a bunch of farmers who wore feed caps, work boots, and overalls.

"I want to tell you right off," she began in a consciously earnest tone, "that I understand better than anyone how important it is to respect privacy and personal pain." She lowered her voice dramatically. "Because I, too, had the experience of seeing my own personal tragedy turned into a movie." (NBC, a thirty-five share.) She paused to take a quick temperature reading of the room but couldn't make out what was going on behind those cornflower blues that stared emotionlessly into her Semitic browns. "A few months before I was to be married, my fiancé was in a surfing accident and"—she paused for effect—"broke his neck."

She couldn't believe what she was doing. Prostituting her personal tragedy to seduce these American Gothics into giving her the rights to their story; blatantly manipulating them into trusting her, when the minute they signed over their rights, they would lose all control, no matter what she promised. "I don't want to exploit anybody," she continued. "I want to protect your privacy so no one will suffer more than they already have."

A lean-faced man with weather-beaten cheekbones the color of plums nodded imperceptibly. "We don't want people thinkin' our kids were bad," he said softly. "They were just kids, having a good time."

"The only villain in this story, as I see it, is booze," Josie interjected, thinking she could use a drink right now. "It's the story of a town, one big family, which from the minute I got here is what I *felt* your circus was." She was making herself cry. "It's a story about trust and the power to go on."

Some of them nodded, but nobody said a word, and Lowell, the consummate salesman, born-again diplomat, asked if there were any questions. No. There were no questions, and they all filed out of the room like the Light Brigade.

"Do they hate me?" She turned to Lowell in a fit of paranoia.

"Not at all." He laughed. "You're just *different* from what they're used to." You mean *Jewish*, Josie wanted to say. "They'll come round," he continued. "Don't you worry." Then he put his hand on Josie's shoulder. "Come on. I want you to meet Mike Wilson, the head trainer."

Mike Wilson was like every gym coach, favorite counselor, all-round good guy Josie had ever known. If the town fathers looked on her with suspicion, Mike was like a proud uncle who wanted to talk about all *his* kids. "It was like losing one of my own," he said, looking up at two teenagers flying like doves in the air. "What happens up there is a natural bonding when you're holding another person fifty feet in the air." Josie followed his gaze up to a beautiful blond girl and a bare-chested boy who was hanging by his legs. "When these kids lock hands, there's a power stronger than any glue." As if on cue, the girl swung into the air, did a half turn, and somersaulted into her partner's iron grip. "It's a power called trust."

Josie felt a shiver. She could already see the promo—*a power called trust.*

"Watch this." Wilson kept his eye glued to the fliers, who clung so closely, they looked like one person. Then the girl, a vision in white, with long blond hair pulled tight back into a ponytail, slid in a slow circular motion down the rope—Eve dancing with the snake—until she was resting on Adam's crotch, transferring her undulating dance from the rope to his body, which she slithered down until they were face-to-face, almost kissing. Josie held her breath, mesmerized by the sexual tension between these (probable) virgins. She hadn't seen anything so hot since her last porno at the Pussycat Theater, only this was happening live and in midair. Suddenly, the girl let out a blood-curdling scream and plummeted toward the earth like Rima of the jungle. Josie gasped, convinced that the young virgin would splat all over the concrete floor, but the second before she hit, her partner yanked the rope up and held her like a tethered swan dangling from her slender ivory ankle.

"Fantastic!" Josie cried out.

"Not a bad trick." Mike smiled from ear to ear.

" 'Not a bad trick'?" Josie guffawed. "I thought she was going to die."

"Meet Tammy and Brian." Mike beckoned the pair over. They seemed much younger and shier on the ground. "This here's a famous Hollywood writer," he said proudly. "She's gonna write a TV movie about circus."

"Oh wow." The two corn-silk children bobbed their heads like dashboard dollies.

"That was the most wonderful act I've ever seen," Josie gushed. "How'd you do it?"

"Wanna try?" Mike asked as Brian and Tammy smiled bashfully.

"Who, me?"

"Yeah, you."

"You mean up there?" Josie pointed to the top of the tent with a shaky finger.

"Yeah. Brian and Tammy'll help you. Won't ya, kids?"

"Sure," they said in unison.

Josie looked at Mike. Mike looked at Josie. They were all waiting to see what she would do. Josie wondered if they put everybody through this test or just the Jews.

"Okay," she said, kicking off her shoes. "I've always wanted to fly." She felt a rush of energy, an intoxicating flash of immortality as she grabbed the flimsy rope ladder and followed the bare-chested boy up to the top of the tent, the wooden rungs digging into her arches, the rope burning her palms.

"Don't look down," Brian said, but it was already too late. Josie felt a wave of nausea sweep over her. The last time she'd been above fifty feet was in an elevator.

"Are you okay?" somebody asked, but she didn't dare look to see where the voice was coming from.

"You're almost there," Tammy coaxed, guiding Josie onto the narrow pedestal and quickly snapping a safety rope around her waist.

"How you doin' up there?" Big Mike called from below. But Josie didn't hear him; her head was swimming, her ears echoing with the sound of cars rushing through a tunnel. She couldn't get enough air into her guppy lungs. Beads of perspiration broke out on her brow and her armpits were dripping.

"You're doin' jes great," Tammy said as she pulled the trapeze closer to the pedestal. Closer, but not close enough. "Okay, then," she said, looking at Josie, who had stopped breathing.

"Okay what?" She could hear panic in her voice.

"You have to jump," Tammy said with a smile.

"Jump?" Josie looked across the chasm of space to the slender bar. This could be it, she thought looking down. I could die.

"You can do it," Brian said, stepping onto the platform, which was hardly big enough for one, much less *three* fliers. "Just keep your eye on the trap and go," he said, and dived into the air, grabbing the catcher's trapeze in his hands and flipping over so he hung by his knees.

Josie willed herself forward, arms outstretched, as if she were walking the plank. It wasn't too late to wimp out. But she had too much pride to climb down.

"Go on," Tammy said, giving her a little push.

You bitch, Josie wanted to say, but before she could speak, she was falling, plunging, lunging, *flying!* Up to the top of the tent and back again, pumping her legs like she was a kid swinging in Central Park, straining to touch the big top with her toes, bending her head back so everything swirled—lights and music pulsing in her brain. She was Mary Martin in *Peter Pan*, soaring above the earth, loop-de-looping between Jupiter and Mars. "Look at me, way up high, like a bird in the sky. I'm FLY–ING."

"Okay," Mike shouted. "Let yourself go!" Josie shot through the air into Brian's herculean hands, feeling her heart fly out of her chest, her scalp tingle, her arms grow out of his like they were connected by a single wing. It didn't matter that he was just a boy and she was old enough to be his *much* older sister. Higher and higher she flew, clinging to him for life, never wanting to let go.

"Okay." Mike cupped his hands over his mouth. "It's time to come down."

"I can't," she cried, trying to unclench her fingers.

"Pull your legs up and drop onto your butt," he yelled.

But every time she willed herself to release, her fingers froze and she couldn't let go.

"Let go, Josie. Drop!" Brian forcibly pried open her rigor-mortised fingers.

"Oh, God, no." She freaked, feeling herself fall through the air like Icarus from the sun, feathers flying, her legs and arms flailing gracelessly. She felt herself bounce off the net and thought she would fall to the concrete floor, but Mike scooped her up and set her down gently. She clung to him as if she were a child asleep in the backseat of the car, so her father would have to carry her up to bed.

EIGHT

It had been a very bad day. Josie had heard that morning at a breakfast meeting with her newest agent, a compact little man with nappy hair and a Ben Turpin mustache who usually spent more time talking about *his* problems than her career, that Disney had passed on her circus script.

"But why?" she asked, pushing away her fruit salad and morning-glory muffin.

"Because Walt didn't like it."

"Walt's dead."

"Doesn't matter."

Josie pictured Walt Disney stuffed and mounted. "What did the boss say?"

"That he loved the script but hates the circus."

"How can he hate the circus?"

"He just does."

"Then why'd he commission the script?"

"He thought it was about hockey."

"Hockey?" Josie started to laugh, as much at herself as at the doofus who was president of Disney, because whenever she was surprised by *anything* in Hollywood, she smacked herself in the head for being surprised. "It doesn't matter if it's about hockey or racing or flying, for Christ's sake. It's a story about family and community, trust and the power to go on. It's got heart and danger, tragedy and–"

"Hope," her agent said, finishing her sentence with a bored yawn. "But it didn't make his ass wiggle."

" 'Didn't make his ass wiggle'?" Josie wasn't sure she'd heard him right.

"That's what he said."

"Geeze, what did Flipper do to his cock?"

"Oh, Josie," her agent said, spitting out a horse pill. "We've got to get you to do comedy."

"He's not the first studio executive to think with his ass. . . ."

"Now, now," he said, wagging a manicured finger an inch from her nose. "Let's not get nasty."

"Why not?" she shot back. "I really care about this script. Even you said it's the best thing I've written since *Prostitute.*"

"But I'm not the president of a studio."

"You will be one day." She smiled, sinking into his Pierre Deux–upholstered lawn chair.

"This is nothing personal," he chirped. "You made your money."

"All rejection is personal," Josie said. "And I need *more* money."

"Don't worry, darling," he said, picking up his Princess phone the second it rang. "Two minutes." He held up his fingers and began to negotiate a deal (for another client) at twice Josie's fee, which made the jealousy monster inside her chest rear its fire-eating head and devour her from the inside out, until she felt herself getting smaller and smaller. She turned her face toward the sun, trying not to listen, and thought how much she hated the constant glare of eternal summer, the obsession (hers, as well) with money and status and deals and celebrity, and then she turned and stared at her agent and realized she felt about him the way a hooker feels about her pimp–hating him for needing him, afraid to get him mad, knowing the minute she wasn't "hot," he'd give the best tricks to someone else (which is what he was doing now).

One of the keys to success in the trade was getting your next gig before you finished your last, but the flood of assignments since *The Wave* had slowed to a trickle, and Josie could feel her agent pulling away. Nothing cleared a room faster in Hollywood than the smell of failure. In fact, the only smoke that didn't send people stampeding for the door was the blue smoke you blew up their asses.

Josie eased the car onto Sunset Boulevard and glided down the gentle hills and sweeping curves, glimpsing the landscaped driveways and oversized mansions, happy to be looking without having to make conversation. She was dreading the next meeting, where she and Gus would have to pitch themselves as the perfect parents to Mrs. Binger of the Bide-Away adoption agency. It was one thing to be passed on for one lousy script but another to be turned down for a baby.

"I see from what you've written that you had a rather strained relationship with your mother," Mrs. Binger said. She was a tall, thin woman in her early forties with milky skin and dyed blond hair, so stiff and shiny, it looked like meringue.

"I don't know if I'd say *strained*," Gus answered calmly, although Josie could tell from the (more than usual) jiggling of his left leg that he was nervous. "But it was very hard after my father died. I was only twelve."

"And you, Mrs. Housman," she said, flipping through the pages of Josie's "assignment" to write a candid description of her relationship to her parents. "You said you thought your mother *acquiesced* to your father. What exactly do you mean?"

"That she gave in a lot. Didn't stand up to him."

"Was that a problem?"

"In some ways," Josie said, fearing if she said too much, which she usually did, she'd queer the deal.

"How so?"

"I don't know. Sometimes, I think she didn't protect us."

"Was he abusive?"

"Not physically."

Mrs. Binger was looking at her with *Village of the Damned* blue eyes, which made her squirm, because she was sure Mrs. Binger could tell how much Josie hated her.

"He had a temper."

"Did he ever hit you?"

"We got a slap on the behind every once in a while, but both my parents did a very good job. I had a very happy childhood." She could feel her temperature drop to zero, a sure sign that she was getting mad, because she had to keep a lid on her anger literally to cool down. This was worse than the worst pitch meeting, when you know before you start that the buyer has already made up his mind and it isn't you he wants. "I think my parents were typical of their generation," Josie continued, her teeth chattering. "My father was the boss. But I'm very different from my mother."

"How so?" Mrs. Binger leaned forward.

"I'm more of a bitch." She didn't mean to say that, but there it was, a giant pea up Mrs. Binger's nose.

"Really?" She shifted in the Windsor chair.

"I don't mean *bitchy* or cruel," Josie said, trying to recover. "I'm just not a pushover."

"You mean you're more *aggressive*?" Mrs. Binger asked, and Josie felt her nostrils flare and blood pressure jump from 90/60 to 180/100.

"I didn't say *aggressive*," she snapped, hearing her father's words echo in her ears.

"I think what Josie's saying is that she's not afraid to speak her mind, and I'm not threatened by her," Gus said, swooping in for the rescue.

Josie could feel her stomach twist into a pretzel as she fought an overwhelming urge to reach across the desk and rip out Mrs. Binger's throat. Who the hell was this tight-assed bitch with the Martha Hyer hairdo and watery blue eyes to tell them they couldn't be parents? What gave her the right to try and psychoanalyze them? Look at all the "natural" parents who screwed up their kids—psychiatrists and child experts the worst.

Gus slid his hand into her lap and gently pressed her hand, and she thought she might shatter into a million shards of ice.

"I think what you're trying to find out," he said in a measured tone, feeling the same distaste for this social worker/bureaucrat but not wanting to blow the interview, "is whether we have a stable marriage. And I think having gone through all we have since my accident—even getting married and making a good life at all—says a lot about us as a couple and as individuals. Josie *is* very strong and impatient and passionate. She's also loving and funny and very smart."

"I appreciate that," Mrs. Binger said with her tight-assed smile. "We'll be in touch."

"You mean 'Don't call us; we'll call you'?"

"That's right." Mrs. Binger stared at Josie with icy eyes.

Gus struggled to stand. It was hard for him to rise from a seated position, as if God had intended him to remain on all fours.

"And man took his first step," Josie announced in her best Charles Kuralt voice as he hauled himself up again, fell back into the chair, stood up, sunk down again, got up—until he gained enough momentum to defy the law of gravity and hold himself steady, taking a step and then another as if he were walking on glass.

If Josie's uncontrollable anger hadn't ruined it already, Gus's calliope imitation didn't help much, either. The minute they were in the car, Josie flew into a rage. "If we were like everybody else," she cried, "we wouldn't have to go through all this shit. We'd just have a baby and bumble along like everyone else."

"But we're not everyone else," Gus screamed back. "And you damn near blew it in there."

"Oh sure, blame me."

"I'm not blaming you, Josie. I'm just trying to tell you that you can't get so angry. It's like any interview with any bureaucrat. She's just doing her job."

"That's what the Nazis said."

"Look at it from her side."

"I don't want to look at it from her side. I don't want to have to write essays or answer questions or prove myself to some professional gatekeeper who's going to tell me I'm not fit to be a mother."

"Nobody said you weren't fit to be a mother."

"That's what she implied. What about that question about whether either of us has ever been in therapy? She was looking straight at me when she said that." Gus was looking at her now. "Why're you looking at me that way?"

"Because she's right."

"What? That I wouldn't be a good mother?"

"No. That you need help."

"Why? Because I'm upset?"

"You're not just upset, Josie. You're mad!"

"You mean mad *angry* or mad *crazy*?"

"Both. What do you expect an adoption agency to do? Hand out numbers like in a bakery. Eenie, meenie, miney, moe? This is what they do. It's a process."

"A process?" She could hear her voice rise to so high a pitch, she hardly recognized it belonged to her. "What's that supposed to mean?"

"This is fucking hopeless," Gus said. "You are out of control."

"Why's it always me?" Josie looked at him with puffy eyes. "What about you?"

"What about me?"

"The whole thing."

"What whole thing?"

"Oh God." A sob broke her voice and she shook her head, not wanting to go on.

"What?" he asked in a whisper. "If I hadn't taken the wave? If I'd dived under? Like you? We'd be the perfect happy family? Is that what you're thinking? Because it isn't true."

"How do you know?"

"I don't. I don't know a fucking thing."

"Neither do I," she said, shaking off her tears and fears like a hound dog shaking off fleas. "I'm sorry. . . ." She looked at him, her face caved in. "I'm so tired of being sorry. . . ." She burst into tears.

"You don't have to be sorry," Gus said, massaging her drooping shoulder. "You just have to be patient."

"Patient." She almost laughed. Patience was not a virtue she'd been taught at home. "You know me, Gus. I'm the kid who sees the shit and not the pony." She wiped her nose on her sleeve. "I'll be okay. . . ."

"That's my line," Gus said. But coming from her, he wasn't sure he believed it.

Albert pictured it before he went to sleep and woke up thinking he was there. The house on the corner of Crystal Street and Belmont Avenue, the biggest house on the block, across the road from the Vanderdam farm and three blocks from the public school. He remembered stopping by the dirt lot where his older sister, Lena, played ball with the big kids, and wanting to join the fun, he had left a pound of butter he'd fetched for his mother under a tree and forgot the time and temperature, only to discover, too late, that it had melted into a shiny pool of grease.

He was scared of his mother. She ran the house like a cossack with an infectious sense of humor and an explosive temper that caught him unawares—a *potch* on the arm, a *zetz* on the head, a kick in the ass. He remembered the day when he was sixteen and she lifted her arm to cuff him and he grabbed her wrist and said, "You can't hit me anymore, Mama; I'm bigger than you." She looked at him with the same dark eyes that had seen her parents butchered in a pogrom, then sensuously caressed his newly shaved face. He felt his insides melt and his temples throb because he loved her so much, he almost hated her, and he wanted to rip himself away from the soft, warm bosom and sweet-smelling kitchen where she nursed a houseful of people, doling out food like love to anyone who was hungry, but forgetting his father, who long ago had grown accustomed to being passed over and who one day quietly got up and left, noticed for the first time because there was an extra place at the table.

Ruth climbed up on the footstool in her big walk-in closet and carefully took down the satin floral box where she kept her old love letters and mementos. She wanted to give her father's watch fob to David, who was getting married at the end of the month to a pretty blond actress with a tight little figure and upturned nose who looked like a dozen actresses Ruth had seen on TV. "He *would* pick a shiksa," Albert said when David sent them a photo. And then added, his eyes eating her up, "But she's sure got a great pair of tits."

Ruth carried the box to her bed, and when she lifted the lid, the smell of sachet and loose face powder, scented stationery tied with faded ribbon and flowers pressed in the bindings of Byron and Yeats rose from the box like a morning mist from a lake. Ruth carefully took out a bundle wrapped in blue tissue paper, so smooth that it looked ironed, and unwrapped an apricot negligee trimmed in ivory lace. She fingered the silk lovingly and buried her face in its folds, inhaling it like a bouquet of spring flowers still sweet with the memory of romance.

Ruth liked being married. She liked being a wife. She had gone through brief periods of wanting a career—getting a degree in child development or special education—but every time she sent for the application or started to register for a class, she found an excuse not to go, preferring to be home for her children at three o'clock, planning meals that Viola cooked, volunteering at the school thrift shop, entertaining, and going away every August when Albert took his vacation.

She pulled a card from the pack of letters she had saved all these years and read the note in her own hand: *I love you in the morning / I love you in the night / I never will stop loving you even when we fight.* And another in Albert's graceful script: *The orange juice's squeezed, the coffee is made. I wish I had stayed in bed, well laid.*

She smiled at the memory of their first apartment on Perry Street, the summers at his aunt's hotel on the Jersey shore, and then as she glanced at him in the other room, sitting in that same green chair as he read his medical journals and the *New York Times*, she felt a thud like someone had slammed a door in her heart. She had begged him not to give up his practice cold turkey, but he wouldn't listen. "You could bring in a younger man and continue to see your own patients," she'd pleaded. "Or teach at the medical school. Or volunteer at Planned Parenthood." But he shook his head and shuffled around the apartment in his worn leather slippers and stained khaki pants—the *Titanic* headed straight for the iceberg.

She bought tickets for concerts, plays, and the ballet, wrote away for brochures to exotic places, country inns, and educational tours. Did anything to cheer him up, even when he snapped at her or froze her out. Like a bird in a fountain, she fluttered and plumped her feathers to distract him, decorated and redecorated the nest to seduce him, twittered over drinks and hors d'oeuvres, but no matter what she did, he seemed lost and alone, looking forward to nothing but his evening meal—although she wondered if she dropped dead tomorrow and Viola was there to cook his food, would he even notice she was gone?

The bride wore a long white dress made out of parachute material and the groom a white tuxedo. It was the ugliest, most expensive wedding Josie had ever attended, held on the Trousdale estate of a hot new director, in a mansion that reminded Gus of the old Penn Station. Two large tents were set up near the pool and Werner Erhard himself was seated next to the bride. David's psychotherapist, a bearded man with a ponytail, puka beads, and a golden *chai*, never left David's side, and Josie was not surprised to learn that he was going with the newlyweds on their honeymoon to Nepal and Jerusalem.

Josie wandered around the grounds with a glass of sparkling cider, her brother having recently gone into recovery after meeting his much younger wife, a nineteen-year-old actress with a trust fund as large as her honeydew breasts, at an AA meeting in Malibu. After a courtship at Esalen and advanced training in est, they had become engaged, although Albert was sure the bride was about four months pregnant, which didn't endear her to her new sister-in-law.

Josie loved her brother but thought him a fool, a chameleon who changed color with every new fad—est today, Shambala tomorrow, Arica yesterday, and ANALYSIS forever. When he was in advertising, he dressed like Beau Brummell, and when he bought a place in Palm Springs, he had different outfits for every sport he played—whites for tennis, greens for golf, spandex for running, English riding boots for polo. But now he was on a spiritual quest, which made him less humble than one would suspect. The world was not just his oyster but also his own personal development deal.

Neither Josie nor Gus knew half the guests, except for the stars whom they recognized from the movies—John Travolta and Meryl Streep, Barbra Streisand and Warren Beatty. Ruth was in heaven, feeling important because she was not only the mother of the groom but elbow-to-elbow with so many stars. Albert sat at the end of the banquet table, a permanent smile on his face, as if he'd died and been embalmed. Amazingly, there wasn't a single guest at the wedding whom he had delivered. After dinner (haute vegetarian), Larry Levin, no longer a television executive but now a major mogul of a mushrooming mega—media empire, rose to give a toast.

"What I have struggled to do most of my life," he said, lifting his glass and peering out at the crowd, "is find a hit television series that has tremendous family values, a certain amount of conflict—one that has trust and respect." He paused to check his notes, and Josie wondered if he thought he was at an affiliates meeting and not a wedding or if he was planning to run for office. "I look to my ol' pal David and his radiant bride," he continued. "Two beautiful people who represent youth and family, the future, if you will. And I think of Ozzie Nelson and Dick Van Dyke, Robert Young and Bill Cosby. I think of Elizabeth Montgomery, Farah Fawcett, and Lucille Ball. I think of how we try to make up the perfect family environment for a hit TV show and how the family events and family responsibilities and family problems we all have to face—episodes, if you will—begin right here and now."

Everyone was looking reverentially at Larry, hoping he'd cast them in his next miniseries, sitcom, or feature film.

"How beautiful." Cindi sighed, wiping away a pearl-drop tear. "Thank you, Larry."

"D'you know how much he's worth?" Ruth leaned over to Josie and whispered in her ear. "About two hundred million. Everybody thought he was a dope growing up, but just look at him now!"

Before she could answer, a band of minstrels, dressed in purple tunics over white tights that, when the breeze blew right, revealed great bulges and sacks of skin, the only "meat" at this vegetarian fair, began to play a medley from the Beatles and Peter, Paul and Mary.

"No Gershwin," Albert piped up over the zither. "How about ' 'S Wonderful'?" And like Merlin the magician, Larry Levin waved his magic wand and the mandolin began to play, accompanied by acoustic guitar, electric piano, and a string quartet.

Albert took Ruth's hand and, without asking, led her to the middle of the dance floor. She was so used to the weight and sway of his body that she followed like a blind woman follows her loyal and trusted dog. Waltzing and gliding as if they were on ice, his knee between her legs, their toes never touching, their faces close enough to kiss, it seemed as if the melody and song came from them rather than that they were following the music. Josie watched her parents with the eyes of a child, enraptured and embarrassed, enthralled and jealous. It was the most romantic moment of the day and needed no ceremony or rehearsal. For even if it was her brother's wedding, it semed to Josie that Ruth and Albert were the bride and groom.

NINE

"You can't turn this down. You'll be the toast of New York. Every producer, director, and movie star will want to work with you. Every advertiser from California to Maine will fight for your time. You'll make more money than you ever dreamed of."

Josie wished Marty the agent was talking to her, offering *her* the perfect job with all the perks and status and money and power. But it was Gus whom they wanted for the job, Gus whom they were begging to head up a lucrative new network. Gus who would be the architect of art and culture on cable TV (even though he could hardly carry a tune and was a better dancer *now* than before the accident).

"I don't know. . . ." Gus hesitated, furrowing his brow. "I've just started a new documentary."

"A documentary!" Marty's face reddened to the color of the corned beef he had brought from Nate 'n' Al's. "You've got your whole fucking life to make documentaries," he yelled. "Your whole life to starve. This is the job of a lifetime. There won't be a person in the country—no, the *world*—who won't do business with you. And that means *me*. I'm not an altruist. I admit it. We can name your price. You'll be the king of cable."

The king of cable, Josie thought. What does that make me? She hated feeling jealous, frustrated, and dependent. She had never been so successful as when she and Gus were a team—"the dog and pony act," they used to joke as they trotted off to every job interview *together*, Josie the freshly groomed poodle with the bow in her hair, Gus the dapple, hobbled pony. But since they had retired their act, except for a couple of out-of-town gigs, no one seemed interested in just one dog—although that was hard for Josie to believe from what she saw on TV.

"We could move back to New York," she said so softly that Marty had to bend forward to hear her over the sound of the waves. "You're the one who hates L.A."

"I don't know," Gus said again.

"What don't you know?" Marty's voice was edged with fury.

"If I want it."

"Why?" Josie asked calmly. "I mean, why *wouldn't* you want this job?" And despite her efforts to be unprepossessing and modest like him, all she could think about was money and power and parties (and a penthouse apartment on lower Fifth Avenue).

Marty waved a dill pickle in Gus's face. "You're like all those fucked-up Commies who're scared of being rich."

"Maybe I'm scared of failure and poverty," Gus said with a smile.

"You've never failed in your life." Marty bit off the end of the pickle with a loud crunch.

"I've never been given anything this big."

"You're walking, aren't you?" Josie said.

Gus looked startled. "I forgot about that."

"Listen to your wife." Marty swung his arm around his new ally.

"You can do what you want," Josie said, not wanting to push. "But I think you should take this job. I think it's perfect."

"You won't see me for nine months."

She wished he hadn't said "nine months," unsure what *her* job would be when they moved back to New York.

"Okay," Gus said.

"Okay what?" Marty asked.

"I'll take it."

Marty sighed like he'd been holding his breath for ten minutes and then kissed Josie exuberantly on the mouth. "Like my mother always said, 'Behind every great woman is a man who's a schmuck.' "

Josie always felt good when she crossed the Triborough Bridge. On safe ground. The familiar gateway to home. She glanced out the cab window to the field at Randalls Island where she'd played soccer in grade school, swayed with the cab as it curved onto the FDR Drive, peered out at the bodega-littered streets in East Harlem, and sailed down Park Avenue, past the Greek Orthodox church and her old private school. She could just as well have grown up in a tiny shtetl, so circumscribed and provincial was her life, the forays with her father to the Lower East Side, the Bronx Zoo, and Coney Island little side trips to the world.

She had always dreamed of living in the West Village, somewhere near the Café Figaro, where she had gone as a teenager to smoke Gitanes and drink inky espresso. The biggest fight of her life had been with her father when he forbade her to go to the Village Gate on the back of Todd Singer's Harley-Davidson.

Coming back to New York felt as comfortable and easy as sliding into an old shoe. The apartment she found on lower Fifth Avenue had a view of Washington Square Park, a tiny penthouse with two bedrooms, one of which she hardly dared herself to wish would be for a child. She hadn't given up all hope (even after the disastrous interview with Mrs. Binger). There were babies to adopt from Texas and Chicago, Korea and Peru. She didn't care where. But the baby she dreamed of even as she blotted him out of her mind crept into her dreams like a phantom confection of spun sugar and clouds, plump and sweet as a ripe apricot; quicksilver that seeped through her eyelids and slid onto the sheets and left her slightly dazed and without memory when she awoke in the morning, a dull ache in her chest and a hollow pain in her womb.

Gus had not yet arrived. Josie moved into the new apartment with a futon and lamp. She didn't want to stay with her parents, who seemed to swim in their apartment like blind fish in the ocean, glancing past each other but never really touching, the light in the rooms murky and gray, as if the sunlight couldn't reach the depths of their sadness. From the moment she stepped into the elevator and pressed the button, she got this sick feeling in her stomach and tried to think of a funny story or joke to tell her father to humor him and avoid any criticism, because no matter what time she said she'd be there, she was always late, her heart beating like a speeding train as she bolted through the door. But this day, he seemed quite happy to see her, which she understood the minute she saw Ezra sitting next to him, his super-8 camera silently filming everything, including her as she rushed into the room.

"Sorry," she apologized, feeling her heartbeat quicken at the sight of Ezra's handsome dark face, his eyes bright with mischief as he lowered the camera. "I didn't mean to interrupt."

"That's okay." Ezra smiled, standing up to greet her, and stared boldly into her eyes. She felt the same magnetic pull she had felt the first day she met him. An invisible undertow. A dangerous riptide. "I hear you're moving back," he said, not taking his eyes from her face, her lips, her neck.

"Yes." She nodded, bringing her hand to her throat to shield her naked skin from his hungry eyes.

"Where's your husband?" he asked.

"In L.A.," she said offhandedly. "I'm going back next week to pack." And then she turned to her father and said as she bent down to kiss him. "How're you doing, Papa?"

"We're going to visit the old house." His voice had a buoyancy she hadn't heard for more than a year.

"What old house?"

"Nine forty-one Belmont Avenue," he said. "Where I grew up."

"In East New York?"

Albert nodded. "Ezra's taking me there tomorrow."

"May I come?" Josie asked, turning expectantly toward Ezra.

"Why not," he said, smiling.

"How're you getting there?"

"In an armored car." He laughed. "It's a pretty rough neighborhood."

"How d'you know?" She thought she sounded just like her father when he challenged her.

"I grew up in Brownsville."

"Where's that?"

Ezra smiled. "I forgot you were a princess."

"What's that supposed to mean?" she asked, bridling.

"Not Texas," he said. She was easy to tease.

"How long did you live there?" Josie asked.

"Till I was twelve."

"Oh, just last year," she said with a toss of her head.

"I was always mature for my age," he said, holding her in his gaze as if imagining holding her in his arms.

"Well, I'm not scared," she said.

"Of me?"

"Of you? No. I was talking about the rough neighborhood."

"We had the most beautiful lilac bush in front," Albert said, interrupting their jousting. "And a big chestnut tree in the back." He was already there in his imagination. "I wonder if it's still there."

They sped across the Brooklyn Bridge on a clear and freezing day, Albert staring out the window with a child's delight at being taken on a special outing, dressed in his tweed topcoat and matching cap, a cashmere scarf around his neck.

Ezra had asked Josie to drive so he could film, reminding Josie several times how much he had paid for his new Mercedes 300D.

"You're not scared we'll be carjacked?" she teased.

"I'll get another one," he boasted as they drove deeper into Brooklyn toward East New York. He talked too much about being rich, as if he doubted he was worth much without his (father's) money. Josie could feel him brush against her neck and shoulders as he aimed the camera, shooting the burned-out neighborhood where he'd spent his first ten years ducking Puerto Rican gangs and a few Italian toughs whose parents had hung on too long but who his mother was convinced were all Jewish. "All those Mediterraneans were Jews," she would say, motioning with a theatrical flourish. "During the diaspora, some went to Italy and the rest to Odessa."

"Looks like a war zone, doesn't it?" he said, scanning the bombed-out landscape and treeless lots.

"Look at that." Albert wasn't listening. "That's where my mother bought her rye bread." He was pointing to an old building with the faded letters PECTER'S BAKERY etched like smoke on the weathered brick. "I can still taste the jelly doughnuts." He breathed in deeply. "She was wonderful, my mother. When I think of all she did . . ." They sped beneath the elevated train, their ears popping as the subway burst out of the ground and clattered loudly above their heads. Albert looked up at the tracks, a shadow falling in stripes across his face. "I remember the day Joey Bartowsky was killed."

"What happened?" Josie asked.

"We used to climb up the metal support beams and sneak onto the trains, but sometimes we were on the wrong side or too far down and had to jump across the tracks. I never saw what happened, but Tally screamed, and when I looked down, there was Joey, his skull cracked like a walnut. His face staring up at me like the underbelly of a fish—a milky blue white, almost gray. I'd never seen anybody my age dead. Tally had nightmares for a year. Made me keep the light on all night long. She still sleeps with the light on when anybody dies, 'cause she says she sees poor Joey's ghost."

Josie felt a palpable joy listening to her father tell his story, as if he were telling it just to her, the way he had told her stories when she carried her clothes into his bathroom and watched him shave and shower. Intimate and close, more real than anything she might find at the end of this magical mystery tour.

"Lock your doors," Ezra commanded as they passed Chestnut Street, Brooklyn, Liberty, and Pitkin avenues, Josie slowing down as they drove through streets with burned-out buildings and rat-infested lots, homeless junkies crouched over fires licking the rims of metal drums, dazed loiterers sucking cigarettes like penny candy, hugging themselves to keep from freezing. As they turned onto Belmont Avenue, Albert opened the window and let the icy gust slap his face while Ezra filmed and Josie yelled at her father to close it. "There it is," Albert cried. "Stop the car."

Josie slammed on the breaks as Albert opened the door. "Wait a minute!" Ezra yelled, but as soon as Josie parked the car, Albert was halfway across the street, prancing like a pony, jumping over potholes as big as craters, so fast that Ezra had to run after him. Rushing headlong toward a memory. For there was no house. No lilac bush. No chestnut tree. Just dirt and debris, the skeleton of a cellar, three stone steps, and a piece of iron gate sticking out of the ground.

Josie cried for him to wait, but he just pointed and beckoned her to follow. "Lock the door," Ezra yelled as he shadowed Albert, who was browsing through the old neighborhood like a Sunday shopper, turning every house and sidewalk crack over in his eye. "That's where Lillian Horowitz lived." He pointed to a trim little house across from the ruins of what had been his home. "And downstairs there was where Mr. and Mrs. Olivier lived."

The names reverberated in Josie's ears. "Wasn't he the one who made the wooden birdcage and fixed Aunt Tally's skates?"

"Felt her up, too," Albert added. "He was an old lech."

Ezra laughed and grabbed Josie's hand, conscious that she didn't pull away but gripped him warmly instead. He wished he could bundle up with her somewhere naked in a bed, beneath a down comforter.

"I'm telling you I could move right back," Albert said. "It looks just the same."

Mom would really love that, Josie thought with a laugh as she watched her father bounce up the stairs of the house next door and ring the bell.

"What're you doing, Papa?" she said with alarm.

"It's okay," Ezra said as he checked the street for marauding gangs and snuck a look at a face peeking at them through the curtain.

"Excuse me," Albert said politely as a thin black man opened the door a crack. "Can you tell me what happened to the house next door?" The man looked at Albert as if he had just landed from the moon, then adjusted the shower cap he was wearing to conk his hair.

"Why d'you wanna know?" he asked suspiciously.

"Because I lived there," Albert said. "Seventy years ago."

The man's eyes widened despite his efforts to give nothing away. "You? You lived there?"

"Amazing, isn't it?" Albert said, touching the man's hand in a gesture of friendship. "It was a wonderful place back then. I used to play stickball with Lillian Horowitz right here." He pointed to the street. "And the people in your house had a big boxer dog used to kill all the cats in the neighborhood until he got run over by a trolley."

"No kidding." The man scratched his head with a long, tapered fingernail.

"But tell me"—Albert bent forward—"what happened to our house. Nine forty-one?"

The man slid his pink tongue across his smooth purple lips and said, "It was abandoned. Then the junkies moved in and started setting fires. Messed it up real bad. They boarded it up, but then the squatters moved in. So the city tore it down. Just came one day with a wrecking ball and bulldozed it into nothin'. I went to work in the mornin', and when I come back, it was gone."

Josie felt like she'd been punched in the belly, so disappointed to miss seeing the house where her father had once lived, to be unable to wander through the rooms she'd pictured in her head, climb the stairs her father had scrambled up and down as a boy, touch the moldings in the kitchen that she imagined still smelled of her grandmother's latkes.

"When was that?" Albert looked wistfully toward the empty lot.

The man thought for a minute. "Just last year," he said. "They come and tore it down. It's a shame, really. It was the nicest house on the block. It must've been real nice when you lived there."

"Oh yes," Albert said as if talking about an old lover. "It was a wonderful house. With a big lilac bush over there and a shed on the other side of the fence." He turned back to his neighbor, who had pulled his ragged sweater closer to his body. "I'm sorry to bother you," Albert apologized, seeing the man shiver.

"That's okay," he said with a little bow. "You could put up another house maybe. It's still the nicest lot on the block."

Albert smiled and nodded his head, but his body seemed to droop like a marionette without a puppeteer. He took Josie's arm as he descended the stairs and leaned heavily on Ezra as they walked back to the car, the cold to which he'd seemed oblivious now seeping into his bones, his euphoria setting with the winter sun.

"Are you okay?" Josie asked with concern.

"Fine," he said, staring back at the lot, a strange calm passing over his face. It didn't matter that the house at the corner of Crystal Street and Belmont Avenue was gone. It was still there for him. The shape of the lot, the rise of the hill, the broken gate, the steps leading nowhere. For Albert, it was home.

Josie didn't remember if she had invited Ezra up, but she knew she never said no. Not once. From the second he pulled her into his soft, wet mouth, her face flushing so hot that she felt she'd opened an oven door, her body falling into his embrace like a sky diver jumping out of a plane. He smelled like sea foam and fried *zeppoli*–crisp and sugary and warm to the tongue. His mother was right. He *did* look Italian with his olive complexion and dark brown hair, and when Josie saw him naked, his back still tan from a winter vacation, she remembered walking into her parents' Cape Cod bedroom when she was little and staring at her father, who lay sleeping after the beach, his flat buttocks the color of squooshy white bread, his back as smooth and brown as caramelized sugar.

Ezra carried her to the rumpled futon and pulled off her clothes like a candy wrapper, running his tongue and lips over her face and breasts, pulling her into his hard body and holding her down like a trapped bird. Everything about him was hard– his cock, his chest, his calf muscles, his biceps. When he lifted her, she felt like Fay Wray in the arms of King Kong. When he entered her from behind, she felt like a cat whose mate holds her still with his teeth in the scruff of her neck.

She liked the weight of him on top of her, luxuriated in his strength and health, watched herself with him as if she were watching her own private porno. He held her arms up over her head and thrust himself deep inside her. She brought her hips up to meet him in a muscular dance, the rhythm coming from sighs and grunts and cries and whispers, their sweat mingling like rain and mud, so slippery that when he lost his way and she reached beneath him to guide him back, he stopped her hand, threading himself into her wetness like a blind eel swimming in silt. "Open your eyes," he commanded. "Look at me." The voice of a stranger. She stared into his eyes, so close to her face, she could see only the glint in his iris like the flash of light in a mirror, a shooting star that is gone before you can point to the sky, and she wondered if he even knew who she was. "Let it go," he whispered as she reared up like a horse spurred over a jump and came with a shiver that rolled over him like a wave tossing them both in its wake.

She didn't know how long they made love, but when they had finished, she rested her head on his chest and felt like she had woken up in the wrong dream, his heft and bulk unfamiliar and strange.

"I've gotta go," he said, thinking to himself that he was always leaving. Like a dog pissing on a hydrant, he left his scent but never stayed long with anyone, although he loved a lot of women and wanted to get married and have kids one day.

"Do you always eat and run?" Josie laughed, thinking that this was as close as she'd ever come to a one-night stand. No three-date protocol, no future or past, no falling in love, although she felt at times as if she had known Ezra in another life or been led to him by an invisible love map. "Don't you want to shower?"

"I like the smell of sex," he said, his hand cradling his head, which was still wet with sweat, his legs akimbo like a pasha seated on a pillow, his heavy round balls moist as moss, the wiry black hair crawling up his belly like ivy. He could still smell her in the room and on his skin, a strong smell of clay and sand that reminded him of the bay at low tide or the woods in April.

"Okay," Josie said, watching him stand above her in the dark. Lithe and graceful. Like a cat. She liked looking at him, running her eyes over his strong, muscular back, studying the way he walked without thinking, bent down, stood up. So easily. Every movement smooth and easy. "You won't say anything to anybody, will you?" she said, feeling a nibble of fear as he pulled on his pants and tucked his tired penis to the side of his leg.

"What about?" He zipped up his fly.

"About this?"

Ezra smiled and shook his head. "Why would I say anything?"

"I don't know," Josie said, feeling foolish. "You've gotten pretty close to my father."

"That doesn't mean I'm gonna tell him I'm fucking his daughter," he said.

"No." Josie let out a nervous laugh, the mere thought making her sick with worry. "It's just that I've never done this before."

"Done what?" He pulled his shirt over his head.

"Had an affair."

"An *affair*?" He made a face. "I wouldn't call it that."

She didn't answer, just lay there naked, her hips and stomach reflecting the moonlight, her breasts white globes that seemed to shine on their own.

"Have you been married long?" he asked, stepping into his shoes.

"Long enough," she said, feeling suddenly guilty.

"And you've never slept with anybody but your husband?"

"Not since I've been married." She didn't know why she felt she had to apologize.

"I don't believe it," he said, pulling her up to him with one strong heave and kissing her warmly and wetly on the mouth, his honey breath filling her nose like elixir.

"It's true," she said.

"Well, don't worry." He slipped on his jacket. "Your secret's safe with me."

And he was gone. Gone like a dream that is so real, you wake up dazed and confused. Gone like a fantasy you sleep with every night but do not recognize when you pass it on the street.

Josie listened as the elevator opened and closed, the way she had listened when she was a girl and her parents went out, her heart falling with Ezra as he floated downstairs and out into the night. She walked onto the terrace, the cold slithering up her legs and wrapping itself around her shoulders like an icy cloak, and stared up at the sky, the stars dull from the veil of moonlight.

She stood there for a long time looking out at the city, the arch of Washington Square looming over the park, the rooftops of the Village unchanged for a hundred years. Then her toes and fingers began to throb with cold, so she went back inside and lay down on the futon, the smell of sex still damp on the sheets. She ran her hands over her body to make sure she was still there and stared up at the ceiling. Ezra's strong body and secretive eyes danced in front of her in a kaleidoscope of colors; then Gus's clear blue eyes and long, slim back, the pencil-thin scar etched like a whisper down his neck shifted with the light. She felt a tug of guilt but pushed it away, not wanting to spoil her pleasure and sense of freedom for having thrown a world of rules right out the window. No rationalizing, regretting, analyzing, or trying to explain. She remembered a day in May before Gus was hurt when they went out to the beach and made love in the dunes, ate steamers and lobsters, and watched the moon rise and wink as if to remind them it had a dark side.

Josie realized she was smiling and crying at the same time, weeping for what they had lost and thankful for Ezra's giving her back a piece of herself. She felt her eyes grow weary and her body sag. She wrapped her arms around herself and curled up into a ball, feeling great relief, as if a wall of pressure had been swept away like a pile of stones from the mouth of a cave.

TEN

Josie knew this was a bad day to shop, but she needed a new dress for the black-tie launch of Gus's cable network. They'd hardly seen each other these past three months, except when they occasionally connected in semiconscious lovemaking, then split apart like amoebas the following morning, rejoining at dinner parties, theater openings, dance recitals, and screenings to which Gus was invited and she was his "date."

She thought of Ezra first thing in the morning when she woke up, a silent alarm that greeted her with the sun, but as the day wore on, she let him slip away like a faded dream. Sometimes, she could feel the pressure of confession cramp her belly like a bad stomachache, but it aways passed even as the words bubbled on her lips.

She took the subway up to Loehmann's in the Bronx, remembering as she trudged through the store to the "back room" what her mother always said: "Never shop for groceries when you're hungry or go to Loehmann's when you're depressed." She *was* depressed, depressed because she hadn't gotten a job since they'd moved back East and depressed because she felt tired and bloated and not herself.

Josie moved like a zombie through the racks of clothes with the labels carefully excised, and she found an empty hook in the communal dressing room, the walls painted a sickly yellow, the fluorescent lights flattening everything except her stomach, which she ignored as she slipped a low-cut black dress over her head and stared at her reflection, wanting to throw up. "Why did I come here?" she wondered out loud, unaware that two elderly, nail-polished, hair-frosted, designer-dressed yentas were watching her like hawks.

"Put it back on," the one with a bust the size of Brunhild ordered as Josie placed the dress on a rising pile of rejects.

"What?" she said, unsure if the woman was talking to her.

"The black one you just discarded." The woman nodded. "It's gorgeous. You just don't know how to wear it."

"Whad'you mean?" Josie looked down at herself in an old bra and panties.

"You've got to wear a slip."

"A slip? I don't have a slip."

"Take mine," the woman said, pulling a black taffeta slip out from under her dress like a magician pulling a rabbit out of a hat or a scarf from thin air. "Go on," she insisted. "The dress doesn't fall right without a slip."

Josie hesitated.

"Listen to her," the other woman commanded. "She used to be a buyer for Lane Bryant."

Josie did as she was told as the woman smoothed and adjusted the black dress with great care, stepping back to see what else was missing. "It needs a little jewelry," she said, taking off a large gold clip-on earring and fastening it above Josie's right breast. "Now do this," she said, bending over and scooping a large handful of flesh and pulling her breasts up so they spilled over her merry widow like a Jell-O mold, her skin smooth and creamy as vanilla pudding. Josie felt a little light-headed as she bent down and imitated her self-appointed personal shopper, impressed (and surprised) by her growing cleavage when she stood up.

"Much better." The woman turned back to her friend. "Don't you agree, Sylvia?"

Sylvia nodded her approval. "What do you think, Berenice? A Calvin? Or a Beene?"

"A Calvin," Berenice said, standing back and folding her arms across her chest and sizing Josie up like a painting. "This dress is simple. Understated. Very classy. I saw the identical model at Bloomies for double."

"Really?" Josie looked at herself but saw only the two *shrekloch* sisters staring back at her in the mirror. "You really like it?"

"Like it?" they cried in unison. "It's gorgeous!"

Josie glanced at the tag. Three hundred dollars! A lot for a dress she'd probably wear only once. "I don't know," she said, hesitating.

"Don't know? I'm telling you. This is a bargain! You can't afford *not* to buy this dress. With a little makeup and new hairdo, your husband will propose to you all over again."

Gus had felt this good only once before in his life—the day he won the city semipro championship game at Griffith Park. It was the bottom of the ninth with two outs, the score tied. Gus on second waiting for the bunt. He remembered the smell of the grass and the taste of his sweat as he ran with the pitch, the third baseman hustling for the ball. He could still hear his heart pounding in his ears as he rounded third base, his chest pumping adrenaline into his blood, his legs propelling him the last ninety feet. He could still feel his legs shoot out from under him to make the slide, could hear the slap of the ball in the catcher's mitt as he dove for the plate through dust and chalk and cheers from the stands to score the winning run.

He had pulled it off again this time, culling the best talent from New York and L.A., spending more money than he could spend making fifty documentaries. He had hit a home run. But the party and glitter were just the afterglow. It was making it happen that gave him a charge. He felt uncomfortable in his rented tuxedo, as if he were at a fraternity brother's Beverly Hills wedding. He had never liked dressing up, didn't care about clothes, even though he knew Josie wished he would dress more stylishly, like her father and brother.

"Fantastic job." Someone slapped him on the back. "Let's do lunch next week." "Hey, Gus. I want you to meet Melanie Breitman." "Hey, Gus, remember me? Danny Mackenzie. We worked together on—"

"I'd do anything to work for you at Prime Star Cable." A tall beauty with a mane of black hair leaned so close, he could smell her maraschino lipstick. "I'm so sick of the shit at the networks, and Hollywood's a joke. What you're doing is—"

Gus suddenly realized he'd lost Josie. She'd been sitting with him at the presentation, had helped him up to the mike. He'd seen her beaming from the audience in her new black dress as he thanked his staff and crew, and he realized just now with a clutch in his gut that he'd forgotten to thank her. He felt a moment's panic as he scanned the sea of faces, but he couldn't swim against the tide of big and little fish darting and ducking, bobbing and weaving in a frenzied whirlpool around his knees.

Even in her Calvin, Josie felt she was dressed in sackcloth. So many beautiful people at the big cable bash that she felt invisible. She watched Gus buffeted by the throngs of well-wishers and ass-kissers, thanking them for their compliments and complimenting them for their hard work, and thought to herself how different she was from him. He wasn't an operator, didn't care about being famous. Didn't keep score. Didn't stay up nights worrying about an imagined insult or passing slight, didn't rehearse tell-offs in the bathtub or write indignant letters. In this sea of sharks, he looked like a butterfish, no more interested in working the room than flying to the moon. As she floated off to her own quiet pool and watched the agents and producers, actors and researchers, old friends and strangers who pretended to know him, she remembered how she had felt when she went backstage with her father and the ballerinas clustered around him, their tulle tutus and diamond ear bobs obscuring him from her view like clouds over the moon.

As she swam away from the party on her way to the bathroom, she half-expected to see Sheri sashaying down the hall, her S & M spike heels clicking on the marble, her red curls poking out from a lace mantilla like Belle Watling in *Gone With the Wind*. Josie laughed to herself. The only difference between Sheri and half the whores at this party was that she had served time; and the only difference between Josie and the rest of the guests was that she didn't feel she deserved to be invited.

Surprisingly, there was nobody in the ladies' room except a uniformed attendant, a middle-aged black woman wearing a pink waitress's uniform with white apron who dispensed paper towels and miniature bars of soap. What a terrible job, Josie thought as she adjusted her dress, which seemed to fit more snugly than it had two weeks ago.

"When're you expecting?" The woman smiled at her as she handed her a towel.

"Expecting what?" Josie asked.

The woman looked at Josie with surprise and embarrassment, knowing even if she were right, she'd made a mistake. Josie pressed. "What did you say?"

"Nothing, ma'am," the woman said, fumbling.

"No, you asked if I was expecting something."

The woman lowered her eyes and bit the smile off her lip. There was no way she could get out of this if she wanted a tip. "I thought you were pregnant."

"Pregnant!" Josie let out a loud laugh. "I've been trying to get pregnant for years."

"Oh, I'm sorry," the woman said.

"You don't have to apologize." Josie washed her hands as the attendant quickly handed her a towel. "It's not your fault I can't have kids."

"Well, you could've fooled me." The woman crumpled the used towel and wiped every droplet of water off the sink.

"Do you have any children?" Josie asked.

"Oh, yes." The woman smiled. "I've got five girls."

"How old?" Josie asked, the smell of disinfectant making her queasy.

"Monitha's sixteen and Tonya's just twelve." She counted on her fingers as she listed the other three.

"We're trying to adopt," Josie said, feeling heavy and sad. Like she'd swallowed wet sand.

"That's good," the woman said, running her eye over Josie's undeniably (to her) pregnant belly. "But if I was you, I'd check it out. You sure got that look about you."

Josie glanced at herself in the mirror, not sure what she expected to see. She had put on some weight, but she couldn't remember when she'd had her last period, having long ago stopped circling dates on her calendar or keeping charts of her temperature.

She thought fleetingly of Ezra, whom she hadn't seen since that night, although she thought about him the way you think about a wonderful meal, remembering everything but the taste. And she'd stopped blaming Gus for her infertility, choosing instead to accept it as her fate. The childless daughter of an obstetrician.

But what if she *were* pregnant? The thought gave her a lovely chill like an ocean breeze on salty wet skin. A tingling in her scalp. Her heart caught. Because if she wasn't pregnant like all the times before, she was sure she was dying of ovarian cancer.

"Cancer?" Her doctor pulled his rubbery fingers out from between her legs. "You don't have cancer." He peeled off the surgical gloves and threw them away. "You're a good four months pregnant."

"How can that be?" Josie slid up the examining table, crinkling the paper gown that made her feel like a badly wrapped package.

The doctor, a benignly handsome man with reddish hair, freckles, and eyelashes the color of bleached flour, looked at her with bemused disbelief. "Isn't your father Dr. Albert Davidovitch, the obstetrician?"

Josie nodded.

"Well, I guess it's the shoemaker's children who go barefoot," he said, laughing. "Why don't you get dressed and come into my office."

Josie sat very still. She could feel the blood course through her veins like fuel being pumped into the tubes, pipes, and cylinders of a Mercedes engine. She cupped her hands over her smooth convex belly and felt something stir inside her bones, so gentle, so invisible, that she wasn't sure if it was a butterfly's wing or a baby's sigh.

Pregnant? It was impossible. But if it was true . . . She jumped off the examining table and ripped off the paper gown, threw on her clothes and slipped into her shoes as she was running, running out of the office and into the street, stopping at the first phone booth to call Gus.

"He's in a meeting," his secretary said.

"It's important." She could hardly wait for him to pick up the phone. "I'm pregnant!" she screamed before he had time to say hello.

"You're what?"

"I'm pregnant." She was laughing.

"You're kidding."

"No. Four months."

"I don't believe it."

"I'm due in September. Oh Gus . . ."

He let out a hoot, a yelp, a *geschrei*. "Fantastic!" he cried. "Josie's pregnant!" he repeated to whoever was in his office. "Oh baby, this is great!"

Josie sailed across the park, remembering a speech from *A Midsummer Night's Dream* that had reduced her professor to tears when he read it aloud in class because his wife had just given birth to a son.

> *When we have laugh'd to see the sails conceive*
> *And grow big-bellied with the wanton wind;*
> *Which she, with pretty and with swimming gait*

Following (her womb then rich with my young squire),
Would imitate, and sail upon the land
To fetch me trifles, and return again,
As from a voyage, rich with merchandise.

Josie skipped and ran and leapt down Fifth Avenue, across the bridle path and up to her parents' apartment. Ruth was away. She had gone to New Orleans to visit a cousin, as much to escape Albert's unrelenting depression as to see a distant relative she had not spoken to in years.

Josie pressed the elevator, thinking she could fly up faster on the wings of her heart, so excited to tell her father and see his face when she said the words *I'm pregnant,* hoping that the news would pop him out of his depression like a chick from an egg and that he would throw his arms around her and kiss her on both cheeks.

The newspaper was still outside the door. Strange, but, like all clues, only meaningful in retrospect. She picked up the paper and opened the door. The apartment was dark and stuffy, as if no one had opened a window in weeks. She felt uneasy as she stepped into the center gallery, her mother's gloves lying neatly on a mahogany table near a picture of Josie and David when they were kids.

"Papa?" she called as she tiptoed down the hall, feeling like Prince Charming cutting a path through prickles and vines. She peered into the little room where he sat all day long, but he wasn't there. "Papa," she said again. "Where are you?"

She hesitated before entering her parents' bedroom, memories of groping blindly toward them when she had nightmares, feeling the walls with her hands, the darkness thick as velvet, her fear dissolving as she climbed into the sweet, warm sheets, her father's hairy legs tickling her backside as she rested her head on the soft cushion of her mother's breast.

He lay curled in a fetal position, the blanket pulled up under his chin. Josie tiptoed closer and peered over his shoulder. In his arms, he cradled a picture of his mother, her large brown eyes and high cheekbones, unsmiling mouth and widow's peak staring out into the distance with dreamy detachment. Josie placed her hand gently on his forehead. "Papa," she said softly, her lips brushing his ear. He was still warm but hardly breathing. "Papa, are you all right?" She shook his shoulder, but he didn't move. "Papa," she said more loudly. "Can you hear me?"

She slapped his face tentatively at first, not wanting to hurt him. "Wake up!" She hit him harder.

Josie felt the ground beneath her give way, like in a dream when you are falling and jerk yourself awake to catch the fall, your heart pounding like a drum. She ripped the covers off and saw a dark amber stain beneath the nightshirt her mother had made for him. At first, she thought it was blood, then realized from the acrid smell that it was urine. The last squeeze of life before the body let it all go. The shallow breathing and lukewarm skin like tepid bathwater. Milky blue. He was dying. Dying before her eyes. Of a stroke or heart attack, she didn't know, but she knew she couldn't waste time, that it was up to her to save him, and though she scanned the bedside table for some clue—empty pill vials or a note—her mind was a whirling dervish as she grabbed the black rotary phone and dialed 911 with trembling fingers.

The paramedics shone a light into his eyes, clamped an oxygen mask over his mouth and nose, and swung him like a koala bear onto a stretcher.

Josie's voice cracked when she heard Gus on the other end of the phone.

"What's the matter?" he said, knowing instantly that something was wrong.

"It's Papa. He's dying," she said, choking.

"Where are you?"

"At the apartment. But we're on our way to the hospital."

"I'll meet you there."

"No. It'd be better if you went out to the airport and met my mother. She's due to arrive in a couple of hours."

"Are you sure?"

"Yes." Josie nodded to herself, thinking how terrible it would have been for her mother to find him curled up in bed like a dead squirrel. "I'll be all right. The paramedics are here. Just meet her at the airport—Delta flight twenty-two—and call my brother."

They raced up Madison Avenue, sirens screaming, horns blaring, their own private rocket. Josie stared out at the people on the street, so used to noise and racket that they barely flinched, and wished she could be any one of them now, remembering the last time she was inside an ambulance, racing from the beach to the hospital, her life suspended, happiness interrupted.

She pictured herself as a little girl walking out of the big nine-room apartment without telling her parents and setting off to see her grandmother, whom she knew lived three blocks away in an old people's home that had once been an elegant mansion. The uniformed doorman let her in and pointed the way to the sweeping marble staircase that seemed to carry her up effortlessly, the brass banister cool in the palm of her hand. Her grandmother was sitting in front of a tall leaded window, the same afghan her father slept with now draped over her shoulders, staring out at a garden full of peonies she could not smell. Josie remembered the look on her face when she'd turned at the sound of Josie's little-girl feet, her eyes opening wide, as if she'd seen an angel, her arms reaching out to take Josie into her lap. She remembered the feel of her large sagging breasts and the smell of her lavender cologne and the loud smacking sound of her kisses as she buried her face in Josie's curls and breathed in deeply as if smelling the peonies that hung heavy and wet with pink rain.

"He has a living will," Josie told the resident as they whisked

Albert into the emergency room, down the same hall from where they'd made their great escape with Ezra. Her stomach did a little flip when she thought about him. "He had a minor stroke last Christmas."

"How old is he?" asked the doctor, a hirsute Israeli with a yarmulke bobby-pinned to his thick hair.

"Seventy-nine," she said, realizing with a shock that his own mother had been seventy-nine when she tried to kill herself. "He wouldn't want you to do anything *heroic*."

"I understand," the doctor said, hooking him up to an electrocardiograph machine in the harshly lit room of stainless steel and cold blue walls. Like an unrefrigerated morgue. "He probably had a massive stroke. We won't do anything extraordinary to prolong his life."

"He's turning blue," said a young intern, who had joined the cast and crew of what seemed to Josie a bad television movie. "He's not pulling in enough air, so he'll probably go into cardiac arrest or fibrillation."

Blue? Josie thought he looked more gray, like the giant tuna she'd seen gaffed and left to die on a splintery sun-bleached pier in Provincetown. She had never seen anybody die. Except in the movies. And Albert looked nothing like a cowboy lying in the dust, his head propped on a rock or piece of wood. No last words. No cough or blood spurt before his head slumped to the side.

She looked up at the heart monitor, which, like the bouncing ball over the words of a song, was beating in perfect four/four time. He sucked in a great draft of air and pushed it out like a bellows, fighting for every particle of life, every bubble, like the fetus inside her, a little goldfish in a sack of water, sipping oxygen from her blood—just like her father.

She could feel herself detach, as if she were watching him from above, holding her breath for as long as he held his, until she couldn't hold it anymore, counting the heartbeats on the screen, wondering which one would be the last. She stared at his fluttering eyelids so pale and blue with delicate veins, his bushy eyebrows flecked with gray, his forehead smooth and waxy like a marzipan pear. She touched his cheeks and ran her finger across his lips, as thin in death as they were when he was angry. She tried to ready herself for the final gasp, the death rattle, but it never came, and she thought how hard it was to die.

She couldn't even cry, though she wanted to drape herself across his chest and pound him back to life. To blow air into his mouth and pump him up like a rubber doll. To save him as he had once saved her when she was ten and couldn't breathe, her throat constricted from strep throat. He had whisked her into the bathroom and bent her over the sink, then turned the hot water on full blast and thrown a towel over her head. She could still remember the hot steam boiling the sickness out of her throat, melting her eyeballs, the sweet taste of air and the relief of breathing. To know he would never let her die—although she learned many years later that he had been terrified he might have had to perform a tracheotomy for the first time since medical school. She never knew he was afraid. Not for a moment. No panic. No show of emotion. He was so competent, so capable, so in control. It was he whom she wanted to be like when she grew up.

Josie prayed he wouldn't die before Ruth got there, that he would wait a little longer. The thought of her mother's trembling lips and tear-filled eyes made the lump inside Josie's throat swell and a sob break through the wall she'd built around her heart. But before she could even whimper, the quiet waltz of impending death, the peaceful vigil of her father's rising chest and dancing dots above his head, switched into a madcap tarantella with doctors and nurses rushing in from holes in the wall like an army of worker ants advancing to save their queen.

"What's going on?" Josie said, frightened by the urgency in their voices and the frenzied scuffle to save him.

"You've got to leave now," an intern who looked about twelve years old said as he yanked the gurney away and began to push it toward a sink in the corner.

"What's wrong?" Josie said, refusing to budge.

"We've found high levels of barbiturates in his blood and urine."

"Whad'you mean?" she asked, knowing exactly what he meant.

"He's overdosed," the doctor with the yarmulke said. "We've got to pump his stomach."

"But wait—" She stretched her arms out to protect her father.

"Get out of the way." A nurse pushed her.

"No." Josie grabbed the gurney. "Why're you going to save him now?"

The yarmulked doctor and the baby-faced intern turned and stared, as if she were holding an Uzi to her father's head. As if she were a murderess.

"He wants to die," Josie cried out. "We know that now."

They grabbed her roughly by the arms, pulling her off the gurney. She held tight, her fingers digging into her father's unfeeling arms. "Why are you doing this?" She spit out the words as they pried her off him. "He's seventy-nine years old, for Christ's sake! You were happy to let him die when you thought he'd had a stroke!"

It all made sense to her now—the stuffy apartment and eerie neatness of his room, his mother's portrait, as if he had wanted her to hold his hand as he took the final voyage.

The Israeli doctor grabbed her arm and a Jamaican nurse held her waist, and together they chucked her into the hall like a cowboy being thrown out of a saloon. Josie scrambled up to her feet, tears of outrage sprouting from her eyes, fear, anger, and embarrassment setting on her like a pack of dogs. She tried to look through the door, but they had pulled a curtain, so all she could hear were the shuffle of white shoes on hospital tile and the sound of running water. "Oh God," she cried as her father's retching filled her ears. Great heaves and groans that buckled her knees, so that she slid down the wall and wept, her chest and throat exploding, her head throbbing with confusion. Nothing in life had prepared her for this. To be the gatekeeper, the judge, the executioner of her father. She wanted him to live even if she knew he wanted her to let him die, the words of his mother echoing in her ears. "Why did you save me? Why didn't you let me die?"

Josie felt the tears on her cheeks, the warm salt stinging her chin. Her head was pounding so hard, she thought her brain would shatter her skull. Her shoulders heaved with all the pain she could no longer stifle.

How could he have done this? Her father. How could she fight to let him die? Her father. How could she be angry at him for something she couldn't understand? How could he leave her without saying good-bye? "I'm sorry, Papa," she sobbed, cupping her hands over her ears to block out the sound of vomiting. "I didn't know."

Then somebody touched her arm so softly, she wasn't sure she felt it. "He could live another fifteen years, you know." Josie turned her swollen eyes up to the pale, flat face of a balding doctor. "People can live productive lives well into their nineties."

"But he doesn't *want* to live into his nineties," she said, too tired to jerk her arm away from his patronizing touch. "He wants to die."

The doctor half-closed his eyes and shook his head slowly like a lizard lazing in the sun. "I know," he said.

"You don't know anything," Josie shot back, burying her head in the sling of her arms, scared if he didn't go away, she'd hit him.

"Where is he?" Josie heard her mother's voice and saw her walking toward her, dressed in her royal blue coat with the shiny black buttons. She looks so pretty, Josie thought. So put together. Like when Ruth used to come to pick her up at school. Class mother. President of the PTA. Always neat. Even in the morning in her Viyella robe and terry-cloth slippers, a Kleenex stuffed in a pocket or sleeve. She never wore pants, which she thought were sloppy. Not even in the country.

"Is he dead?" she asked, her voice quivering but not breaking.

Josie shook her head and glanced at Gus, who stood with his arm protectively around Ruth's shoulder. "They saved him," she said.

"You mean he's still alive?" Ruth didn't understand.

"They pumped his stomach." Josie swallowed the bile rising in her throat. "He's in a coma."

"Oh God." Ruth swayed and grabbed Gus to keep from falling. This was a mess too big to wipe away with a damp cloth.

Josie led her into a room marked DO NOT ENTER, where Albert lay with tubes threaded through his nose and throat, a panel of flashing lights and blinking monitors keeping him alive. Next to him, a nurse stood guard.

"Oh God." Ruth placed her hand on Albert's forehead—the cool hand that Josie could still feel on her feverish brow—a single tear falling on his hair. The room had an icy glow that reminded Josie of Christmas, except there was no tree or presents, just knobs and plugs and pulsing dials that beeped and belched in syncopated time. "This is exactly what he didn't want," Ruth cried, her shoulders slumped as if she were carrying rocks on her back. "This is his nightmare."

"What a fuckup!" David strode down the hall, bleary-eyed and unshaven, up all night on the red-eye from L.A., but dressed in an Italian leather jacket as soft as butter, Gucci loafers, and custom-made jeans. He shook his head. "I can't believe he did this. I can't believe he could be so cruel. What did he expect? That Mom would walk in and find him dead? Some welcome.

The bastard. Why didn't he check into a hotel or jump off a fucking bridge."

"He's scared of heights," Josie said straight-faced.

"Jesus fucking Christ." David rubbed his hand over the stubble of his chin. "What do they say? I mean, is he gonna make it?"

The neurologist was an old colleague of Albert's, a man with a beard like Trotsky's and thick bifocals. Ruth called him by his first name, as she did all the medical moguls at Mount Zion, thinking that familiarity would confer some special treatment.

"He's in a deep sleep," said Nathan "Nat" Berkowitz. "The drugs are like a cloud over his brain, but when they lift, he'll be fine."

"Fine?" David almost shouted.

"Physically," Nat added. "I'm not talking about his depression."

"Well, maybe we should talk about his depression," he insisted.

"Not now, David." Ruth spoke to him as if disciplining a difficult child.

"Is there a chance he won't come out of it?"

Nat nodded. "He could develop pneumonia."

"He has a living will," Ruth said. "He wouldn't want to be kept alive."

"There's nothing I can do now," Nat explained.

"Why not unplug him?" Josie asked.

Nat shook his head. "You don't understand. A living will means nothing in a suicide."

"What do you mean?"

"Because it's *reversible*. A living will is applicable only in cases of *irreversible* damage. Suicide is not terminal."

Josie laughed. "Suicide not terminal?"

"It's like hypothermia," he said. "It can be undone."

"Maybe next time, he'll stick his head in a freezer," David said with a contemptuous laugh.

"How long will he be in the coma?" Ruth asked, ignoring David's remark.

"We have no way of knowing," Nat said. "His vital signs are strong. It depends on how many pills he took and what." He turned to Josie. "You never found the vials?"

She shook her head, wondering if she would have saved him had she known. Imagined reading a note and sitting down in the rocker near his bedside table where she had carved her initials when she was ten, and waiting and rocking to the sound of his death rattle. "What happens when he wakes up?" she asked.

"Surprise!" David shouted, throwing his arms in the air. "We could all dress up like angels." He had always been able to make Ruth laugh whenever she was angry, but not now. She covered her face with her hands and melted, her shoulders heaving with silent keening. "I'm sorry, Mom," David said, gently massaging her back. "It's just so fucking awful."

Ruth sat up straight and dabbed her eyes with a white linen hankie. "I don't want anyone to know," she said, fear darkening her eyes.

"Know what?" David and Josie asked in unison.

"Anything about this." She was too ashamed to say the word.

"So what're we supposed to say?"

"That he had a stroke."

"And if he recovers?" Josie asked. "Without any neurological impairment."

"Then it's up to him."

"But Mom," Josie began. There had always been guilt—what Jewish family was without it?—but never shame. Shame was for Catholics. "*You* didn't do anything. There's nothing for *you* to be ashamed of."

Ruth shook her head to fight back the tears. "I don't want it discussed outside the family." Her voice was steady and positive. "Do you understand?" She stared at Josie.

"I don't agree."

"I don't care." Ruth's eyes flashed. "It's nobody's business."

"There's nothing to do now but wait," the doctor said, getting up wearily. "He could still die."

Josie lay next to her mother in her parents' double bed, her growing belly pressed up against her mother's back, her arms encircling her protectively. She hardly slept all night, aware that she was lying in the hollow of her father's shadow, etched after years of sleeping in the same position. She could feel the ridges of his bones as if she were lying on top of him in a shallow grave, holding her mother the way she imagined he had once held her. Strangely sexual, everything topsy-turvy, she her father in the bed where he had slept with her mother for more than forty years, the same bed where she had lost her virginity and where she had sought safe haven as a child.

Josie dreamed she was climbing a huge sand dune that rose directly from the sea. In her hand, she clutched her address book, filled with the names of everyone she knew and the name of her unborn child. A gust of wind blew the pages out of the book like birds in flight, a burst of white, but she was too scared to chase them because the wave was racing toward her, climbing twelve stories high. She clawed the sand, her legs deadweight, but at the summit saw her father, his white hair whipping around his head like Moses or King Lear. She grabbed the bottom rung of a ladder that appeared from nowhere and pulled herself up to where he stood. But when she got to the top, he had disappeared.

Josie awoke from her sleepless night more tired than when she had gone to bed. Feeling hungover and bruised, she padded into the kitchen, where her mother sat hunched over a cup of coffee, a wad of Kleenex in her hand. Her face red and splotchy, her hair uncombed. Josie rested her hand on her drooping shoulders. "The mornings are always the hardest," she said.

Ruth tried to hide her tears in the sodden tissue.

"Go ahead and cry, Mom," Josie said.

"How could he have done this?" Ruth wept. "I don't understand."

"He was desperate," Josie said.

"But why? It's not like he has cancer or was in any physical pain. That I'd understand."

"He's been planning this since the day he stopped working," Josie said. "Even before."

"I told him not to sell his practice. I told him he should continue seeing his old patients, even if he brought in a younger man. Or teach. He could've taught at the medical school. But no, he was always so positive. Never listened to anything I said. Even when I told him to buy this apartment." Her carefully modulated anger cracked her voice like an adolescent boy's.

She scanned the large sunny kitchen with the pictures of friends and family and David's faded drawings. "He's such a fool," Ruth said, biting her lower lip to stem the tears, as if crying were a sign of weakness.

"Why don't you just cry, Mom? It's okay. You can be angry, for Christ's sake! He wasn't thinking of you or me or David when he did this. He just checked out. He didn't think about who he was leaving behind. Has he ever put anybody ahead of himself? Ever?" she asked.

"Yes," Ruth said with melancholy eyes. "His patients." Josie didn't answer. "I've been married to him for forty-two years," she continued. "And he's never going to change." Her hands were shaking as she brought her tepid coffee to her lips. "I don't like to hear you talk about him like this." Her tone was stern.

"Why? Because I'm saying what you're thinking?"

"No." Ruth's voice was steady. "Because he's your father."

Josie felt the blood rush from her head to her stomach and thought she would faint. She gripped the edge of the table.

"Are you all right?" Ruth asked, seeing the color drain from Josie's face.

"I haven't had a chance to tell you," Josie said, holding on to the edge of the table to keep from passing out. "I'm pregnant."

Ruth lifted her dark face like a sunflower to the sky. "Oh, Josie," she said, smiling. "How wonderful! You're pregnant. Oh, darling, when did you find out?"

"About eighteen hours ago," Josie said, glancing at the clock above the stove.

Ruth got up and wrapped her arms around Josie, feeling her daughter's stomach with her hands as if she could see the baby with her fingers. "I thought you were pregnant." She smiled. "I even said something to Papa, but he pooh-poohed me. I can always tell, but I didn't want to say anything in case you weren't. I'm so happy, darling." She took Josie in her arms again and felt what she always felt when she held her grown children, felt their bulk and long limbs, felt how strong and big they were, and she thought it almost impossible that these giants had once fit so snugly inside her womb, wedged like widgets between her hips and heart. "When are you due?"

"September twentieth."

"Gus must be thrilled."

Josie nodded. "I wanted to tell Papa . . . ," she said, feeling her eyes fill with tears, the tears she'd been holding back for so long. "That's how I found him."

"Don't worry, darling," Ruth said, smoothing Josie's hair away from her eyes like she'd done a thousand times and would continue to do for a whole new generation. "Let me fix you something to eat."

They all stood around Albert's bed—Gus at the foot, Ruth at the head, Josie and David side by side. Josie thought that Ezra should be there, too, recording it on film. You couldn't script a scene more dramatic than this. She had wanted to see him again, was even hurt he hadn't called, blurring the line of fantasy and reality—after all, she was a married woman. But now, all that seemed trivial and unimportant as she waited for her father to awaken and respond to more than his name, which is what he had done that morning—the fifth day of the Big Sleep.

Josie held her breath. David clutched her hand.

Albert's eyelashes fluttered; his bushy eyebrows twitched. He tried to focus through crinkled eyes, and Josie thought how bizarre it was to be witnessing her father's rebirth, as if the Great Producer in the sky had spliced together *Sleeping Beauty* and *Return of the Living Dead*.

"Albert?" Ruth whispered into his ear. "We're all here."

"You're alive, Dad," David said, his lips quivering.

Albert tried to speak, but instead of words, staccato sobs, more like an animal caught in a trap than a man delivered from the jaws of death, pierced the stagnant silence of the room, and Josie wondered if these were cries of joy or sobs of disappointment and pain. Ruth kissed his forehead. "Can you hear me, Albert?" she whispered between gulps. "Do you know where you are?"

He nodded slowly, then closed his eyes, tears seeping out of the corners like a day-old kitten.

"Oh, Albert," Ruth said softly, and seeing him turn toward her with what she hoped was love, she rested her head on his chest, waiting for him to make some move as Josie watched and prayed that he would touch her mother, caress her cheek, do anything to show he cared. Then slowly and deliberately, as if he'd heard her silent prayer, Albert moved his IV'd hand gently up Ruth's back and ran his fingers through her hair.

ELEVEN

Josie felt the baby somersault inside her, a knee poke her below the ribs, an elbow nudge her behind the navel. Sometimes when she floated between sleep and dreaming, she imagined herself inside herself, swimming weightlessly in a sac of water, peering at her unborn child to see whom he looked like. She touched her hard, round belly, which was stretched tight as a kettledrum, and shifted in the uncomfortable ladder-back chair in the office of the hospital-appointed psychiatrist who had been assigned to Albert's case, where she sat with her mother and brother to discuss how to keep someone alive who wanted to die, how to make someone eat when he wasn't hungry, how to talk to someone who was voluntarily (or involuntarily, depending on how you viewed it) mute. Although "alive," Albert hadn't spoken, eaten, or made eye contact for two weeks, his body drooping like a plant in need of water, his eyes unseeing, his hair dull as slate.

The doctor wore a dark gray suit that hung on him like mourning cloth and a narrow maroon tie that reminded Josie of the loose red skin above the capelike chest of a vulture. His office was "decorated" in hues of brown and burnt orange, with a large macramé wall hanging the likes of which Josie hadn't seen since the sixties, a Danish modern brown tweed couch, and a black leather chair. (In years to come, she would learn that this was what most New York psychoanalysts' offices looked like— brown, Danish modern, macramé, Eames chair, bad woodcuts, and two-year-old copies of *The New Yorker*.) In the corner was a large grandfather clock (an Ethan Allen repro) that ticked so loudly, Josie wondered how many of his borderline patients had thrown themselves out the window when it chimed the hour. She immediately resented this man as much for his predictably bad taste as for his bloodless manner, as if he had no passion, even if he had to possess a modicum of *com*passion to fulfill his therapeutic duties.

"Why couldn't we just take him home?" David asked, crossing and uncrossing his legs as he always did when he was nervous.

"Because he's not eating, and if he goes home, he may starve himself to death," the doctor said.

"So?" Josie didn't mean it to sound so cavalier. "I mean, if he wants to die, how can we force him to eat?"

"You can't." The doctor turned his thickly hooded eyes toward her. He was a strange-looking man with a long, sallow face and a nose like a proboscis, with a few stray hairs peeking out from the nostrils. "I suppose you could just let him die, but it can take a long time."

"How long?" David asked, looking nervously at Ruth, who sat folded into herself as if in a cocoon, her legs crossed doubly around themselves, her arms limp in her lap, her back hunched over as she twisted and untwisted a damp hankie.

"It can take three weeks or more," he said as he trained his eyes on Ruth. "And it's not a very pleasant thing to watch. He can go into kidney failure, go blind—"

"I couldn't do that." Ruth shivered, the ghoulishness of the conversation making her want to run out, as if she were at a horror movie at the Thalia.

"No," the doctor said kindly. "I don't think you could."

"What are our choices?" Josie asked.

"Electroshock," the doctor said as if reading off the specials from a menu.

"Electroshock!" David cried, visions of *Cuckoo's Nest* and *Frances* playing in his head. "Forget it."

"It's very effective in cases like this," the doctor said in a soft voice. "It's not like in the movies."

"What's it like?" Josie asked, glancing at her mother, who seemed to be shrinking before her eyes.

"It's been refined over the years," the doctor said as he uncrossed his spidery legs. "The patient is lightly sedated and given a series of treatments—no more than twelve." David groaned. "It's painless."

"How do *you* know?" David snapped. "Have you ever had shock treatments?"

The doctor ignored the question. "When the patient awakens, he has no memory of what happened or why he's there."

"You mean that he doesn't remember anything?" Josie felt the baby kick her as if to say, I'm here, when all she could think was, Who do I have to fuck to get off of this picture?

"That's right." The psychiatrist nodded. "That's why it's so effective. The patient forgets why he's depressed, which allows us to feed him."

Josie pictured her father as a large white goose, a funnel in his throat, his liver plumped for foie gras, his brains blanched and smothered in caper sauce. It was unimaginable that he would not want to eat, that food, like sex, would no longer be the source of his (like her!) greatest pleasure. She drifted away from the ticking clock and lugubrious conversation to a week in August twenty-five years before, when she had gone with her parents to Provence and watched her father taste a tart of *fraises des bois*, their perfume moving him to tears. She could still remember everything they ate—*feuilleté de ris de veau, poulet à l'estragon, haricots verts*, a Grand Marnier soufflé—and how she and Albert had studied the menu every night before they went to sleep, their bellies bulging with the previous meal, only to dream about the next meal and the next after that, until all the days and meals were eaten, leaving Josie twelve pounds fatter, with stretch marks on her hips as testimony to their incestuous culinary orgy.

Ruth spoke for the first time. "What are our other choices? I mean, aren't there pills he could take to cure the depression? Or some kind of shot?"

"In the head," David added, sounding just like Albert when he was annoyed.

"I understand how difficult this is," the psychiatrist said. "But I think electroshock is the method of choice."

The method of choice, Josie repeated to herself. *The patient. In cases like this.* As though he were talking about a stranger. Not a man. Not her father.

They waited numbly for somebody to speak.

"I guess we have no choice," Ruth said.

"I think it's the most responsible thing to do," the doctor replied.

"Do you want more time to think, Mama?" Josie squeezed her mother's hand. "You don't have to decide right now."

"What's the point of waiting?" Ruth said, nodding her assent as the doctor whipped out a pen and handed her a form to sign, as if she were buying a used car.

"Will he know what's happened?" Josie asked, feeling guilty that no one was consulting Dr. D.

The psychiatrist shook his head.

"So someone will have to tell him," she said, not daring to look at her mother or brother.

"Isn't that your job?" David addressed the psychiatrist. Like he was talking to an employee. "Or do you just plug him into the wall after you zap him?"

"I understand your anger," the doctor said. "But I think he would hear it better from one of you."

"Okay," Josie said, looking from her mother to her brother. "Who?"

"I've got to go back to L.A.," David said, getting up and pacing. "I can't stay away any longer. I've already postponed production for a month."

"If you want me to—" Ruth couldn't finish the sentence as she looked at Josie with dark-circled eyes.

"That's okay, Mom." Josie held her stomach with both hands. "I'll do it."

"You don't mind, do you, Josie?" Ruth said. "I think it'd be better if he heard it from you."

Her father was sitting near the window in the psychiatric "sunroom," an open space that were it not locked and filled with people in pajamas and felt slippers would have looked like the skylit gallery of the Frick Collection. Even Dr. D. was beginning to look like an El Greco, his face elongated and his hands too big for his body. He turned at the sound of her footsteps.

"How pretty you look, darling," he said sweetly, and Josie felt a wave of love wash over her like liquid balm. "You're pregnant."

"Yes." She smiled, taking his hand and holding it over the invisible foot of his unborn grandchild. "Six months," she said, sitting down near him in a turquoise Naugahyde chair. "How are you feeling?"

"Oh, fine. Just fine," he said, looking out at the park.

"Do you know why you're here, Papa?"

He shook his head.

"D'you know where you are?"

"I'm in the hospital," he said, turning to face her.

"But do you know why?" she repeated.

"No," he said, waiting for her to tell him.

"Because you tried to kill yourself." She spoke very slowly and clearly, as though she were talking to a child.

"I did?" He seemed amazed.

"You took a lot of pills," Josie said. "Mama was away and I dropped by the apartment after I found out I was pregnant. I wanted you to be the first to know."

He leaned forward. "Go on."

"The paper was outside the door and all the lights were off in the apartment. I called your name, but you didn't answer."

"Where was I?" he asked.

"In your bed. You were unconscious. If I hadn't come, you would have died." She faltered, remembering the scene she wished she could forget. "I tried to wake you, but you were dying. . . . Mama would've come home and found you curled up in bed like a dead squirrel."

"There was a squirrel in the bed?" He looked confused.

"No." Josie laughed. "You were in the bed. You just reminded me of a squirrel."

"Then what happened?"

"I called the police."

She could see him try to bend his mind around the holes burned in his brain like those on a scorched pot holder. "Why?" he asked.

"Why what?" She was confused.

"Why did you save me?"

"Because I didn't know you wanted to die." She could hear the high pitch of defensiveness in her voice. "I didn't know you'd taken pills. I thought you'd had a stroke. There were no signs. No vials. No note. Do you remember any of this?" He shook his head from side to side. "When I took you into the emergency room, they were going to let you die, but when they found barbiturates in your blood and urine, they pumped your stomach and revived you."

Albert's eyes sparkled beneath his magnificent brows. Josie felt like a shaman conjuring the spirits around the fire, mesmerizing her father with the story of his near death. For a man who had so artfully engineered his life, he had failed miserably to exit gracefully.

She stared at her father, the man whom she had feared her whole life, whose approval she had worked so hard to earn and whose love she had tried so painfully to trust, whose success she had longed to emulate, sitting in the sun-filled psych ward of the same hospital where he had delivered thousands of babies and been so happy, his memory shocked out of him, his anger cauterized and in its place an unrecognizable sweetness.

"That's the most fantastic story I've ever heard," he said. "Will you tell it to me again?"

"Josie!" Ezra called her name as she whirled past him on her way out of the hospital's revolving doors. "Josie, wait!" He dashed after her, not sure whether she was avoiding him or if she hadn't heard him call her name.

She turned and smiled, happy to see him before she had time to censor her thoughts or feelings, the same strong physical attraction—like a drug.

"It's me, Ezra," he said.

"I know." Josie wanted to embrace him. "How did you find out?" She held back.

"Your mother called and said he wanted to see me." He quickly ran his eyes over her belly and noticed the gentle bulge, which, without asking or thinking or knowing why, he touched. "You're pregnant," he said, surprised that she didn't move away.

"Yes."

"That's great."

"We're thrilled." She felt the same discomfort she always felt when Gus and he collided in her head.

"When?"

"September twentieth," she said.

"My birthday!" Ezra exclaimed, and without a word, he pulled her into his arms, feeling the bulge of her belly and smelling the ocean in her hair, a smell that always turned him on. "I got into UCLA film school," he announced.

"That's terrific," Josie said, feeling a mix of relief and sadness that he would be so far away. He was always lurking in her day-dreams. "When do you leave?"

"Next week."

"Congratulations," she said, and started to go.

"Josie." Ezra took her hand. "Did he have a stroke?" She didn't answer. "What did he do, try and kill himself?"

She looked amazed. "That's not the official story," she said.

Ezra held her in his gaze, staring long and hard at her face, his eye caressing her pregnant belly, and said, "I won't tell."

They kept him in the hospital for twenty-one days, but as soon as he got home, all Albert thought about was killing himself. From the minute he woke up until he went to bed, his mind working like a motor he couldn't shut off. He could be doing anything—eating (they were right about shock treatments—his appetite had returned), reading (although he found it hard to concentrate), getting dressed (he wore the same stained khakis and polo shirt)—but half his brain was somewhere else. He needed a plan. Even though he was a doctor, there was a limit to the number of barbiturates he could prescribe, and not all of them for himself. He'd already figured out how he could write dummy prescriptions for each member of the family. No one would know. But he still had to be careful. He couldn't botch it a second time.

"Maybe you *wanted* to be caught," Josie said, sounding just like him. "Maybe you wanted to live."

They were so much alike. That's why they fought. Analytic, direct, born flirts. Albert remembered watching Josie with grown-ups when she was just a little girl—the way she cocked her head to one side and listened with intense dark eyes, inviting intimacy and confession. She combined a certain coyness with brute determination, which had made him nervous when she reached puberty. He always sensed a strong sexual drive in her, and though he never asked, he was sure the "friend" who had needed an abortion was Josie.

Albert waited for Ruth to leave so he could count his pills. How ironic, he thought, that she still works at the same hospital where I no longer have privileges. They hardly spoke these days, Ruth having given up trying to lead him out of his depression like Theseus with too short a string. Had he become such a Minotaur, devouring all pleasure in fits of rage, shutting people out because he was jealous of the past—and terrified of the future? He didn't care anymore. He had never really cared what other people thought. He had nothing to live for without his work; the spine of his life was broken. He didn't need an excuse.

Albert waited to be sure Ruth wouldn't come back for something. She was always forgetting things when they went out—her gloves, a hankie, her cigarette lighter. It was a tic that had always annoyed him. Having to wait while she rushed back into the apartment to find the thing she'd forgotten, holding the elevator button open until the buzzer sounded and he had to let it go, watching her light the cigarette she would rub out on the street before hopping into a cab.

His closet smelled of winter wool—sweet and pungent like the inside of a humidor. His custom-made Church shoes were neatly stacked in a wooden shelf David had made for him in middle school shop and a faded drawing of a ballerina Josie had given him for a birthday years ago was taped above his bureau.

He grabbed a footstool and climbed up shakily, teetering for a moment as he reached for the shoe box where he stashed his drugs, thinking with a laugh how funny it would be if he fell and fractured his skull preparing to commit suicide. He was tempted to call his sister Lena to share the joke. They had the same zany appreciation of the absurd. It was Lena who had called him in a panic in the middle of the night to say she was bleeding to death, when what she was hemorrhaging wasn't blood, but borscht. And it was Lena who had climbed to the top of Chichén Itzá, froze in panic, and had to be carried back down by two Mayan guides. Then he thought about Lena playing backgammon at the Jewish Home, hiding her pennies underneath the rug, her humor and looks fading into senility, and he was doubly sure that what he was doing was right.

Albert spread the contents of the box onto the bed and rolled his hand over the vials. He checked the issue dates and counted the pills like a miser counting his gold. Seconal, Valium, Dalmane, Nembutal, Darvon, Demerol. He had enough drugs to kill the entire Upper East Side. Now all he had to do was pick a time and place.

Josie's water broke at half past nine on September 16, four days before her due date, a gush of salt water, a stab of pain. All the techniques and exercises she had practiced flew out the window as she picked up the phone to call her doctor but instead dialed her father.

"Why're you calling *me*?" he asked, making her feel foolish for secretly wishing he would rush up to the hospital like she had seen him do with all his other women and deliver her!

"Now what do we do?" Gus said, rummaging through the closet for the tennis balls, hard candy, rope, and ice bag the Lamaze coach had instructed them to pack a month before.

Down the elevator and into a cab, the pains strong enough to double her over and make her clutch Gus's hand.

"Are you okay?" he asked fearfully, never having seen a baby born except from a distance when he was in the South and a sharecropper's wife was giving birth to her tenth child.

This was the moment Josie had been waiting for, the grand finale, the Easter show at Radio City Music Hall, every kick hitting her in the groin. Legs up and into the stirrups. She could hear women screaming in the halls. "Aiiiyee, aiiiyeee, Mom-mmeeee. Oh God. No. Please. Help me!"

Gus fed her ice chips and rubbed her back, looking at her helplessly as she cried and threw up.

The doctor had not arrived, probably having his last demi-tasse and brandy at La Caravelle before moseying up to the hos-pital in time to catch the baby.

Josie thought she was going to die. With every excruciating push, she felt a truck hit the wall of her vagina, each urge collid-ing with raw pain, clean and inescapable. Thank God I'm in a hospital and not in a field, she thought. "Don't let me die," she screamed, digging her fingers into Gus's hands. "Please God," she repeated. "I don't want to die!"

So this was what she had been waiting for, dreaming about, rehearsing her whole life. This was what made her special. Except her father wasn't there. The gentle doctor whom so many women loved was nowhere to be found.

"Go ahead and push." Gus urged her on, the green surgical cap and mask falling comically over his eyes and ears. Except it hurt too much to laugh.

"I can't," she cried, holding back because each push felt like her crotch was being pummeled with a fist. And with every con-traction, she thought about her father splitting the duck up the middle with shears. "I can't do it," she said, weeping.

"You're doing fine," a Filipino nurse encouraged her. "I can see the head."

Gus wiped the sweat from her face and whispered, "I love you" into her ear, when all she could yell was, "Get it out!" She marveled that her mother had done this *twice*. Why, she won-dered, would anybody do it again?

"You're almost there." The doctor swooped in like Superman, all smiles and glaring light. "Just one big push." And Josie gath-ered all her strength, her neck muscles tightening like a bow, the pain so dense that it had no end, and pushed with trembling thighs and shallow breaths until all thoughts of dying gave way to life and she felt herself swim to the surface of her pain like Gus had fought to keep from drowning.

He held her head and cried, "Look up at the mirror. You can see it now." And there between her legs she saw a space as big as a tunnel, a softball of hair instead of a train barreling out, a scrunched-up face, a blind man, slippery and wizened, staring out like Rumpelstiltskin. With one orgasmic cry, she pushed, the pain propelling her to the height of power as the rest of him, wrinkled and wet, his umbilical cord like stuffed *derma*, his delicate balls swollen like purple quail's eggs, slid into the doctor's hands. "It's a boy!" Gus cried, and wept into the soft, damp hollow of Josie's neck.

They placed her son on her breast, his head too heavy for the little body, his crablike fingers clawing blindly for her tit, his toes like peas. He cried, more a squeak than a squawk, and when he latched on to her nipple, she saw he had a tiny birthmark on his shoulder, the same little ink drop on the love map she had inherited from her father, a capital city somewhere in the universe.

Josie never knew if Gus or Ezra was his father. Nor did she care. At times, she saw Ezra's soft, sweet lips and Gus's dark blue eyes. Sometimes, she saw her father's brow. She laughed when her mother swaddled her grandson, whom they named Daniel, and said with uncharacteristic wit, "This is as close as you'll ever come to having your own penis. . . . Life is easier for a boy."

Josie's world was molded around her baby from the moment she felt her breasts swell, throbbing with milk and leaking viscous blue sugar when he cried, to the quiet time when the city slept and she felt that she and Daniel were the only two people in the world. Even crushing fatigue was assuaged by the simple order of her life—rising every four hours to feed him, rocking him back and forth, taking him into bed and feeling him nestle in her arms, sweet-smelling like a loaf of freshly baked bread. All her ambition seemed to fade, each day passing without her questioning that what she was doing was exactly what she wanted.

For a while, Daniel's presence seemed to soothe her father and give her mother hope. Josie watched Ruth hold the baby across her knees and rub his back hypnotically, swaddle him tightly and lay him on his side to sleep when he was fussy, kiss him so often that his cheeks glistened. She was the pro, the maternal muse, pouring all her love into her grandson and lavishing him with extravagant generosity and affection while ignoring the telltale symptoms of Albert's depression. Albert, too, seemed to forget his kamikaze mission when he lifted his grandson, no bigger than a plump capon, and snuggled him in the crease of his neck, the baby's little kitten face peeking out over his collar. Josie felt a pool of light warm her stomach and spread through her body as Albert closed his eyes and swooned, breathing the baby's perfumed skin as if it were a perfect rose, feeling the warm, moist breath tickle his ear. Josie couldn't tell if his ecstasy was real or a put-on. He'd always been a ham, and as he waltzed around the room singing the same Yiddish lullaby he used to sing to her when she was little (even though Daniel was a boy, so the words didn't make sense)—"*Oy, meydl, meydl, meydl, ich hob dir azoy lieb; meydl, meydl, meydl, ich'l far dir geyn in grieb*"— Albert cooed and vamped, to the baby's delight, and that of anyone else who was watching. Then he suddenly lost interest and handed him back to Josie, his eyes dimming like a candle that had no air.

Josie's skin and hands went cold when he turned off like that, and she remembered the feeling she'd had as a child when they played a game in the living room, where he would pretend not to see her sneak into his big green chair as he picked up the paper and sat down on top of her, popping up with feigned anger as she laughed and cried with pleasure, begging him to do it again and again. "More, Papa, more!" she cried, sweaty with excitement, trying to pull the paper out of his hands and climb back into his lap. But he was finished, the phony anger now real, so real that he once pushed her away with such force, she fell backward and cut her head on a glass coffee table.

Gus was smiling and saying no at the same time when Josie wheeled eight-month-old Daniel into the apartment from an afternoon romp in Washington Square Park.

"What was that?" she asked, plopping the baby on Gus's lap.

"I was just asked to be the head of KRBZ." (The cable job having long since gone up in a blaze of critical success, but without enough profits to satisfy Wall Street.)

Josie felt her stomach drop. How could she leave her parents now? "What're you going to do?" she asked.

"I told them no."

"Why?"

"I figured you wouldn't want to leave your—"

"Why'd you figure that?" she said, cutting him off.

Gus looked at her to make sure she wasn't joking. "Would you be willing to move to San Francisco?"

"I don't know," she said, her mind a whir of memories of their first trip to California. "Do you want to do it?"

"It's a great job."

She saw herself strolling around Berkeley with Daniel on her back, growing flowers and vegetables in her own garden, writing in a studio in the woods. "Is it yours if you want it?"

Gus nodded, meeting her eyes in a confident stare.

"Then let's do it."

"Are you sure?"

She didn't tell him about the recurring nightmare she'd been having, where she was caught in a fire in her parents' apartment and didn't know whom to save first—her baby or her father. "Yes, I'm sure."

Ruth folded Daniel's miniature clothes, his soft cotton jump-suits and fresh-smelling nightshirts, his tiny socks hardly big enough to hold an egg, and placed them in a suitcase, lingering as if she were laying them in the grave.

"You'll come and visit us," Josie said, trying to console her. "Papa, too."

"We'll see," Ruth said wearily.

"What's there to see?"

"How can I leave?"

"He'll be all right."

Ruth didn't answer. Josie could feel herself weakening, sway-ing beneath a weight of guilt. She was abandoning her mother. "You can't spend your life watching over him," Josie said.

"That's easy for you to say." Ruth's lips tightened. "Look what happened the last time I went away."

"It wasn't your fault."

"If I had been there . . ."

"He would have found another way."

"And now?"

"I don't know," Josie said. "But you have a life, too."

Ruth swallowed hard, fighting the sickness that pressed her heart. A life? Her life had always been with him and with her children. Now they were all leaving.

Josie draped her arm around her mother's drooping shoulders and pulled her into a tight embrace, feeling how much smaller she was, as if Albert's depression had ground her down a size.

"It's so sad for it to end this way," Ruth said, fishing a tissue from her sleeve. "I'm not saying we didn't have problems. What marriage doesn't? But we had a wonderful time. When I think about the summers on the Cape, the meals. The beach picnics. The trips to Venice and France. Thanksgiving. Christmas. Birth-days." She was smiling. "God, we had fun!" Then the tears rolled down her paper white cheeks despite her efforts to control them, and Josie could feel her throat tighten. "You think you know somebody after all these years," Ruth continued. "All we shared. But now I'm not sure."

"Of what?" Josie felt like she had swallowed half a chicken.

"Of anything. I can't reach him anymore. He's like a shell of his former self. Like one of those snake skins you find in the desert—all the markings and scales in place, even the shape of the coils, but there's nothing there. Just a skin."

The last time Josie saw her father, he was sitting in the same green armchair with the afghan draped over his knees, reading about Schliemann's excavation of Troy.

"If I hadn't been a doctor," he said, "I would've been an archaeologist."

"There's still time." Josie smiled. "Have you ever been to Greece?" He shook his head and closed the book. "You'd love it," she said.

He nodded silently and fixed Josie with a stare that made her squirm. But instead of criticism or gratuitous advice, he asked her, "Will you help me?" She sighed with relief, surprised and flattered that he would turn to her.

"Of course I'll help you, Papa. What do you want?"

"To die," he said without emotion.

Josie felt like she'd been hit between the eyes with a two-by-four. Like she'd been duped. "How can you ask me that?" she cried.

"Because I have nobody else to turn to," he said. "It's all I think about from the minute I wake up until I go to bed. It's like I'm sleepwalking through the day, not tasting or smelling. Not feeling." He looked at her with frightened eyes and for a moment Josie caught a glimpse of him as a little boy. "But I'm scared."

"What are you scared of?" Josie's eyes were burning.

"Of fucking up again."

Josie closed her eyes and breathed a ragged sigh. Was he asking her permission or absolution? Should she call the police and have him committed? Should she tell her mother? Was she sitting in the den having this conversation, or was it a dream? "I don't want you to die, Papa. I want you to live," she said, unaware that she was crying, wanting to get up and climb into his lap as if she were a child. *His* child. But she remained frozen, her mind a jumble of memories and sounds, the ticking clock, the honking, clanging world outside.

"Why won't you get help to stay *alive*?" she pleaded. "Why won't you *try* to get well?"

"I never forgave myself for saving my mother." He ignored her question.

"But you saved her, didn't you? Why? Because you were a doctor or her son?"

"I was a doctor." He sat up straight and proud. "I was *trained* to save lives."

"She was your mother, Papa!" Josie screamed. "You were saving her because you didn't want her to die!"

"I was wrong." He looked at Josie coldly. "I should have let her die."

Josie wanted to run but was frozen in her chair, wanted to scream, So do it, already; stop dragging us through your pain! but the words died on her tongue and she felt ashamed of her anger. She looked at him sitting in his chair, still healthy in body but shrunken in soul, his clothes clean and neatly pressed, and felt the blood throb behind her eyes and her throat swell with fear. Was there nothing she could do to save him, to convince him that life was still worth living, that he still had them? But she just sat there, mute, feeling as he felt. Locked in her own private pain. Then she rose slowly and walked over to his chair. She reached out her arms to him and said, "May I kiss you good-bye?" He stood up easily and pulled her into his chest, hugging her so hard, she could feel his supple fingers press into her spine, could smell the wet-wool, sweet-and-sour smell of him fill her nose. She wished she could stay there forever if only to keep him alive, but his body stiffened and he pulled away.

"Good-bye, Papa," she said, thinking she would see him again, her mind too big a trickster to let her believe this was the final good-bye, the thought too unbearable as she walked toward the door. One last look as he slumped back into his chair, the heavy door closing behind her, the whoosh of air behind the elevator. She pressed the button with numb fingers and rode down in slow motion, wanting to run back and grab him around the knees, to hold him, hit him, kiss him, scream. But she kept going—out of the elevator and down the marble lobby stairs, past the doorman and out into the sunlight. She crossed the street and looked up at the window that had been her room and thought of her father standing in the doorway, seeing nothing but darkness across a threshold he was scared but determined to cross. She felt weak at the knees and leaned against a building to keep from falling until the tears came, warm and clean, blurring everything but the jumbled memories of the family seated around the dinner table, her father at the head, a carving knife in his hand.

The day after Josie arrived in California, her mother called to say her father was dead. She had found him in the back room with the afghan pulled up over his head. There was no note or empty vial. Nobody knew exactly how he died, but everyone was told it was a stroke.

On what would have been his eightieth birthday, she and her brother, David, Ruth, and Gus rented a boat not far from the beach where Gus had been hurt, and threw Albert's ashes into the ocean—although it would have been more fitting to strew them on the empty lot between Crystal Street and Belmont Avenue.

That night, Josie dreamed she was thirteen, standing in front of her piano teacher's house. It was a sunny day and she felt confident and pretty, her clean hair tied back in a ribbon that matched the pink sweater Ruth had knit for her. She buzzed to be let in, but before the door opened, she turned around and saw her father in the street, backlit so brightly, she had to squint.

"Hello, darling," he said, so sweetly that Josie felt dizzy with love.

"Papa!" she cried out. "What're you doing here? I thought you were dead."

He didn't speak but continued to smile, then turned and walked away. She wanted to go after him, but just as she was about to run, her piano teacher buzzed her in and she turned away. "Oh God," she cried out, so loudly that Gus shook her awake. But all she wanted was to go back to sleep so she could see her father.

Josie tried to imagine what Albert had thought before he died. What was the final picture before all went black—a purple anemone, his mother's hand, Ruth's amber eyes? She wanted so badly to see him again, to touch his face. Just one more time. And then she remembered, as clearly as the blue lights dancing across the ceiling, a cold winter night when she was five and her father and she had walked around Lake Placid, where they had gone on a family vacation before Albert discovered the hotel was restricted and checked them out the next morning. She could still feel her small mittened hand in his strong leather glove and hear the crunch of their footsteps on the dry, clean snow. In the distance were pine trees festooned with blue lights, and as they walked together, their breath made wisps of smoke in the icy air. Just she and her father. Warm and snug. The lake as vast as an ocean, the shoreline studded with tiny blue lights. No noise but their footsteps and the sound of their breathing.

A NOTE ON THE TYPE

This book was set in a version of Garamond, a type
named for the Parisian typecutter Claude
Garamond (ca. 1480–1561). Garamond, a
pupil of Geoffroy Tory, based his letter on the
types of the Aldine Press in Venice, but he
introduced a number of important differ-
ences, and it is to him that we owe the letter
now known as "old style."

Composed by Creative Graphics,
Allentown, Pennsylvania
Printed and bound by Haddon Craftsmen,
an R. R. Donnelly & Sons Company,
Bloomsburg, Pennsylvania
Designed by Anthea Lingeman